PRAISE FOR SUSAN STOKER

"I will read anything Susan Stoker puts out . . . because I know it's going to be amazing!"

—Riley Edwards, *USA Today* bestselling author

"Susan Stoker never fails to pull me out of a reading slump. With heat, action, and suspense, she weaves an incredible tale that sucks me in and doesn't let go."

—Jessica Prince, *USA Today* bestselling author

"One thing I love about Susan Stoker's books is that she knows how to deliver a perfect HEA while still making sure the villain gets what he/she deserves!"

—T.M. Frazier, *New York Times* bestselling author

"Susan Stoker's characters come alive on the page!"

—Elle James, *New York Times* bestselling author

"When you pick up a Susan Stoker book, you know exactly what you're going to get . . . a hot alpha hero and a smart, sassy heroine. I can't get enough!"

—Jessica Hawkins, *USA Today* bestselling author

"Suspenseful storytelling with characters you want as friends!"

—Meli Raine, *USA Today* bestselling author

"Susan Stoker knows what women want. A hot hero who needs to save a damsel in distress . . . even if she can save herself."

—CD Reiss, *New York Times* bestselling author

THE SAILOR

DISCOVER OTHER TITLES BY SUSAN STOKER

Alpha Cove Series

The Soldier
The Sailor
The Pilot (August 2026)
The Guardsman (March 2027)

Game of Chance Series

The Protector
The Royal
The Hero
The Lumberjack

Ace Security Series

Claiming Grace
Claiming Alexis
Claiming Bailey
Claiming Felicity
Claiming Sarah

Mountain Mercenaries Series

Defending Allye
Defending Chloe
Defending Morgan
Defending Harlow
Defending Everly
Defending Zara
Defending Raven

Silverstone Series

Trusting Skylar
Trusting Taylor
Trusting Molly
Trusting Cassidy

SEAL of Protection: Alliance Series

Protecting Remi
Protecting Wren
Protecting Josie
Protecting Maggie
Protecting Addison
Protecting Kelli
Protecting Bree

Rescue Angels Series

Keeping Laryn
Keeping Amanda
Keeping Zita
Keeping Penny (May 2026)
Keeping Kara (July 2026)
Keeping Jennifer (November 2026)

The Refuge Series

Deserving Alaska
Deserving Henley
Deserving Reese
Deserving Cora
Deserving Lara
Deserving Maisy
Deserving Ryleigh

SEAL Team Hawaii Series

Finding Elodie

Finding Lexie

Finding Kenna

Finding Monica

Finding Carly

Finding Ashlyn

Finding Jodelle

Eagle Point Search & Rescue Series

Searching for Lilly

Searching for Elsie

Searching for Bristol

Searching for Caryn

Searching for Finley

Searching for Heather

Searching for Khloe

Delta Force Heroes Series

Rescuing Rayne

Rescuing Aimee (novella)

Rescuing Emily

Rescuing Harley

Marrying Emily (novella)

Rescuing Kassie

Rescuing Bryn

Rescuing Casey

Rescuing Sadie (novella)

Rescuing Wendy

Rescuing Mary

Rescuing Macie

Rescuing Annie

Badge of Honor: Texas Heroes Series

Justice for Mackenzie
Justice for Mickie
Justice for Corrie
Justice for Laine (novella)
Shelter for Elizabeth
Justice for Boone
Shelter for Adeline
Shelter for Sophie
Justice for Erin
Justice for Milena
Shelter for Blythe
Justice for Hope
Shelter for Quinn
Shelter for Koren
Shelter for Penelope

Delta Team Two Series

Shielding Gillian
Shielding Kinley
Shielding Aspen
Shielding Jayme (novella)
Shielding Riley
Shielding Devyn
Shielding Ember
Shielding Sierra

SEAL of Protection Series

Protecting Caroline
Protecting Alabama
Protecting Fiona
Marrying Caroline (novella)
Protecting Summer

Protecting Cheyenne
Protecting Jessyka
Protecting Julie (novella)
Protecting Melody
Protecting the Future
Protecting Kiera (novella)
Protecting Alabama's Kids (novella)
Protecting Dakota
Protecting Tex

SEAL of Protection: Legacy Series

Securing Caite
Securing Brenae (novella)
Securing Sidney
Securing Piper
Securing Zoey
Securing Avery
Securing Kalee
Securing Jane (novella)

THE SAILOR

SUSAN STOKER

Published by Montlake, Seattle

www.apub.com

EU product safety contact:
Amazon Media EU S. à r.l.
38, avenue John F. Kennedy, L-1855 Luxembourg
amazonpublishing-gpsr@amazon.com

ISBN-13: 9781662527302 (paperback)
ISBN-13: 9781662527319 (digital)

Cover design by Hang Le
Cover photography by FTAPE LIMITED
Cover image: © Carlos Banyuls / Shutterstock

Printed in the United States of America

THE SAILOR

Chapter One

Marit Phillips had had high hopes for her new job working on a lobster boat in Rockville. However, she'd only been there a week and unfortunately, some of the same issues she'd had while working down in Portland had already started. But at least this time her boss, the captain of the *Wave Rider*, seemed to be genuinely happy to have her on board.

Eliot Sullivan was around fifty years old and, like a lot of lobster boat captains, had been working on the waters around Maine since he was a kid. It was in his blood, as people liked to say, and he'd been successful enough this year not only to hire a second crew member for his boat, but to actually *need* another pair of hands.

His son, Jonah, was a little older than Marit, and he worked just as hard as his dad. In the week she'd been working for the father/son duo, she'd laughed more than she had in years.

In fact, the comparison between the overall working atmosphere here and the one she'd left behind in Portland couldn't have been more different. Even though both cities were in Maine, Rockville seemed to be a lot less cutthroat, which was a relief. In Portland, she'd walked on eggshells every moment she was on a boat and didn't relax until she was home, behind the locked door of her apartment.

It was no way to live, and making the decision to move to the smaller town up the coast had been risky. But so far, Rockville had more than met her expectations . . . despite the minor rumblings of the last couple of days.

Because of course, not *everyone* was happy to see her on the docks.

She knew from experience that many lobstermen still had long-held and deeply ingrained prejudices against women working on the boats. Some didn't think women were strong enough to do the physical work required to haul lobster pots in and out of the water all day. Others felt it was bad luck to have a woman on a boat. And still others were just assholes who wanted to keep all the money to be made in the lobster industry to themselves.

For the most part, Marit had learned to ignore the naysayers, those who wanted to see her fail. Who would delight in seeing her slink off with her proverbial tail between her legs. But . . . she couldn't deny the fact that a narrow-minded jerk was the entire reason she'd left Portland.

Thorne Deaton.

Even thinking his name made the hair on the back of Marit's neck stand up. The man was dangerous. Though no one else seemed to think so, which she honestly didn't understand. Her previous boss actually told her that he was harmless after she'd brought up some of the things he'd said to her when no one else was around. Insisting he was simply "blowing off steam" and that she shouldn't worry.

But Marit had learned a long time ago that there were different expectations because of her gender. She was well aware that as a woman in a male-dominated profession, she had to work harder and longer than the men around her, and if she made any mistakes, they would be held against her for months.

Thorne owned a lobster boat named *Sea Men Rule*. It was a misogynistic name at best, pornographic at worst. Of course, most of the men she worked with thought it was hilarious and couldn't understand why she was so offended. But it wasn't just the name of his boat that had set Marit on edge. Thorne was a big man—over six feet tall, and he outweighed her by at least a hundred pounds. He was loud, brash, and loved to embarrass others, men *and* women.

Most people thought he was a joker, a good ol' boy, and for some reason, they let him get away with things that would get other lobstermen heavily fined, like constantly having oversize lobsters in his catch—including the occasional breeding female.

That was one of the most egregious mistakes you could make . . . the females with eggs attached to their bellies were the future of lobstering. And any lobsterman worth his salt knew to notch the tails of those females and throw them back.

But weirdly, the other lobstermen—and even the odd enforcement officer—let Thorne get away with that shit.

Marit didn't understand it, and she'd actually confronted Thorne at one point about his questionable fishing practices. He hadn't liked that, and from that moment on had made it his goal to make her life miserable.

He'd succeeded. So much so, she'd left Portland and moved farther inland to mid-coast Maine.

Thankful to have left Thorne behind, Marit still wasn't surprised she'd begun to experience some of the same discrimination she had while in the bigger city, but thankfully not on the same level as she had with Thorne and his buddies. At least . . . not yet.

She'd started working almost as soon as she'd arrived in town. With Eliot's help, she'd also found a tiny apartment, but she hadn't had time to actually unpack much yet. With Rockville's Lobster Fest starting in a week, she'd been working long hours on the boat with Eliot and Jonah to catch as much as they could. Everyone wanted as many fresh crustaceans as possible, since apparently people from throughout Maine, and even the country, flocked to the small town to enjoy all the activities the festival had to offer, which included cooking contests, running races, live entertainment, crafts . . . and of course, lobster.

The excitement for the looming festival was infectious, and she loved living so close to the heart of the town. Her new apartment was two blocks away from the main street, and she enjoyed being able to walk to work, as well as the choice of family-owned restaurants for picking up dinner on her way home.

So overall, Marit still had far fewer complaints and was much happier since making the move. She made good money, especially since she was single. She'd always invested responsibly, and she didn't have a lot of needs or vices. At twenty-eight, she thought she was doing more than all right, as far as making a living. She loved what she did, loved being on the water, even when weather conditions were less than ideal. And she truly enjoyed *most* of the people she worked with. The majority were hardworking, down-to-earth men.

Exceptions like Thorne Deaton were few and far between, thank goodness.

It was the end of another long day, and she'd gone to use the restroom as soon as she, Eliot, and Jonah returned to shore. She was returning to the *Wave Rider*—hoping to avoid more of the dubious looks she'd received from a couple of lobstermen on her way to the public facilities—when she saw a man standing on the dock next to the boat, talking to Eliot and his son.

He turned and eyed her up and down as she walked toward the trio. Usually that kind of visual inspection irritated her, but Marit didn't see any judgment in his eyes . . . or any leering, for which she was thankful.

"Hi," she offered as she approached.

"Marit, this is Zachary Young. He's a local boy who recently moved back home after doing a stint in the Navy. He owns The Lobster Buoy."

Marit's eyes widened. "Oh my gosh, really? I *love* that place!" And she wasn't simply being polite to the man. That lobster shack had some of the best food she'd ever eaten—and she considered herself a lobster expert, considering how much time she'd spent around the creatures.

Eliot went on to explain to the newcomer that she'd just started working for him, and that she'd moved up from Portland. She held out a hand to the man, wishing she was taller, as he was a giant. He towered over her five-two frame by more than a foot. Her head barely came to his shoulders. But she'd long gotten over being intimidated by men who were taller than her . . . simply because just about everyone over the age of twelve was taller than her.

"Marit Phillips," she said, introducing herself. "It's nice to meet you."

"Zach."

Zach's hand closed around hers—and she was surprised to feel a jolt move up her arm when he touched her. That had never happened to her before, and she had no idea what it meant.

She kept the smile on her face, not willing to give any hint that this introduction was different from the dozens of others she'd had in the last week. Eliot seemed to delight in introducing her to anyone and everyone he knew, so she'd met a lot of people recently.

But none had caused a reaction like this man.

When she pulled her hand back, Marit couldn't stop herself from taking a step backward, wanting to kick herself for letting even that small sign of discomfort show. She was known for being stoic; she'd learned not to let her true feelings show because they could and would be used against her . . . at least, they had in the past.

She listened as Eliot and Zach discussed how many lobsters he wanted, and as they chatted about the upcoming weather for the Lobster Fest. It was supposed to be sunny but not too hot, which was perfect for the vendors at the festival.

Eliot packed a crate full of lobsters for Zach, and without thought, Marit reached over and picked it up. It was heavy, but she'd been hauling lobster pots in and out of boats for years. It was no heavier than those. "I'll help you load up. Lead the way," she told Zach.

He stared at her for a beat, and she wanted to kick herself. This man didn't need her help. He could've easily carried the crate himself. But she was curious about the guy who'd caused such a reaction with just a simple handshake. Wanted to get to know him better.

Which was shocking. When was the last time she'd had the slightest interest in a guy? Years. It had been *years*. She'd been too busy working. And therefore, the men she saw the most were the ones she worked around every day . . . and they weren't exactly the type she envisioned for her future.

She didn't want to marry a lobsterman. She had nothing against them. She just assumed that, eventually, she'd get to a point in her life where the physical demands of working on a boat would become too much, and she'd transition to another career. And while she'd always be grateful for working on the boats, she wasn't sure she'd want to be around them forever, especially if she could no longer do the work. If she married a lobsterman, she'd end up tied to them for life.

To Zach's credit, he didn't ask if she could handle the crate of lobsters, he simply gave her a small smile and a nod as he leaned over to pick up the second, smaller box Eliot had loaded up for him.

They walked along the dock, toward the parking lot. Marit was at a loss as to what to talk about, now that Eliot and Jonah weren't there to contribute to the conversation.

She glanced over at the man next to her. Zach Young was good looking, there was no doubt. He was tall and slender, with dark hair and hazel eyes. He had a beard . . . well, it wasn't exactly a beard, but it wasn't a five-o'clock shadow either. It was the perfect amount of facial hair. Not scruffy at all. His biceps bulged as he shifted the box in his arms, and she couldn't help but notice his hands. The one closest to her looked a little rough, had a couple of small scars . . . and it was huge.

Of *course* her brain decided to go there. She was well aware of the correlation between the size of a man's hands and his . . . wait, was it his hands or feet?

Glancing down, she saw that Zach's feet were also large.

Before her mind could go somewhere inappropriate—or, to be honest, fall even deeper into that topic—she noticed he was limping. It was subtle, and if she hadn't been paying attention, she wouldn't even have noticed.

"Are you all right?" Her gaze swung up to his face.

He frowned. "Yeah, why?"

Marit second-guessed her question. She had a tendency to speak before thinking, which she was regretting right now. Men didn't like when any kind of flaw was pointed out. "Just checking," she said vaguely, quickly trying to come up with something else to say.

"No, why do you ask?"

Shoot. Fine. She'd just ask and get it over with. "You're limping. Not a lot, but . . ."

To her surprise, he grinned. "Didn't think it was noticeable."

"It's not. Not really," Marit was quick to say. "I'm just used to observing others."

He tilted his head at that, as if trying to figure out the deeper meaning behind her words. He was obviously intelligent and quick. Because there *was* a deeper meaning behind her need to study others. As a small woman, she always wanted to be ready to react however a situation merited. Whether that meant getting out of the way of a fist swung by a drunken lobsterman in a bar, or clearing the area of ropes that a careless coworker had coiled wrong on a boat . . . or figuring out what kind of mood one of her brothers was in so she could respond accordingly.

Not wanting to go *there*, she pushed thoughts of her siblings to the back of her mind, where they usually resided.

"Had two knee surgeries when I was in the Navy. Every now and then they ache. Especially when I've been standing for a long time. It's one of the reasons I got out of the military. Spending all that time standing in the galley was hell on my body."

"And you've been standing a lot lately, I'm guessing. Getting ready for Lobster Fest."

"Bingo," he said with another grin. "Not as long as you, though, I'm guessing. Working on a lobster boat isn't easy."

Marit couldn't help it, she chuckled. "I think that's an understatement."

"But you're good at what you do."

Her brows came down at that. "How do you know?"

"Because Eliot's not an idiot. He wouldn't hire someone who was incompetent."

"I've only been working for him a week," Marit protested.

"He'd know after one day if you were going to work out," Zach said with a small shrug.

"Have you known him long?"

"Years. He's been here as long as I can remember. I always saw him when I came home on leave from the Navy, and now that I'm home for good, I won't buy lobsters from anyone else if I can help it. I know he's not breaking any rules when he's on the water, he's not trying to sneak in larger-than-allowed lobsters, and he genuinely cares about the industry. The fact that you're still on his boat after a week tells me all I need to know about your work ethic."

His words felt good. Really good. The tingles she felt when she'd shaken his hand returned . . . tenfold. "When did you get back? To Maine, that is?" They were approaching a blue Ford Explorer that had a few dings but was still fairly new.

"This past spring. My dad died, and my brothers and I all decided to move home to help my mom out on Lobster Cove . . . that's the name of the property she lives on. Of course, my almost sister-in-law calls it *Alpha* Cove, because of the vibes my brothers and I give off . . . not to mention the other men who work at the various businesses there."

Marit's mind was already spinning. There was a lot of info in what he'd just said. Her brain was bursting with questions, wanting to know all about Lobster Cove, his mom, and of course, the businesses on the property. She wasn't thrilled with the fact that he had brothers, but that was her own prejudice. They were probably perfectly nice guys . . . maybe.

"This is me," Zach said unnecessarily as he put the box he was carrying on the ground next to the back of the Explorer and reached to open it.

When he opened the hatch, Marit saw the back of his SUV was full of fresh vegetables and other bags she assumed held food from the local grocery store. Zach turned and reached for the crate she was holding, making it seem as if the box weighed nothing, and placed it into the only available space in the cargo area. He placed the box he'd been carrying on top of the crate and shut the hatch. Then he turned to her.

Marit was suddenly tongue tied. She wasn't sure what to say. For the first time in years, she wanted to prolong her time with a man she'd just met. It was an unsettling feeling, and she had no idea why *this* man. Why now.

"You live around here? In town, I mean?"

Disappointment crept in at the question, as he hadn't seemed like the kind of man who would proposition a woman after just meeting her. But then again, she didn't know him. Not at all.

"Sorry, that sounded bad. I just . . . I'm sure you have stuff you need to do on the boat, and I need to get back to The Lobster Buoy and finalize my menu for tomorrow, but I was thinking maybe, if you live near here . . . I live a few blocks from town . . . maybe we could meet up and have dinner or something? It would have to be later. Around seven. And that might be *too* late, and I'd understand. You probably have to get up early to go back out onto the water. It was just a thought . . ."

He sounded so unsure. It was cute. This larger-than-life man stumbling over his words when he was asking her out.

Wait, *was* he asking her out? Would this be a date? She didn't date. Not really.

But for this man? She'd make an exception.

Marit had a feeling she'd do a lot of things she wouldn't normally do for Zach Young. He'd had that much of an impact on her with that handshake. Of course, he might eventually disappoint her. Might proposition her after dinner. Might ask to walk her home, then push her to invite him inside.

Disgusted that she was basically sabotaging this . . . *whatever* this was before it even started, she blurted before he could take back the offer, "Yes! I mean, yes, I live near town. I could meet you somewhere."

"Awesome. How about the Fog Bar and Café?"

"Where? I've never heard of it."

Zach looked surprised. "You haven't? It's right downtown. On Oak Street?"

"The only thing I've seen on Oak is Rock City Café . . . they have the best coffees. They aren't open before I head to the dock, but I often stop in and get one on my way home."

"Shoot. I hate that some really good restaurants I used to love aren't around anymore. I've been back for a few months and haven't even realized it wasn't here anymore."

"What about Rock Harbor Pub and Brewery? It's typical bar food, but filling."

"Perfect. Seven okay?"

"Yeah." Marit felt shy all of a sudden. A date. She had a *date*. It was almost surreal that she'd met this man less than ten minutes ago, and now she was making arrangements to meet him for dinner.

Zach smiled at her for a beat. Then asked, "You like lobster?"

Marit couldn't help it. She rolled her eyes. "No, I'm allergic."

He looked shocked.

She laughed. "Kidding! Yes! Of course I like lobster. I've made my career out of the creature."

"Right. Sorry. My plan is to make lobster and asparagus risotto as the special tomorrow at The Lobster Buoy. You want to try it and let me know what you think? I could bring you a sample. I know we're going out to eat, but . . ." His voice trailed off.

"Sure. I mean, I've loved everything I've tried from your shack, so I'm sure that'll be just as delicious. And for the record, I think it's cool that you've gone high-end, but you've also kept your prices reasonable. I, for one, appreciate that. Lobster rolls get old."

"I agree. When I decided to move home, I swore up and down that there was no way I was opening a lobster shack. They're a dime a dozen around here, and the last thing I wanted was to serve lobster rolls . . . and here I am, with a lobster shack."

"But not serving lobster rolls?" Marit asked with a smile.

"Well, I am. But I'm doing it my way. Fancy-pants lobster rolls."

"I haven't tried one yet, but now I think I need to."

She realized what she was doing . . . prolonging their conversation. She really did need to get back to the dock to do her fair share of the cleanup and to get ready for tomorrow morning. But this was the first time in ages that she was really enjoying talking to a man.

"Well . . . I'll bring you some risotto tonight, and you can give me your honest opinion. If it sucks, I expect you to tell me."

"Oh, I have no problem telling it like it is. I don't beat around the bush." Marit felt obligated to warn him about that.

"Good. I don't like when people say one thing but mean another. It's exhausting."

Relief spread throughout her. "Right. And now I need to get going. I'll see you later."

"Yes, you will," Zach said firmly.

Marit began to back away.

"Thanks for the help with the lobsters."

"You're welcome. See ya."

"See ya," Zach echoed.

Marit forced herself to turn and walk back toward the boats at the docks. She couldn't resist glancing over her shoulder toward Zach and his car, fully expecting to see him pulling out of the parking spot—but to her surprise, he was standing exactly where she'd left him. At the back of his SUV, staring at her.

Her cheeks turned pink, and she lifted a hand to wave at him . . . like a complete dork.

He smiled back at her and lifted his chin.

She sighed. Jeez, that was such a manly move. When she read about men doing that in the romances she sometimes read, she always thought it was super cheesy. That no one actually did that in real life. Boy, was she wrong. And it was hot.

As she stomped in her rubber boots back toward the dock, she couldn't keep the grin off her face. Moving to Rockville had been a necessary thing for her health and safety . . . and not only had she found a boat to work on where she felt comfortable and welcomed, she had a *date*.

Marit wished she had someone to share her giddiness with. To ask about the Young family, make sure they were good people. Eliot seemed to like Zach, but she didn't feel comfortable asking him, especially around Jonah. She'd gotten the feeling her coworker had a crush on her. She didn't encourage it, simply stayed friendly and kept things work oriented.

She hadn't made any good friends back in Portland either, and she was too new to Rockville to have met anyone outside the small lobstering community. She'd have to work on that.

It was too soon to say how tonight would go. But Marit was cautiously optimistic. She'd enjoyed the small bit of time she'd spent with Zach, and he did have Eliot's respect. And there was that reaction she'd had when they'd touched. Hopefully they were all good signs. Time would tell.

Chapter Two

Zach couldn't stop thinking about Marit Phillips. He'd met many women like her while he'd been in the Navy. Women who'd worked in male-dominated fields and flourished. Fighter pilots, mechanics, shooters, aircraft-handling officers.

But there was something a bit more . . . *vulnerable* about Marit.

Her eyes spoke to him. Drew him in. Made him want to get to know all her secrets and slay all her dragons. It was more than obvious she could slay her *own* dragons, but that didn't mean Zach wanted her to *have* to. It was a confusing thought, but he couldn't shake the belief that there was much more to Marit than most people bothered to get to know.

She was a tiny thing, but a dynamo. Clearly strong as hell. Tough. She had to be, in order to work on a lobster boat.

His mom would love her.

Zach blinked at the thought. From what he'd gleaned at first glance, Marit was a lot *like* his mom. And that idea should turn him off . . . but he was a mama's boy. He was the youngest of four brothers, the baby, and he'd been spoiled throughout his childhood. It didn't mean his brothers didn't pick on him mercilessly, but it *did* mean his mom went out of her way to cook his favorite meals more often, send him letters every week when he was deployed, and generally treat him like her favorite son.

That wasn't true; Zach knew that. She loved each of her sons equally. But he and his mom had a special bond. Once his brothers were out of the house, and it was just him and his parents, Zach and his mom grew even closer than they'd been before. He wouldn't trade that time for anything. He missed his brothers, but he'd reveled in the one-on-one attention.

He'd learned a lot about Evelyn Young during that time, and even more since. She was stubborn, hardheaded, hardworking, and she had a huge heart.

It was crazy that after knowing Marit Phillips for such a short time, he already suspected that she and his mom were cut from the same cloth. He couldn't wait to find out for sure.

He also couldn't remember the last time he'd been on a date. It had been way too long. But there was no denying he hadn't wanted to say goodbye to Marit that afternoon. He probably would've seen her the next day when he went to the dock to get more fresh lobsters for the shack, but in the moment, tomorrow had seemed like too far away.

He was very curious about her. Zach met a lot of people working in the food industry, and most of the time he made small talk and forgot about them a second later.

Marit was different. She intrigued him, and that was part of the reason why he'd asked if she wanted to go out for dinner. He wanted to get to know her better. A woman working on a lobster boat was unique, and he wanted to hear all about how she'd gotten into the profession and how she'd made her way to Rockville.

But more than that . . . he hadn't been as physically attracted to anyone as he was to Marit in a very long time.

It wasn't as if he didn't enjoy a woman's company. He did. With the ladies, he prided himself on being considerate, kind, and respectful . . . exactly as his parents raised him to be.

And as the youngest, he'd also gotten a lot of advice from his brothers on how to be a good lover. Zach hadn't had any complaints in that department.

But since moving home, he hadn't had time to think about sex at all. He'd been too busy helping around Lobster Cove and getting The Lobster Buoy up and running . . . and profitable.

The second he spotted Marit, however, something clicked inside him. It was a weird feeling, being almost desperate to talk to a woman. To experience those tingles he'd had when he'd first touched her.

For a moment, he thought she was going to turn him down when he'd asked her out. The immense relief he'd felt when she'd agreed made him realize something about this woman was different.

She was sexy in a subtle way. He wasn't sure many people would agree with him, especially considering how she was dressed that afternoon, in her fishing attire. But her strength was intriguing. If the way she hefted that crate of lobsters was any indication, she was most likely very muscular under those layers of protective clothing. And even though she was tiny, Zach bet she could hold her own against anyone who dared take her for an easy mark . . . physically or otherwise.

Her white-blonde hair was also unique in itself. Her sky blue eyes shone with intelligence, and her lips . . .

As Zach drove toward the parking area near his lobster shack, he squirmed in his seat, thinking of how those plump lips might look wrapped around his cock.

The thought was as arousing as it was startling. He just wasn't the kind of man who walked around thinking about sex all the time. Especially not lately. He was almost uncomfortable with how desperately he wanted to get to know her . . . in bed and out of it.

He parked in a space that was thankfully relatively close to The Lobster Buoy and turned off his engine. Closing his eyes, Zach took a deep breath. He couldn't rush this. Couldn't fuck it up. Marit seemed a bit skittish, and so he needed to go easy. They might have dinner tonight and find out they weren't compatible at all. Physical attraction was one thing, but Zach was done with one-night stands. True, he wasn't old at thirty, but he wanted what his parents had. What his older brother had found with Britt. Love. Respect. A relationship that could stand the test of time.

Could he have that with Marit? It was way too soon to tell. But he hadn't been this interested in a woman in . . . ever? It was crazy, as he knew nothing about her except that Eliot respected her and she worked on a lobster boat and enjoyed eating the beasts she caught every day.

A relationship with her wouldn't be easy, as they both worked long, irregular hours. Her on the water and him in the food industry. But they did have lobsters in common . . . maybe they could work with that?

Zach opened his eyes and blew out his breath. He was reaching and he knew it. Just because she caught the lobsters he loved to cook didn't mean a relationship between them could work.

Baby steps. Dinner tonight. Get to know her better. Bring her home to meet Mom.

So much for baby steps.

That last thought hit Zach hard. He was pretty sure his mom would love Marit, but what if she didn't? What if the women didn't get along? That was a hard line for him. Whoever he ended up with had to love Lobster Cove as much as he did. Had to enjoy spending evenings hanging out with his family.

Knowing he was thinking too hard about a simple date, Zach opened his door and slammed it behind him as he strode to the back of the SUV. He had risotto to make. He needed to think about *that*. Not about a future relationship he may or may not have with a woman he'd just met. And he had to make sure not to rush things either way. Taking Marit home to meet his family was a big deal, and not something that should happen on a first date.

Definitely not.

~

"You want to visit Lobster Cove? We could have dinner there. I'm sure my mom would love to meet you, and she loves my risotto."

Zach wanted to take the words back the second they left his lips. What had he *just* been thinking earlier today? To be cool. To take things slow. And here he was, inviting Marit back to his family property three seconds after seeing her for the second time in his life. He was an idiot.

He was running a little late by the time he'd gotten to Rock Harbor Pub and Brewery. Marit was waiting for him outside the bar and grill with a frown on her face. The restaurant was closed for a private party. He'd blurted out the suggestion about going home with him without even thinking about what he was saying.

"Um . . ." Marit said, biting her lip in indecision.

Zach wanted to say all kinds of things to convince her. Wanted to promise that his mom was awesome, and admit that she'd already said she'd love to meet her . . . because *of course* he'd already told his mom about the woman he'd met this afternoon. Explain how beautiful Lobster Cove was and promise it wasn't that far away—even if it would take twenty or so minutes to drive there.

Instead, all he could do was stare at her in awe . . . and lust.

He'd been attracted to this woman when she was wearing several layers of lobstering gear. But in jeans and a T-shirt? She was perfection. He was right, she was plenty muscular; he could see her defined biceps thanks to the short sleeves of her shirt. Her thighs and ass filled out her jeans perfectly, making his mouth water, and her tits looked like a nice handful. *His* handful. Which was bigger than average because of his size.

She'd also put on a bit of makeup, just a little, to highlight her long lashes and make her plump lips even more desirable. All in all, this woman hit all the right buttons for Zach, and it was taking a large amount of control on his part not to blurt out how fucking beautiful she was.

"How far away is it? I'm meeting Eliot and Jonah at five tomorrow morning."

"About twenty minutes. Not that far."

"Your mom's not expecting us though, right?"

"No. But I can call her on the way and tell her we're coming. Trust me, she won't have an issue with us coming over. I'm the baby of the family, she always wants to see me." Zach smiled, letting Marit know he was kidding . . . kind of.

Marit looked back in what he assumed was the direction of her apartment, then down the other end of the street. He could practically hear her thinking. About to suggest maybe they find another place to eat here in Rockville. But now that he'd offered, Zach found he really wanted to bring her to Lobster Cove. To the heart of his family.

"Mom hasn't tried this particular risotto. I told her about it earlier today, and she mentioned coming by to get some. If we go tonight, I can save her a trip to Rockville. I know she wants to spend the day making pastries tomorrow."

Shit. And now he was trying to influence Marit, when he'd *just* told himself he wasn't going to pressure her. For a second, he was positive she was going to decline.

Then he saw the decision in her eyes a split second before she spoke, and his knees went weak with relief.

"Okay. Why not. I never do anything but work and go home. I'll come. Should I drive?"

"Since we both have to come back to town, I'm happy to drive. That is . . . if you feel comfortable with it?"

Marit met his eyes then; she had to tilt her head back in order to do so. "Are you going to try to hurt me?"

"No." The answer was quick and heartfelt. Zach meant it in more ways than one. He would do his best not to hurt her tonight, or any other night, in any way.

"You should know that I'm no pushover. I've taken many self-defense classes. With my size, I've had to be sure I can protect myself. I can and *will* do whatever it takes to disable anyone who dares to think I'm an easy mark. And I already know your knees are your weak point. I can have you on the ground in seconds if you decide to try to overpower me."

Instead of being offended, Zach actually found himself turned on by her words. She was confident and, as promised, not afraid to tell it like it was. And knowing she could defend herself?

Yeah. He liked that.

"Good," he said fervently. "If I do anything out of line, I give you full permission to take me to the ground. It would serve me right."

Marit tilted her head as if trying to read his mind. To see if he was being honest or not. Then she nodded. "All right. Let's do this. But I probably need to be home by ten."

"That works for me, as I need to get up early myself to make the risotto for the shack, as well as help Jack get the other menu items cooking. I'm parked at my apartment, you can either wait here and I can swing by and pick you up, or you can walk with me." Zach held his breath, hoping she'd decide to come with him. He didn't want her to risk having second thoughts and bolting on him before he could get back to the restaurant to pick her up.

"I'll walk with you. It'll do me good. I do a lot of standing on the boat. I need to walk more."

"Same," Zach agreed. "Standing at the shack, cooking and serving customers, has been hell on my workout schedule."

"Jack is your employee?" Marit asked, as they started walking toward his apartment.

He had a container of risotto he'd brought for Marit in his hand, and he was suddenly very glad he'd packed more than he thought she'd eat. There was more than enough for his mom to try, as well. "Yeah. He's in his mid-fifties, a veteran, and grumpy as hell." He chuckled. "It's a good thing I don't need him to work directly with customers because I'd be bankrupt in a week."

"He can't be that bad," Marit said with a small laugh.

"The other day, he went out to get more rolls because we ran out, and when he came back it was especially busy. He walked up behind a woman with two small kids and growled 'Move,' instead of saying

'Excuse me.' He scared the kids and they started crying. The woman was offended, of course, and she stormed off. And that's just one incident."

Marit giggled. "Oh my," she said.

Zach returned her smile, loving the carefree sound of her laugh. "Yeah. He's a great cook. Can follow directions to a tee and doesn't try to deviate from any of the recipes I give him. Which makes him invaluable. But dealing with customers . . . let's just say it's not his forte."

"You like him," she observed.

"I like him," Zach agreed. "He's got some amazing stories from his time in the Marines, and he's a tough old bird. Doesn't care what others think of him, and he doesn't need a lot of material things in his life. He's single, lives in a trailer, and there's a heart of gold underneath the gruffness he shows to the world. He rescues injured and stray animals. Rehabilitates the wild animals if he can and releases them, and finds good homes for the dogs and cats."

"He sounds amazing. A lot of the guys I've worked with in the past sound like him. Rough around the edges and not politically correct, but if push came to shove, they'd give you the shirt off their backs."

"Exactly," Zach said. "Which is why I put up with his . . . not-so-great customer-service skills."

They approached the small lot behind the house where Zach's studio apartment was located, and he went to the passenger door, opening it for Marit. She nodded at him in thanks and sat. Zach went around to the driver's side and put the bag he was carrying in the back seat, then climbed behind the wheel.

On the way to Lobster Cove, he kept up a running commentary about the area and the places they passed along the way. Marit was quiet, nodding and looking interested in what he was telling her. When they pulled onto the curvy road that led to his childhood home, Zach told her all about the wreck Britt and his mom had endured not too long ago. About how the brakes in the CR-V were cut and the steering tampered with.

"Oh my gosh! They're okay?" Marit asked.

"Yeah. Thankfully it was high tide, not like now. If they'd gone off the side during low tide, things could've been a lot worse. We aren't sure when the court date will be for Otis and Camden, for the kidnapping and attempted murder of both Mom and Britt, but you can bet we'll all be there when it happens."

"Wow," Marit breathed.

"No one fucks with my family and gets away with it," Zach said earnestly. "The Youngs are tight. Which is why my brothers and I all came home after Dad died. Mom couldn't run all the businesses on the property herself. Chad was the one who had the idea, and honestly, it hasn't been without its ups and downs, but I'll never regret coming back. I love Maine, and I love my family. It's been nice to get to know my brothers as adults."

"Are they going to be here tonight?"

Zach heard a note of . . . something . . . in Marit's tone. He wasn't sure what it was. Trepidation? Regret that she'd agreed to come with him? Fear? Whatever it was, he didn't like it. Not one bit.

"Probably just Chad. After the shit went down with Otis—who was Mom's accountant—she made the decision to end the Lobster Cove Rentals business. Chad and Britt will move into the larger of the guesthouses on the property, a two-bedroom, after this tourist season is over. They're living in the main house right now. Knox and Linc have their own places near Rockville."

Marit nodded.

"Have you met my brothers?" Zach asked, pressing a little to try to figure out why she seemed so nervous.

"Not that I know of. Why?"

"No reason. They're good men. Knox was in the Coast Guard, and he works for them now as a contractor. Linc was a fighter pilot in the Air Force, and he . . . well, he doesn't do much right now, as far as a job. He helps at Lobster Cove, and he's busy fixing up the old house he bought. He was medically discharged, so he has a good pension from the Air Force. And Chad was in the Army."

"Huh. Four branches of the military?" Marit asked.

Zach grinned. "Yup. But of course, the Navy is the best."

To his relief, she chuckled. "I'm sure if I ask your brothers, they'll all disagree."

"Of course they will. But they're wrong."

Whatever it was he thought he heard in her tone was gone now, which was a relief for Zach. But he still wondered what seemed to worry her about his brothers.

"Here it is," Zach said, as he approached the long driveway that led to Lobster Cove. He and Marit had been talking so much, he'd forgotten to call to tell his mom they were coming by. He knew she wouldn't care, though. She'd be overjoyed to see him, and even more so to meet Marit.

Zach smiled when he saw the sign by the road. It was old, but he loved it. It was nostalgic, seeing it every time he came home.

He drove slowly, letting Marit take in everything as he approached the house. He tried to see it all through her eyes, but he had no idea what she was thinking as she looked around.

There was the auto body building, with cars parked neatly around the bays. The now-empty boat storage facility and yard, the two small rental houses in the distance, and of course, the main house. The sun hadn't set yet, and it currently glinted off the water in the cove. Every time he came home, Zach was struck once more by the beauty of the property. He'd grown up here, and he knew he was a lucky son of a bitch.

Then his stomach rolled as he took in the number of cars parked in front of the house. He'd told Marit that his brothers most likely wouldn't be here, but he'd been wrong. Both Knox's truck and Linc's SUV were here.

"Before we go in, I have to tell you something," Zach said seriously, after he'd turned off the engine. It was likely he had about a minute to talk to her before someone came to the door to welcome him home. There were sensors around the property letting his mom know if someone came down the driveway, so she knew he was there by now.

"Yeah?" Marit asked with a small tilt of her head.

Ignoring how adorable that was, Zach went on. "My brothers are here. I didn't know, I swear. And I have a feeling something about them makes you nervous. So we can leave right now if you want. This is our first date . . . at least, I hope that's what this is . . . and the last thing I want is to do something that makes you reconsider agreeing to a *second* date. Do you want to leave?"

The fear he thought he'd seen in her eyes earlier flared bright and strong now, before she controlled her emotions. She bit her lip and looked toward the house. Zach held his breath. He was curious as to why everyone was there, but he'd leave with Marit in a heartbeat if that was what she wanted . . . needed.

"It's okay," she said after a moment's hesitation.

"Are you sure?"

"No. But yes. I . . . I had two brothers."

She didn't elaborate, and Zach said, "I'm sorry for your loss."

Her gaze whipped back to his in surprise. "Oh, they aren't dead. They're just dead to *me*. I don't talk to them. Don't *want* to talk to them. Would prefer to pretend I don't have any siblings."

It was Zach's turn to be taken aback. "Okay."

Marit sighed. "It's a long story. I'm sure your brothers are good. Cool. Fine."

"They are," Zach reassured her, making a mental note to have a word with Knox, Linc, and Chad to tell them to go easy, give Marit space. He didn't know her story, why she had such a bad relationship with her own flesh and blood, but he wasn't naïve enough to think that everyone got along with their family. Hell, Britt's mother was the devil incarnate, so he understood that sometimes families weren't as close as his own.

"Zach! We were about to call you to come over. Get in here! Who's that with you?" Knox stood on the porch, hollering.

"You can change your mind at any time," Zach told her quickly. "I mean it. No matter what's going on, say the word and we're out of here. No questions asked."

She looked at him with a startled expression on her face. "So if we get to the porch and I change my mind, you'd turn around and leave?"

"Absolutely."

"Why?"

"Because I don't want you to be uncomfortable. Because I want to get to know you better. Because my family can be overwhelming at times. Because seeing that look of uncertainty on your face makes me want to do whatever I can to wipe it away and see you smile again. Because there's something about you, Marit Phillips, that's different from any other woman I've taken on a date."

"Oh."

"Yeah, oh. Shall we do this?"

"What are you guys doing in there? You aren't making out, are you?" Knox yelled across the yard, laughing hysterically at his own words.

Zach opened his door at the same time Marit did, and he heard his mom call out from inside the house, "Knox Young, behave! And stop yelling like a heathen!"

He chuckled, and when he looked over at Marit, he saw her lips quirk upward a tiny amount. Seeing that small smile made him feel a little better.

After grabbing the risotto, he met Marit at the front of his SUV and they walked toward the porch together. Zach ached to put his hand on the small of her back but resisted the urge. It was too soon. Too soon for a lot of things—like meeting his entire fucking family, but that was what it was at this point.

"Hey! I'm Knox. I'm the smart one of the Young brothers. What are you doing with *this* reprobate? You're much too pretty for Zach."

Zach could've sworn Marit inched closer to him at Knox's greeting, before visibly relaxing her shoulders and lifting her chin.

"He makes a mean lobster roll," she retorted.

Knox snorted and put a hand over his heart. "Foiled again because I can't cook worth a darn."

Zach glanced at Marit. "He burns water," he told her with a straight face.

"He's not wrong," his brother said with a chuckle. When Marit and Zach climbed the steps and reached the porch, he held out a hand. "Knox Young. It's nice to meet you."

"Marit Phillips," she said as she shook his hand.

"What're you doing here?" Zach asked, as he leaned in and gave his brother a one-armed hug.

"You'll see," Knox said mysteriously. "Come on. We really *were* just about to call you."

Zach gave in to the need to put his hand on Marit's back as he urged her forward behind his brother. The touch was fleeting, really only his fingertips brushing against the small of her back, but it was enough to send those same tingles that he'd felt the first time he'd touched her zinging throughout his body once more.

The smell of gingerbread filled his nose, and Zach inhaled deeply. His mom usually only made her gingerbread cookies on special occasions, and he wondered anew what was afoot.

"Zach!" his mom exclaimed, as she made a beeline for him. She hugged him with a surprisingly strong grip, then let go faster than usual. "Introduce me to your friend," she ordered, as she turned to Marit.

"Mom, this is Marit Phillips. She works with Eliot Sullivan on the *Wave Rider*. Marit, this is my mom, Evelyn Young."

"It's so nice to meet you, Marit," his mom gushed. "Welcome to Lobster Cove!" Then she leaned in and gave Marit a longer hug. They were about the same size, his mom only a couple of inches taller than Marit. Her light-gray hair almost matched Marit's white-blonde color.

But Zach could see how uncomfortable Marit was with the affection. His mom was a hugger. She was very touchy-feely, but it was obvious Marit wasn't.

"All right, Mom. Enough," Zach said gently, putting his hand on his mom's elbow. Not to pull her away from Marit, but as a warning.

His mom wasn't stupid, and she immediately let go. "Sorry," she said with an easy smile. "I'm a hugger. I forget that others aren't. Come in, come in. I'm making cookies."

"I brought a lobster and asparagus risotto for Marit and you to try, but I didn't make enough for everyone."

"It's okay. I grilled up some ranch chicken and green beans. We were just sitting down to eat when you got here. Great timing, son."

"Hey," Lincoln said from the kitchen, where he was spooning the fresh green beans into a bowl.

"Hey, bro. Marit, that's Linc, the oldest. And that's Chad, and his girlfriend, Britt."

"It's nice to meet you," Marit said politely.

Thankful that both his other brothers could see how uncomfortable Marit was with all the attention on her, they simply returned her greeting before going back to what they were doing. Chad continued to set the table—with two additional places—while Britt approached Zach and Marit.

"You work on a lobster boat?" she asked with a friendly smile.

"I do," Marit agreed.

"That's so cool! I've always wanted to go out on one. I haven't had the chance since I've been here though."

"Maybe after the summer season is over, I could ask if Eliot would take you out for a bit."

"Really? That would be awesome! Chad! Did you hear? Marit's going to take me out on a real live lobster boat!"

"I heard, Peach. I mean, you're standing right there." He grinned at her.

Britt rolled her eyes and turned back to Marit. "You get used to their smartass-ness . . . kind of."

To Zach's relief, Marit seemed to relax a little more. He wasn't sure if it was just the presence of another woman around her age that made her not quite so tense, but he was grateful.

"Come on, everyone sit. Except you, Zach. You need to dish up that risotto so Marit and I can try it," his mom ordered.

"It's not fair that you didn't bring enough for all of us," Knox grumbled.

"If someone had invited me for dinner—which it seems that you were going to have without me—maybe I would've brought more. As it is, you can always come down to The Lobster Buoy and get some tomorrow," he told his brother.

"But the line is always so long," Knox whined.

Linc nodded. "Which means little bro is doing all right for himself. Give it up, Knox. You'd eat a corn dog someone dropped on the street if it meant you didn't have to cook for yourself."

"Not true," Knox argued. "Maybe a donut. Especially one from Ruckus Donuts. But not a corn dog. Gross!"

Everyone laughed. Probably because they knew Knox wasn't really kidding. He had a huge sweet tooth, but couldn't cook or bake worth a damn.

Turning toward Marit, Zach whispered, "Okay?"

She knew what he was asking without him having to expound. She nodded. "I'm starving and everything smells delicious."

Of course she was hungry. She'd burned a lot of calories hauling pots all day.

Zach still wanted to know what was up with his family, but as always, they wouldn't let him in on whatever was going on until they were ready. Until then, he'd enjoy spending time with his loved ones and getting to know Marit better.

Chapter Three

Marit couldn't believe she'd volunteered to take Britt on the *Wave Rider*. First off, it wasn't her place to invite people onto Eliot's boat. Second, she wasn't sure she wanted to prolong a relationship with anyone associated with the Young family. She liked Zach, had been attracted to him from the first moment she'd seen him, was *still* attracted to him . . . but the fact that he had three brothers made her very uneasy. Made her less sure about getting involved with him.

She had a bad history with brothers. Starting with her own. But over time, those bad feelings extended to *any* brothers. Unfair, she could admit . . . but she couldn't help that the very word itself was a constant reminder of the awful men she'd left behind. The ones she tried hard to forget.

If she'd met any one of the Young men individually, she likely wouldn't have any issue with them. It was seeing them together, acting all . . . chummy, that set off the bad memories in her head. Making her remember her own brothers, always ganging up on her.

Forcing her thoughts away from the past, Marit did her best to enjoy dinner, concentrating on the here and now.

And to their credit, Chad, Linc, and Knox weren't behaving like her brothers. First off, they were clearly being respectful of her boundaries. They could tell she was nervous—whether they knew it was because of *them* or not, she couldn't say. But they didn't press her to talk. Instead, they made jokes and picked on each other throughout dinner, but in a friendly way. Not in the mean-spirited, hateful way that she was used to with siblings.

Also, watching them take care of their mother was . . . a revelation. They made sure her water glass was always full. When she dropped her fork on the floor, Linc jumped up to get her a new one. They patiently waited while she took her fill of the food—along with Britt and Marit, actually—before any of them dug in, and the compliments on her cooking were plentiful and sincere.

Overall, their respectfulness and attentiveness surprised her. It was as if the brothers were wired to see to the needs of the women at the table before their own. It was a shock for someone like Marit, who'd been looking after herself from a young age. Who lived and ate alone as an adult . . . and even before.

By the time the meal was nearly over, Marit reluctantly admitted she may have been wrong about this particular set of brothers.

And as it turned out, Zach had brought more than enough of his lobster and asparagus risotto for everyone to sample. It was so damn good, Marit thought she'd died and gone to heaven. Creamy, rich, and whatever Zach had used to spice it complemented both the rice and the asparagus.

"This will be gone in a heartbeat," she told Zach honestly. "As soon as the first person tries it, they're gonna exclaim about how amazing it is, and everyone else in line is gonna forgo the stupid lobster roll they were going to get and buy this instead."

"Oooh, what if you put this on *top* of the lobster roll? That would be amazing!" Britt added.

"I don't know, a huge bowl of this would be enough all by itself," Linc countered.

"Of course it would, but if you could get them to buy both a lobster roll *and* the risotto, you'd make twice as much," Britt suggested.

"But then you'd need to change the name. And what the hell *is* risotto, anyway?" Knox asked.

Everyone laughed.

Marit secretly agreed with him. But "rice with asparagus" didn't sound nearly as fancy or appealing.

"You ready for Lobster Fest?" Chad asked.

Zach snorted. "No. I remember from us growing up and going to the festivals how crowded and busy they always were. And from what I understand from other vendors, it's just grown since then. I'm second-guessing how many lobsters I need to buy each day to meet demand and what items I want on the menu. I want stuff that's quick and easy to make to keep the line moving, but it needs to be different . . . special. Not typical."

"I have faith in you," Evelyn said. "You're going to do great, son."

"Thanks, Mom."

"You need help?" Linc asked.

Marit glanced at Zach's older brother in surprise.

"If you're volunteering, yes," Zach was quick to say.

"You paying in food? Because if that's the case, I'll talk to my boss and see about getting some time off to help too," Knox said.

"The rental houses are booked for next week. I mean, of course they are," Chad said. "But I'm sure Britt and I can still find some time to come by and do whatever needs doing, as well."

"You guys are the best. Thank you. I'll definitely let you know if I need some extra hands."

Marit's chest felt tight. It was more than obvious this family was a true unit. She should've known that when Zach said he and his brothers had moved back to Maine because their mom needed help. But actually seeing the closeness and cohesiveness and willingness to help each other was a whole other thing. Something she had no experience or familiarity with.

Even on the lobster boats, competition was a big thing. Everyone was competing against everyone else. For the best lobsters, the biggest catch, and to work on the best boats. True, when a disaster happened, lobstermen tended to work together, but after the crisis was over, it was right back to being cutthroat.

"Mom, I'm gonna take Britt out to the beach so we can look for sea glass. You need any help before we head out there?" Chad asked.

Evelyn quickly shook her head. "No, I think with all the help around here, you guys can have a night off from dishes."

"Oh, but we can still help," Britt protested. "It's not a big deal."

"No, you two go on. We got this," Linc assured them.

Chad pulled Britt up from her seat and took her hand in his. "Come on, Peach. Before they change their minds and make us mop the floors or something."

Britt laughed. "As if you've mopped in the last month or so."

Chad smiled at her and they headed for the door that led to the back deck. Marit had spotted stairs off the deck earlier, so she assumed they'd head down to the beach that way.

The second the door shut behind them, Evelyn shoved her chair back and grabbed her plate. Knox and Linc did the same, both of them grinning.

"Come on, Zach! Get your and Marit's plates in the sink so we can go watch," his mom said urgently.

"Watch what?" Zach asked, sounding confused but obediently standing and reaching for her plate.

"He's doing it! He's proposing to Britt!" Evelyn said with so much glee, Marit couldn't help but smile.

"Holy shit, he is?" Zach asked.

"Language. And yes! We need to give them a second to get to the beach, but then we can sneak onto the deck and watch!"

So that was why the whole family was here. It was obvious Zach had no idea, but his other brothers were in on the secret.

"Why didn't anyone tell me?" he grumbled, as he brought their plates to the sink. "I would've made a cake or something."

"And totally given away that something was up," Linc countered. "It's bad enough Mom couldn't help herself and made her gingerbread cookies. It's a good thing Britt doesn't know she only makes those on special occasions. And for the record, I didn't know until Mom called and ordered me to come over for dinner tonight. I almost said no, because I have stuff to do on the house, but she insisted and ended up spilling the beans on why she wanted me here."

"Same with me," Knox agreed. "I was supposed to work late, but managed to get off on time and came straight here."

"I was going to tell *you*, but you weren't answering your phone," Evelyn accused, giving Zach a look.

Marit almost laughed when he wrinkled his nose in obvious chagrin. "I was working," he said simply.

"Right . . . so, now you know. Come on, everyone stay quiet on the deck. We don't want Britt to suspect anything. Linc, you're going to take pictures, right?"

"Yes, Mom. I got it."

"She has to suspect something's up," Knox said, as they all made their way toward the deck door. "It's not as if they've ever actually found any sea glass on our beach. There just isn't much glass in our cove."

"True. But I think she's gonna be pretty happy with the rock she finds this evening," Evelyn practically cackled.

"Please tell me Chad didn't go down earlier and hide a ring in the rocks on the beach," Zach asked. "With his luck, a seagull or eider duck has stolen it by now if he did."

Evelyn smacked Zach on the shoulder playfully. "Of course not. It's in his pocket."

"You've seen the ring?" Linc asked their mom.

"Of course. I helped narrow down which one he wanted to give her."

Marit couldn't help but smile at the exchange between mother and sons. But she felt like an outsider. She wasn't sure she should be here for such an intimate moment in this family. Though it wasn't as if she could tell Zach she wanted to leave. She had a feeling if she asked, he wouldn't hesitate. He'd leave before seeing his brother propose to Britt if that's what she wanted to do.

It was a strange feeling to have. To know that someone would willingly give up something important to themselves, just for her.

She wasn't sure what to do with that knowledge. Especially after only knowing Zach for such a short time.

She pushed the unsettling feeling to the back of her mind and followed the others out onto the deck.

The land the house sat on was gorgeous, of that there was no doubt. Marit saw water views every day, all day. She'd thought she was immune to the beauty of coastal Maine. But she was wrong. The sun was just starting to set, the trees around the cove were in full bloom, and there was a slight breeze, making the temperature comfortable, if not a little cool for her in her T-shirt.

She could see Chad and Britt wandering hand in hand on the pebble beach, beyond the deck where they were all standing. Every now and then, the couple would stop and lean down to inspect something on the ground, then continue meandering along slowly.

Then, as Marit and the rest of the Youngs watched, Chad reached into his back pocket and subtly dropped something behind him. He immediately called to Britt and pointed to whatever he'd surreptitiously dropped. She joined him, crouching to take a look . . . and by the time she'd stood up and turned around, Chad had gotten down on one knee.

Marit could hear Linc snapping pictures with his phone as the scene played out in front of them.

One of Britt's hands flew up to her mouth as Chad took the other, holding the ring he'd pulled out of his pocket and sliding it onto her finger. They all saw Britt nod, and then she threw herself at Chad. He kept them both from falling to the ground, holding Britt in his arms. He swung her around in a circle, then stopped and took her face in his hands. He said something before lowering his head to kiss her.

It was a long, intimate kiss that clearly showed how much the couple was in love.

Marit wasn't a romantic woman. She'd lived too hard a life to have so much as a romantic bone in her body. But standing on the Youngs' deck in the waning light of the day, watching two people she'd just met—and found she actually liked quite a lot—pledge to spend the rest of their lives together . . . it made her long to find someone who loved her as much as Chad obviously loved Britt. To find someone who understood her, who would support whatever it was she wanted to do with her life.

Someone she could laugh with, cry with, and simply coexist with peacefully in the same space.

And it was that last bit Marit wasn't sure she'd ever find. It had been her experience that peaceful coexistence was the hardest part. Her own family couldn't figure out how to do that. How could she find it with someone who didn't share her blood?

But then again, she was watching proof that it *could* happen. At least for some people.

"That was beautiful," Evelyn said as she sniffed.

Knox handed her tissues he'd obviously brought outside with him, prepared for his mom to cry at watching one of her sons get engaged.

Then Linc let out a whoop, scaring the crap out of Marit. Knox joined in, yelling exuberantly and clapping enthusiastically. Zach whistled, adding to the cacophony of excitement. Evelyn clapped as well. Then yelled, "Please tell us she said yes!"

"Of course I said yes!" Britt yelled back. Then she threw her head back and laughed as Chad spun her in a circle once again.

This was . . .

Marit couldn't wrap her mind around what was happening. Intellectually, she understood, but it was so far from anything she'd ever experienced. Genuine happiness and camaraderie between siblings. Chad wanting to share this intimate and huge moment with his family. Allowing himself to be vulnerable in front of those he loved. What would've happened if Britt had said no? But she supposed he had to have been pretty sure she was going to agree to marry him, if he chose to ask in such a public way.

She thought about her own brothers. They would've no sooner invited her to be a part of asking a woman to marry them than give her a helping hand if she was hanging off a four-hundred-foot cliff, ready to plunge to her death. They'd be more likely to stand by and berate her for being idiot enough to get herself into that situation in the first place.

She felt like an interloper here. Zach had brought her home thinking it would be a quiet dinner with his mom and one brother. He had no clue they'd be witnesses to a marriage proposal.

"This is awesome," he said, turning to Marit with a huge grin on his face.

She did her best to return his smile, but she had a feeling it missed the mark when his grin slowly disappeared. He stared at her intently, as if reading her mind and knowing she was two seconds from bolting off the porch and going to sit in his car.

Before she could blurt out that she wanted to go home, Chad and Britt returned to the deck. Everyone took turns hugging the newly engaged couple while Marit stood back, feeling even more awkward and out of place. She was surprised when Britt actually hugged her too. She didn't say anything, but Marit could literally feel her happiness.

The atmosphere on the deck was thick with excitement. She sensed nothing but genuine pleasure for the couple.

"There weren't any boats in the cove blowing their horns, and there's no lobster dinner, but I did manage the beach, the ring, and my family cheering from the deck," Chad told Britt, as he wrapped an arm around her waist and pulled her into his side, once everyone had gotten their hugs out of the way.

Britt laughed. "It was perfect. Having your family here was the icing on the cake."

Again, Marit felt as if she was in the twilight zone. The comparisons between this family and her own were like night and day, and she was struggling to wrap her mind around the dynamics. No wonder Zach had wanted to come home to Maine to help his mom. If Marit had been as close to her brothers as the Youngs were to each other, she had a feeling her life would be much different.

"We have one more thing to share," Chad said with a huge smile on his face, as he looked down at his fiancée.

"You're pregnant!" Evelyn blurted excitedly. "Please tell me I'm going to be a grandma!"

Everyone chuckled.

"We're pregnant!" Britt confirmed. "Well . . . we *think* we are. It's a little too early to know for sure, but I missed my period and the line on the test was faint, but still there. I've already scheduled a doctor's appointment, but if we're right, we'd be due in April!"

Instead of whooping with joy, Evelyn burst into tears.

She was immediately surrounded by her four sons, all clearly panicking at seeing their mom cry as they tried to console her and figure out what was wrong.

"I'm so happy!" she exclaimed finally, as the tears continued to course down her cheeks. "You all have no idea how long I've waited for this moment!"

"Actually, we do," Linc said dryly.

"Yeah, it's not as if you've been subtle in your hints that we all need to find women and settle down and give you grandbabies," Knox added.

"Well, at least Chad listened to me," Evelyn grumbled, as she wiped her cheeks.

Everyone laughed again.

Marit had already taken a step backward toward the door to the house. She needed to get away from all this happiness. Her emotions were all over the place. She was honored that she'd gotten to be a part of Britt and Chad's big evening, but she *really* felt like she shouldn't be there.

As if he could feel her pulling away, Zach said, "Happy for you, bro. You too, Britt. Thank you for sharing your moment with us. But unfortunately, Marit and I need to get going. We both have to get up at the crack of dawn tomorrow. Her to go lobstering, and I need to get to The Lobster Buoy and start cooking. If you need anything, give me a yell. We'll talk soon."

Before she could blink, Zach was leading her back through the house toward the front door. She'd had just enough time to give her thanks to Evelyn for the dinner and let the others know it was good to meet them.

Being polite in public was one thing her brothers had always insisted on . . . behind closed doors, that was another story.

Zach didn't say anything as he led her to his car. When he'd taken her hand in his, she couldn't say, but she was grateful. It felt like if he wasn't holding on to her, she'd splinter into a thousand pieces.

She wasn't sure why she was struggling so much with everything that had happened and what she'd witnessed. She'd always thought she was pretty tough. She could withstand freezing temperatures on a lobster boat, spend hours doing the backbreaking, monotonous work without complaint, and she could hold her own against men a foot taller and a hundred pounds heavier than her.

But emotionally? She was obviously a freaking mess.

She kind of zoned out while Zach was driving back toward Rockville, lost in her own mind. Trying to sort through her emotions without much luck. It wasn't until she felt the car stop that she blinked and looked around.

They weren't in Rockville. Zach had parked in a tiny gravel parking lot of sorts, and she could see a sign indicating they were at some kind of conservation area.

"I know it's late, but I thought maybe you could use a walk to clear your head. It's about half a mile to the shore from here. There's an easy trail. Flat. So even though it's almost dark, it won't be dangerous. You want to walk? Or have me take you home?"

Looking over at Zach, she saw he was staring at her with a concerned expression on his face. His brows were drawn together into a frown . . . and she felt guilty. He should be on top of the world. His brother was engaged and he was apparently going to be an uncle. Instead, he was clearly able to read her like a book—and was worried about her.

It was a weird feeling. To have someone *see* her so clearly. Marit was used to fading into the background most of the time.

"Walk," she said quietly. Maybe he was right. Maybe it would help settle her mind.

Zach nodded and opened his door. She did the same and they met at the back of his car. As if they'd done it a hundred times before instead of just once, Zach took her hand in his and started off for the path between the tall grasses.

"I'm sorry," Marit blurted as they headed out.

"For what?" Zach asked, not sounding put out in the least.

"For making you leave your family early. For crashing what was an intimate family event tonight."

"First, you didn't make me leave. We *do* need to get up early, and trust me, my family has a way of sucking you in and making you forget what time it is. If I hadn't taken that moment to escape, we could've been there until three in the morning.

"Second, you didn't crash anything. My mom was thrilled to meet you and to have you there, and Chad and Britt were in their own world. There could've been an entire circus watching and it wouldn't have changed how special that moment was for them. Besides, you weren't the only non-family member there. The guests currently renting the cabins were watching from the path along the shore. You didn't see them?"

Marit blinked. "They were?"

"Yup. Chad knew they were there. He waved to them on his way back up to the deck. Trust me, he loves the attention, and he had no problem with you being there."

That actually made Marit feel a little better. She nodded.

"I hesitate to bring this up, because it *is* our first date after all, but . . . you want to talk?"

She didn't play dumb. Zach was smart. He'd obviously seen her reticence and semipanic at being around his brothers.

She was collecting her thoughts when he continued.

"I know we just met, but there's something about you, Marit. Something different from any other woman I've met. I felt a connection with you that first time I shook your hand. And tonight, I could see your distress. If there's something about my family that's bothering you, please tell me. You said you hadn't met my brothers before tonight, but I can't think of any other reason why you'd be so nervous around them."

Marit had never met a man like Zach. Someone so astute. Who wasn't into playing games. Wasn't following any kind of playbook for getting to know a woman. He laid his thoughts out there. She actually appreciated that. She'd spent too much of her life trying to second-guess and anticipate what others might be thinking or what they were planning on doing.

"My parents died when I was twelve. Boating accident. My brothers were saddled with the task of raising me. They were extremely resentful and bitter that they had to look after me."

"Shit, Marit. I'm so sorry," Zach said softly.

They were still walking along the grassy path, and Marit stared straight ahead as she spoke. Maybe if he learned about her past now, it would save her some heartbreak later when he decided he couldn't deal with her baggage.

"How old were they? Your brothers, when your parents passed?"

"Eighteen and twenty. I was an oops baby. A preemie at that. I think Maxwell and Maverick also resented the attention I got when I was little, because of my health issues. And when my parents died, they felt forced to become my guardians because of pressure from the community we lived in."

"Where was that? Maine?"

Marit shook her head. "No. Out in Oregon. I moved away from there as soon as I could, and went as *far* as I could. All the way to Portland, Maine."

Zach squeezed her hand but didn't say anything. Which Marit appreciated. He could've tried to justify her brothers' behavior by saying they were young and probably mourning their parents. Or by saying they'd done their best to become parents to an almost teenager. She'd heard all the excuses for Max and Mav—and she knew none of them were true.

The truth was, they were simply two bullies. Two men who loved having power over others. And having control over and responsibility for their little sister was something they alternately reveled in and resented.

"Max and Mav fought all the time. With each other, with the manager of the grocery store, with the postman, with my principal, with me. They told me all the time how worthless I was. How things would've been easier if I'd just died when I was born. How Mom and Dad's deaths were my fault."

"That's bullshit!" Zach blurted. "How was a boating accident your fault?"

Marit shrugged. "It wasn't. But that didn't stop my brothers from saying it anyway. They did everything they could to tear me down. And when I refused to bend to their will, they made it their goal in life to break me."

Zach squeezed her hand again, and just that little show that he was there, listening, empathizing, helped her to continue. She almost never talked about this stuff. She might as well get it all out now.

"The thing is . . . I know people say that blood is thicker than water. That you should love your family unconditionally. That they're the people you'll know the longest in your lifetime. But Max and Mav . . . they taught me that family means *nothing*. They showed a good face in public when they had to, but at home, they made my life miserable. Forced me to do all the cleaning and cooking, and yelled at me the entire time I did any of it. Smacking me when I dared to back talk them. My grades were C's at best, simply because they didn't leave me any time to do my homework or study. Of course, they called me stupid as a result."

"Where are they now?" Zach asked.

"No clue. And I don't *want* to know. I don't want them to know where I am either. As far as I'm concerned, I have no family. I'm better off that way. But I think I'm doing just fine without them. Better than if I'd had to continue to deal with them, actually.

"Anyway . . . when I heard you had three brothers . . . it threw me for a loop, for obvious reasons. I have some baggage when it comes to family."

"I understand."

Once again, she appreciated that he didn't immediately start explaining how great *his* family was. How his brothers were nothing like hers. He didn't need to state the obvious.

"I love this spot," he said, as they came to the end of the path. In front of them was another cove. Not Lobster Cove, as they'd driven too far from the house for it to be the same area. There were lights from a few houses across the water, and there was a boat moored in the middle of the cove. It was beautiful. Quiet. Peaceful.

"I've been on the water most of my adult life," Zach told her. "Of course, most of that time I was in the belly of a huge ship making meals for the thousands of sailors and Air Force personnel aboard, but one of my favorite things to do was go up on the outer decks at night when most people were sleeping and stare at the stars. It reminded me so much of home. How my brothers and I used to sleep on the beach, or the back deck, and look up at the stars and brag about all the great things we were going to do with our lives.

"And while I think each of us did do some amazing things, coming home was the best decision we've ever made. Being with Chad, Linc, and Knox again . . . it's like a part of me that went missing when Linc first left home for college is finally whole again. I'm sorry you didn't have that with your brothers. But, Marit . . . that's *their* loss. They will never know what they're missing, and that's sad."

For the first time in her life, a little bit of weight seemed to lift from Marit's heart. Zach was right. Her brothers had always treated her as if she was a burden. Less than them. But the truth was, she'd made it. Thrived on her own. She was damn proud of all that she'd accomplished. Sure, she'd had a shit adolescence, but that didn't mean the rest of her life was shit too.

"Yeah," she agreed quietly.

"You want to sit for a minute?" Zach asked, gesturing to a bench sitting on the shoreline.

Marit nodded.

It was dark now, but the moon was full, giving them plenty of light to see where they were walking without the need of a flashlight. The July evening was mild on the water, and Zach's hand in hers felt . . . good.

It was a lame word, but Marit couldn't remember a time when she'd felt this relaxed. And that was saying something, considering she'd just had a very stressful night and just talked about her nasty brothers for the first time in years.

As she sat next to Zach, she realized it was the man next to her who was making her feel relaxed. He didn't judge. Didn't feel the need to fill the air between them with words. He was simply existing in this beautiful place with her.

She couldn't help thinking of Lobster Cove . . . and the fact she'd despaired of ever finding someone to just coexist with peacefully, the way Britt and Chad had found each other. Was that really less than thirty minutes ago?

Her stomach twisted at the thought, a combination of nerves and excitement.

Turning, Marit studied Zach. He was staring out over the water with a serious expression on his face. She realized anew how handsome he was. He could have any woman he wanted. So why he was with *her*, why he'd asked *her* out, she had no idea. But she felt lucky.

It was a strange feeling. She'd felt as if she'd gotten the short end of the stick for most of her life. Between her health issues when she was younger, her short stature, her parents dying, her shit brothers, the issues she'd had in Portland with Thorne Deaton, she'd always felt decidedly *unlucky*.

Now, after spending the evening with people who obviously loved each other deeply, seeing their loyalty to each other, being a witness to Chad and Britt's engagement, seeing Evelyn so happy about becoming a grandmother, and now sitting here at some unknown cove, her hand in Zach's . . . she felt extremely fortunate.

"What are you thinking about so hard?" she blurted, wanting to know what was going through Zach's head to make him look almost ferocious.

"How much I want to bash your brothers' heads in."

Marit blinked in surprise. Her lips quirking upward, she grinned, then she began to laugh.

Zach glanced at her. "I'm serious."

"I know you are," she said, still chuckling. "I was just sitting here thinking how lovely your family is. And then you come out with that."

He shrugged. "For what it's worth, it takes a lot to get me riled up. But make no mistake, Marit, I won't sit back and let those I care about be abused in any way. Verbally, mentally, or physically. I hate that you had such a piss-poor experience with your family."

Every word out of his mouth made Marit like him even more. She'd already been impressed that he seemed to always say what he was thinking, didn't play games, was loyal to the extreme. This violent side of him didn't scare her in the least . . . because she had an innate feeling she'd never see that anger turned toward *her*.

As she stared into his hazel eyes, she felt her body stirring. She wanted Zach. Wanted to know how it felt to have all that intensity he demonstrated when he talked about defending those he cared about, centered totally on her.

Marit licked her lips and her nipples hardened as his gaze dropped to her mouth. He shifted just a touch closer, and she wanted his lips on hers more than she'd wanted almost anything in her life.

She leaned into him and lifted her chin.

Zach's free hand came up and caressed her cheek in a barely there caress. "May I kiss you?"

Shit. She was a goner. All that other good stuff she already liked about this man, and now he was asking for consent? That feeling of being lucky came back tenfold.

"Yes. Please."

Zach leaned closer, taking his time. Heightening the anticipation. He licked his lips, and Marit was almost panting with how much she wanted this. Him.

"If you go out with me, you're probably going to see a lot of my brothers. My mom. I'm a mama's boy. Is that going to be an issue?"

He didn't need to warn her. She definitely understood that he and his family were a package deal. She wasn't sure she could do it when she'd first learned of his brothers, but now? After spending the evening with them? After seeing everyone interact and not detecting one iota of the traits she'd observed in Max and Mav?

She decided it was about time she tried to get over her fear of family. Logically, she knew that not everyone was like her brothers. Most families were decent and loving. And Zach admitting he was a mama's boy made her want to laugh. She could see how much his mom doted on him. He was the baby of the family, after all.

"Marit?" Zach asked warily, still inches away. His hand had come to rest on the side of her neck while she'd been contemplating his words.

"No, it won't be an issue," she whispered.

As soon as the last word was out of her mouth, Zach's lips were on hers.

She thought he might take things slow. Instead, his tongue immediately demanded entry into her mouth, and as soon as she opened for him, he took control. Tilting her head, tightening his hand on her neck, and moving his other hand to her waist as he devoured her.

The attraction Marit had felt before bloomed into full-fledged desire. The man knew how to kiss. He wasn't shoving his tongue down her throat, but caressing her possessively. Showing her without words how skilled he was when it came to satisfying a woman.

They were both panting when he finally pulled back. But he didn't go far. He kissed her nose. Then her forehead. Then her cheeks. Then he went back to her lips as if he couldn't get enough.

By now, Marit was more than ready to strip off all her clothes and let Zach take her right then and there. It wasn't as if there was anyone around to see them. He could've done anything he wanted to her—and she would've let him. But his hands didn't stray past her neck or her waist. While his kiss communicated how much he wanted her, he obviously wasn't going to attempt to go any further tonight.

One of Marit's hands slipped under his T-shirt, and she dug her nails into his lower back. The other gripped one of his biceps hard as he continued to kiss her. How long they made out on the bench, she had no idea. She only felt regret when he finally stopped.

The smile he gave her was both wicked and tender at the same time.

Marit felt off balance. All this was so new. She'd never wanted to sleep with a man on a first date. But looking into Zach's gaze, she swore she could see their future looking back at her. He was as open with his reverence and desire as he was with his words. This man had way more layers than she guessed anyone would suspect. And he was with *her*.

Just like that, her self-esteem rose. If he liked her, she had to be kind of special, right? He wouldn't still be single at his age if he wasn't picky.

"I like that smile," Zach said, brushing a lock of hair off her forehead.

"You're very good at kissing," she blurted.

"It's not me, it's you. You inspire me," he insisted. Then he turned serious. "Thank you."

"For what?"

"For trusting me not to go too far. For letting me kiss you. For being open minded about my family. They'll grow on you if you let them. I'm not saying they can't be annoying, because they can. But my brothers are good people. Once you win them over, which I think you've already halfway done, they'll have your back for life. No one messes with a Lobsterite . . . that's those of us who belong to Lobster Cove. You need something and you can't get a hold of me, you call Chad. Or Linc. Or Knox. Or Walt or Barry, who work at the auto shop. They'll get what you need or get to you, no matter the situation."

That was intense, but the warm feelings continued to spread through Marit. She nodded, overwhelmed. Yesterday, she'd been alone in the world, and today she felt as if she had a brand-new family. It was strange. And Marit was very aware that this was only her first date with Zach. Things could go south and she could lose everything he was dangling in front of her, but she wasn't going to dwell on that right now. She felt too damn good.

"Shoot. Now I've freaked you out. Come on, let's get you home so you can get your beauty sleep before having to get back on the water in the morning."

Zach stood and reclaimed her hand before they began walking back toward the path.

"I . . . I'm not freaked out," Marit told him as they walked.

He glanced at her and lifted a brow.

"Okay, maybe a little. But in a good way. Be patient with me. It'll take me some time to get used to this. I'm used to being alone."

"You aren't alone anymore."

They were four simple words, but they felt like a promise.

The trip back to Rockville seemed much faster than the one to Lobster Cove, probably because they were halfway back to town in the first place, but also because Marit was relaxed, and not stressed about meeting Zach's family.

"I'd like to drop you off at your apartment, but if you aren't comfortable with me knowing where you live, I'm not sure what to do. I don't want you to walk to your place from my apartment parking lot by yourself. And before you say that you'll be fine, I'm already sure you will be. Rockville isn't a hub of criminal activity. But it's not in me to let a woman walk home by herself. So I'm not sure—"

"It's fine, Zach," Marit said, interrupting him. "You had your tongue practically down my throat and we were completely alone. You could've done anything you wanted to me . . . and you didn't. I trust you."

He looked over at her. "Thank you. That means a lot to me. I'm not going to hurt you, Marit. You have my word."

She swallowed hard, feeling emotional all over again. This night had been full of her emotions careening all over the place. She wasn't sure she liked it. She liked her nice, predictable world.

No. She was lying to herself. Yes, she liked knowing what was coming and what to expect, and tonight had been out of her comfort zone . . . but nice all the same. She'd felt included, and that hadn't happened in a very long time.

After she gave him directions, Zach soon pulled into the small parking area of the house where her apartment was located, and he met Marit on the passenger side of his Explorer. He leaned in and kissed her as if he'd done the same thing countless times before. "I'll see you at the dock tomorrow afternoon?"

"Yeah."

"If you aren't too tired, you want to do dinner again? I can make us something at the shack, and we can go down to the park to eat it. Or if you want something more substantial, we can go back to my place, and I can grill steaks or salmon or something."

"The park sounds great. But can I go home and change first? Maybe I can meet you there?"

He gave her a look, and Marit remembered what he'd just said about her walking alone. It was kind of ridiculous, because this was Rockville and she'd been walking around on her own for years. But it also felt nice that he wanted to make sure she was safe.

"If you text me when you're ready, I'll come here and we can walk together," he suggested.

"Okay." She pulled out her phone, and they quickly exchanged numbers. Even saving his contact info in her phone felt like a big step. She didn't have a whole lot of contacts, and seeing his name made her feel warm and fuzzy inside.

"I'll give you my brothers' numbers tomorrow. And my mom's too. But I warn you, she's forever misplacing her cell, so if you want to talk to her, you should probably call her landline at the house. Oh, and Walt and Barry too. And I'm sure Britt will want to text you as well. She spends a lot of her time out at Lobster Cove and could probably use some girl talk. My mom is great, but having someone closer to her age would probably be welcome."

Marit was proud of herself for not freaking out at the thought of having so many people added to her contact list. It was likely they'd never contact her anyway. Zach was just being nice in suggesting they'd want to have her number.

"I had a good time tonight," Zach said, walking her toward the house. "Thank you for coming with me."

"Your family's . . . nice," she told him.

"Remember that when they're being pains in my ass," he teased.

Then he leaned in and kissed her once more. He lingered a bit longer than he had when he'd kissed her after getting out of the car. But it wasn't nearly as passionate as the kiss they'd shared on that bench by the water. Her belly still did somersaults though.

"See you tomorrow. If you want, text before you head out on the boat. I'll be up."

"I will. Good luck with the risotto tomorrow."

"Thanks. Be safe on the boat."

"Always."

This was ridiculous, and Marit couldn't help but smile. They were both prolonging the goodbye, obviously neither of them ready to part. But she needed some sleep. As did Zach. So she did the adult thing and took a step toward the stairs that led up the side of the house, to the apartment she was renting.

She wasn't really surprised when she reached the top of the stairs and looked down to see Zach still standing there, watching to make sure she got inside all right. She gave him a small wave, and after he returned it, she slipped into her place and shut the door, locking it behind her. She leaned against the surface and found that she was still smiling. Huge.

Tonight had been nothing like what she'd expected. She'd experienced some pretty intense emotions, but overall it had been . . . awesome.

Moving to Rockville had been the right decision. It was tough to leave Portland and a lobstering community she'd worked so hard to fit into, but Eliot was a great employer and Jonah a hard worker. The other lobstermen in the area were a bit standoffish, but she hoped that would change when they saw she was serious about her profession.

And of course, there was Zach. It was hard to believe she'd just met him, but for once in her life, she was going to go with the flow. Try not to overthink things. Time would tell whether or not they worked out, but she was going to be cautiously optimistic for now.

Still smiling, she pushed off the door and headed to the kitchen to get a cup of water before heading to bed. Sleep came fast for Marit, and she drifted off with the same silly grin on her face.

Chapter Four

The week leading up to Lobster Fest went by extremely quickly. Zach found himself spending more and more time at The Lobster Buoy. The crowds were thicker each day, and he and Jack spent most of their time hunched over the cooktop in the shack, making meals as fast as the tourists could consume them.

As a result, he and Marit hadn't been able to spend much time together. She was almost as busy as he was, spending extra hours on the *Wave Rider* catching the lobsters everyone in town wanted to purchase.

They stayed in touch via text, sending an obnoxious number of notes back and forth. Most of the time they didn't talk about anything deep, just shared jokes and thoughts about all the tourists in town.

With every day that went by that he didn't get to see her—except for short periods of time when he went down to the dock to buy lobster—he got more and more irritated. Not with her. With the fact that he very much wanted to spend time with her and wasn't able to.

"I can't believe I'm going to say this, considering I'm the king of assholes, but you're being extra assholey, Zach. Why don't you take the morning off tomorrow," Jack suggested at the end of the day, when Zach was getting ready to head down to the docks.

Looking over at his employee in surprise, he said, "Tomorrow's the first day of Lobster Fest. I can't take the morning off."

"Of course you can. You're the fucking boss. You hired Casey, Bill, and Karen to run the front of the shack and me to keep the food crankin' out. We've got this. Besides, it gets busier in the afternoons rather than the mornings. Go buy some flowers for your girl and spend tonight with her, without worrying about getting up and coming in to work."

Zach stared at the older man. He was an asshole most of the time, but he was a damn good worker. And the lobster hash with fried eggs he'd planned for the special tomorrow morning wasn't difficult to make. Jack could more than handle it. The lobster and smoked gouda quesadilla for day one of the festival was fairly simple too. Zach had already seasoned a large batch of lobster for that dish, and Jack could easily grill the quesadillas quickly if they had an influx of customers before he arrived.

The more he thought about it, the more Zach wanted to take Jack up on the offer. Owning his own restaurant was a hell of a lot of work, even if it was "only" a lobster shack. Having Lobster Fest come around so soon after starting the business made his life that much more difficult, but was a boon at the same time. The increase in income would help keep him afloat during the leaner winter months, when tourists were few and far between.

He should feel guilty about leaving things to his employees, but Zach mentally said fuck it. "Thanks, Jack. I think I'll do that."

"Good. Maybe it'll improve your mood," his cook said under his breath.

Zach hadn't realized he'd been acting any differently. But if *Jack* said he'd been an asshole, he must've *really* been a prick lately.

As he got ready to head to the dock, his mood lifted significantly. He couldn't wait to see Marit. He was sure she'd still need to get up early in the morning, but the thought of sleeping in himself sounded damn good.

"You have my number in case anything goes wrong," he told Casey and Bill, the two high schoolers who were working the front of the shack, and who'd be there in the morning when the festival started.

"Like running out of lobster?" Casey asked with a huge grin.

"Bite your tongue, girl!" Zach said in mock horror. But silently, he did the calculations. Running out of lobster would mean he'd make thousands of dollars in a *very* short amount of time. He could deal with that.

Zach walked quickly through town, which looked as if someone had thrown shellfish all over it, as every storefront and restaurant had used lobster decor to celebrate the festival. Grabbing his SUV at his apartment, he made a spontaneous stop at one of the local businesses before continuing on his way.

When Zach was little, he used to love how Rockville transformed itself for Lobster Fest. Banners with lobsters on them were strung everywhere, and locals seemed to be in a happy mood, despite how many extra people suddenly flooded the town. He and his brothers had spent countless hours entertaining themselves at the festivals: running around the park, stuffing their faces with "fair food," listening to live music, and participating in the various activities. One of his favorites had always been the lobster-eating contest. He remembered Linc winning one year . . . then he'd gotten so sick, he'd thrown up in the parking lot after getting his prize.

They'd done the Codfish Carry competition when they were in elementary school, the Kids' Fun Run, and then the 5K when they'd gotten too old for the kids' race. The parade was always a highlight, as well.

But the most fun activity was the Great Crate Race.

Zach remembered laughing until his stomach hurt at some of the falls people had while attempting to run across the fifty floating lobster crates strung across the harbor. The winner most years was usually a kid, because they weighed less than the adults and the crates didn't sink as far into the water when they ran across them. If someone made it all the way across the fifty crates, they turned around and came back, continuing to run back and forth until they fell into the water.

He could still remember his mom telling him about the year when there was a tie for the winner. Seven-year-old Scarlett Flint and nine-year-old Harrison Page successfully crossed sixty-five hundred crates! Zach couldn't wrap his mind around that. He hoped he'd be able to take some time away from The Lobster Buoy to watch this year's competition.

For now, he was just eager to get to the docks to see Marit. They'd texted that morning, and she'd admitted that she was exhausted. She and the Sullivans were working extra-long hours to catch enough lobsters for their regular customers, as well as the additional haul needed for the influx of tourists to Rockville for the festival.

He didn't bother to change out of the clothes he'd been wearing all day at The Lobster Buoy, knowing Marit honestly wouldn't care that he had some grease stains on his shirt and smelled like fried food. Not when she'd be wearing her lobstering gear.

It took longer than normal to drive the couple of blocks to the pier, and Zach felt lucky to find a parking spot. He made a mental note that he was probably going to have to walk over here for the next few days. He'd bring his dolly to transport the crates of lobsters back to his shack. There would be no parking spots to be found until Lobster Fest was over.

Leaving the purchase he'd made on the back seat of his SUV, Zach hurried toward the *Wave Rider*, happy to see the boat was already parked at the dock. He could easily tell the difference between Marit and the Sullivan men because of her size. She really was tiny, but somehow when he was around her, he forgot all about how diminutive she was—especially compared to him—because she had such a large personality.

As he approached the boat, however, he caught some weird vibes coming from the trio, who were busy packing the lobsters they'd caught into crates for transport.

"Hey," Zach said as he approached.

Everyone looked up, and for a split second he saw wariness on Eliot's face, until he realized it was Zach approaching. Then his expression evened out.

"Oh, hey, Zach. How was business today? You ready for the people tomorrow?"

"Good, and yes. As much as I can be. Were the lobsters cooperating today?"

"Hell yeah. We got an awesome haul," Eliot told him.

Zach thought it was odd the way Jonah didn't look up or say hello. "Hey, Jonah," he said.

The other man glanced up quickly, nodded, then got back to work.

"Hi," Marit said, with a soft smile.

Not thinking twice about his actions, Zach stepped toward where Marit was standing next to a crate of lobsters and leaned over, kissing her briefly before straightening. "Hi," he returned. "You have a good day?"

Instead of responding affirmatively, she shrugged.

Zach frowned. "You didn't?"

"Lucas Pearson," Eliot spat.

Turning toward the older man, Zach asked, "Who?"

"No one. It's not a big deal," Marit said quickly.

But Eliot ignored her attempt at dropping the subject.

"He owns the *Men At Work*, another lobster boat. He ran his mouth this morning about Marit working on the *Wave Rider*. Saying all kinds of sexist shit. Then he followed us most of the morning, commenting on Marit's technique and insisting having her on board was bad luck, that she was gonna bring that same luck down on the fleet. He ended his childish and stupid rant by saying she should've stayed in Portland, that Rockville didn't want no 'sissy girls' lobstering in its waters."

Zach's anger rose hot and fast. "Are you fucking kidding me?"

"It's okay, Zach," Marit said. She'd moved around the crate she'd been filling to put her hand on his arm.

"It's *not* okay," he countered.

"You're right, it's not. But I'm used to it."

"Which is also bullshit!" Zach exclaimed. "You shouldn't be used to that. You're damn good at what you do. I haven't been on a boat with you, but I've known Eliot a long time and he doesn't tolerate incompetence. If you couldn't hack it as a lobsterwoman, you wouldn't be on his boat. I've heard him say more than once how happy he is that he hired you before anyone else could."

Marit's face softened. "Thanks."

"Who is this Pearson guy, anyway? He worked around here long?" Zach asked Eliot. He wasn't ready to let this drop yet. The thought that someone was harassing Marit didn't sit well with him. Not at all.

"No. As far as I know, he arrived at the beginning of summer from the Portland area."

"Did you know him while you were there?" Zach asked Marit.

She sighed. "Kind've. He was buddies with a lobsterman there who definitely didn't like me much, and who made it his goal in life to make sure that I—and I quote—'leave the lobstering to the men.'"

Zach studied Marit. He could see the exhaustion and frustration in her face. He supposed he wasn't all that surprised there were some people who didn't think women could do a difficult job like lobstering, but in this day and age, to come right out and harass her because of it was a little surprising. He'd seen women in the Navy in traditionally masculine roles endure some of the same harassment, and it made his blood boil then, just as it did now. He had no problem with anyone's gender when it came to jobs. If they could do the tasks required, great.

Then another thought occurred to him. "Was that why you left Portland? Because of this other guy?"

Her silence told him all he needed to know.

Zach turned to Eliot. "What did you and Jonah say when this Pearson guy was harassing her?"

To his surprise, Eliot's gaze dropped. And Jonah continued to count lobsters as if he hadn't even heard Zach's question.

"Please tell me you told him to fuck off," Zach growled.

Eliot shrugged. "I did say that Marit's been doing an awesome job," he said a little defensively.

"You have got to be kidding me," Zach said under his breath. He took a deep breath, trying to control his temper. "You can't let this guy get away with this. A bully will always sense weakness, and if you don't stand up for your employees, he'll just continue to berate her and try to get her to quit. Is that what you want? To lose Marit as an employee?"

"No!" Eliot sighed. "You're right. I fucked up. I'm sorry, Marit. I was just hoping he'd go away and shut up."

"He won't," Marit said, the defeat easy to hear in her tone.

Eliot stood up straighter. "Well, if he says anything again, I'll be sure to put him in his place."

"Me too," Jonah agreed, speaking up for the first time.

But Zach was hardly impressed. The two men had blown the perfect opportunity to nip the harassment in the bud. He wasn't so sure it would be easy to get Pearson to back down now. He probably got some sort of high out of knowing how uncomfortable he'd made everyone on the *Wave Rider*. He'd feed on it. Come back for more. Like a predator sensing weakness in his prey.

Fuck.

"I meant to tell you earlier, but my wife has an appointment tomorrow morning, and I need to drive her to Damariscotta," Eliot told Marit. "Which means we won't be able to go out first thing. How about we all just take tomorrow off, since we won't be able to get a full day in? We got enough lobsters today to keep our regulars happy, even with the festival going on."

"Oh, is she okay? Marilyn, I mean?" Marit asked.

It said a lot about her that she'd ask about Eliot's wife, when he and his son had done nothing to defend her against Lucas, and before voicing her pleasure at getting an unexpected day off.

"Yeah. She's been having some pains in her back, and we want to see what can be done about it before it gets any worse."

"Oh, I'm sorry. I hope the doctors can find out what's going on and help her."

"Me too. But no telling how long the appointment will take, so . . . day after tomorrow, here at the dock? We'll head out at our usual time. We might need a bit more time to check the traps, though. Hopefully they'll all be full."

"Of course."

"Go to Lobster Fest. Check it out. It'll be your first time going, right?"

"Yeah. I've heard a lot about it. Even when I was working in Portland."

"It's a good time."

"Thanks, Eliot. I appreciate it."

He waved off her thanks. "You work hard. Damn hard. You deserve a day off now and then."

"I don't work any harder than you and Jonah do," she protested.

"Not sure about that. And Marit?"

"Yeah?"

"I'm sorry for not saying something more to Lucas. I won't let you down again."

"It's okay."

"It's not. The man doesn't know what the hell he's talking about. And for the record, I don't give a damn that you're a woman. All I care about is that the job gets done. And you more than accomplish that."

"Thanks," Marit said.

"I'm sorry too," Jonah added quietly. "I should've told him to go to hell."

Marit's soft heart was on display when she let the younger Sullivan off the hook as well. "It's okay. I'm used to people commenting on my size and gender in this job. You guys have things under control here? You need me to deliver any crates anywhere?"

"No, we've got it. Go, Marit. Have some fun. Sleep in. Relax. We'll see you the day after tomorrow."

Zach was ready to go. He was overjoyed that Marit had tomorrow off, but he still wasn't happy with Eliot and Zach . . . or about the situation with this Lucas Pearson guy. If the guy dared to say one damn word to Marit in his presence, he'd get an earful about being a major fucking asshole.

"Will you drop off my order at The Lobster Buoy?" he asked Eliot.

"Sure thing."

"Thanks." Then Zach took hold of Marit's hand and pulled her down the dock toward the parking lot.

"What's the hurry?" she asked with a small laugh.

"The hurry is, if I don't get away from your coworkers, I might say something you aren't going to like."

She tugged on his hand, and Zach stopped, looking down at her.

"It wasn't that big of a deal. I've heard worse."

"You don't get it. The fact that *anyone* felt it was all right to talk to you that way, and that Eliot and Jonah apparently didn't do a damn thing to shut him up, is wrong on every level. I'm frustrated with them. I'm pissed at Pearson. I feel sick that you had to listen to that garbage. I'm tired, worried about how Lobster Fest is going to go in regards to the shack, and upset that I haven't been able to see you much this past week."

Marit stepped into his personal space and wrapped her arms around him as she laid her head on his chest. Something inside Zach eased as he returned the hug. She felt amazing in his arms. Right. And just holding her seemed to make all the shit rolling around in his head calm.

"I haven't had a chance to tell you yet," he said into her hair, as he continued to hold her. "I'm taking the morning off tomorrow."

Her head whipped up so fast, she almost clocked him in the chin. "Seriously?"

"Seriously."

"That's awesome!"

"Yeah. You want to come over for dinner?" Zach asked. "I haven't planned anything, but I figured I could scrounge up something for us to eat. That is . . . if you're comfortable with that. I know we haven't done much outside of that first date at Lobster Cove. We can try to find someplace to eat, but with all the tourists in town, I'm not sure—"

"Your place is great," Marit said, interrupting him.

"I promise you're safe with me."

"I know I am. Thank you for saying so, though."

"You want to stop by your apartment and change first?"

"You wouldn't mind?"

"Not at all. I could use a shower myself."

She chuckled. "I don't know. You smell like fried food. And seafood."

Her belly chose that moment to growl. They both laughed.

"See? You smell delicious," she told him.

Zach smiled. "Eau de lobster. It's a good thing you don't mind it, since I own a restaurant called The Lobster Buoy."

"I don't mind. As long as you don't mind that *I* smell like raw fish."

"I think we're perfect for each other." It was a simple statement that Zach realized had never been so true with anyone else.

Just like his dad had always told him and his brothers about meeting their mom . . . when you know, you know. Zach had never really believed that, had always thought love was a slow process . . . that you met someone, liked them, went out, got to know them more, had sex to discover if you were physically compatible, and then when you were comfortable enough with each other, you got married.

But this thing with Marit, it was anything *but* what Zach had expected.

"Come on. I'll drop you off at your place, go home, change and shower, then come to your apartment to walk you back to mine."

"I can walk by myself," she reminded him.

"We've had this discussion," he told her with a small shrug.

"Fine. But give me twenty minutes or so."

"That's all you need?"

She tilted her head back even more to meet his gaze. "Do you think I need more?"

"I think you're a woman. And I haven't known many women to be that fast with a shower and a change."

"Well, you know one now."

"Cool. The faster we can change, the more time we get to spend with each other. I've missed you this week. Texting is great, and I've loved the quick calls we've had, but I like being able to see you in person, to hold you, way more."

"Me too," she agreed a little shyly.

"Come on. The faster we get going, the faster I can feed you."

They got into his SUV, and he remembered the stop he'd made before going to the dock. After she sat, he reached into the back, holding up a bag with a grin. "I stopped and got some Ruckus Donuts for dessert."

Marit's eyes lit up. "Oh, I love those things!"

"Doesn't everyone? I'm a good cook, but baking isn't my forte. I'm happy to support a local business and satisfy my sweet tooth at the same time," he said.

"Thank you, Zach."

"You're welcome." Happy that the impromptu stop had brought a smile to her face, Zach turned the key in the ignition and backed out of his parking space.

The trip to her apartment was fast, and Zach mentally went through the things he had at his own place, trying to decide what he could make for her. She needed something filling; she worked at her job, burned lots of calories. Marit wasn't the kind of woman who shied away from eating carbs and a large meal . . . at least, he didn't think so.

After he'd washed the smell of fried food out of his hair and changed into a fresh pair of jeans and a T-shirt, he quickly prepped some chicken parmesan for dinner. He popped the chicken into the oven, which should be ready by the time he and Marit returned.

Then he set out for her place, arriving exactly twenty-two minutes and thirty-four seconds after he'd dropped her off. He went up the stairs to her door and knocked. She answered almost immediately—and it was all Zach could do not to fall to his knees right then and there and beg her to love him forever.

She was wearing another pair of jeans, and a tank top that showed off the muscles she'd gained from working on the lobster boat. It dipped low in the front, giving him what he guessed was supposed to be a hint of cleavage, but was actually more than she probably thought, considering he was so much taller—and looking almost straight down her shirt.

His mouth watered, but Zach pushed the lustful thoughts away. He respected Marit, and it was obvious she hadn't dressed for seduction. He could control his desire for her . . . maybe.

She'd left her long hair down, and it was still damp. It was darker than normal, but when it dried it would be back to its unusual white-blonde color. The ends curled around her tits, framing them perfectly. She looked like a damn angel . . . and Zach wanted to defile her in every way possible.

"You clean up nicely," she said with a smile.

"You too," Zach told her.

"You want me to bring anything over to help with dinner?"

"Just yourself."

"All right. I'm ready."

"No purse?" Zach asked.

Marit shrugged. "I've got a credit card and my ID in the little pocket on the back of my phone case. My keys will fit in my pocket. Don't need much else."

"True. Don't you worry that if you lose your phone, you'll lose your stuff?"

"Not really. When I'm on the boat, I put my phone into a dry bag that's clipped onto a hook in the cabin, so it can't fall overboard accidentally. And when I'm not on the boat, I've always got my phone in my back pocket. It hasn't been an issue, honestly."

Zach nodded.

"What would I carry in a purse, anyway?" she asked, as they headed out.

Zach waited patiently behind her as she locked her apartment door. "I have no idea. I don't know what women carry around with them all the time. I had to look in my mom's purse for something once, and it scarred me for life. I saw a tampon, a bag of pretzels, and a wad of what I thought was used tissues, and I was done. No more purse looking for me."

Marit laughed as they headed down the stairs. Zach took her hand in his when they reached the bottom. He loved hearing her laugh. For all she'd apparently been through with her brothers while growing up, and the harassment in her chosen career, she was a surprisingly happy person. He loved that about her. That she could live in the moment and not dwell on the past.

"Tampons are a normal part of life," she said, when she'd gotten control of herself.

They walked at an easy pace toward his place, which was only three blocks away. It was still light outside, as the sun didn't set until late in the summer. Although all too soon it would be dark at four in the afternoon and stay that way until around seven in the morning.

"I realize that. And I have no problem with tampons or pads. I've bought them in the past and brought them to women when they were having an emergency in the bathroom. I just don't want to think about my *mother* having them or using them. Or having any kind of sexual organs, for that matter."

Marit giggled once more. "You do know that you and your brothers wouldn't be here if she hadn't had sex."

Zach pushed a finger from his free hand into his ear and singsonged, "La la la . . . I can't hear you."

Marit stepped closer and knocked her shoulder into his arm. "Whatever."

Zach smiled down at her. He liked this. A lot.

"You've brought a tampon to someone when they were in the bathroom with a period emergency?"

"Yup," he said nonchalantly. "On a Navy ship, there's not a lot of privacy. And I was walking by a bathroom when I heard someone calling out from inside. I peeked my head in and heard a woman asking for someone, anyone, to get her a tampon. I flagged down the next woman I saw, had her get me one from her room—which, luckily, was nearby—and brought it into the restroom for the other woman."

"Wow. That was . . . nice. You weren't embarrassed?"

"Not really. I mean, like you said, it's a part of life. I don't even know who the woman was either. I had to get to the galley right after that."

"Huh."

Zach looked down at her. "Is that a good *huh*, or a bad one?"

"Neither. Just interesting. What are we having for dinner? I could eat a moose. Not that I've ever had moose, but I'm just sayin'."

"No moose. Chicken parmesan."

"What's your way?"

"Alfredo and lobster sauce. Tons of garlic. And of course, cheese. All the cheese."

"Oh my God, that sounds amazing. Will it take long to cook?"

"The chicken's already cooking. When we get to my place, I'll take it out and finish it up on the stovetop, giving it a quick fry so it has a nice crispy breading, then add the sauce. Then it'll take another ten minutes or so in the oven to melt everything. I *did* bring home some lobster-and-Brie-stuffed mushrooms that we served at the shack today. They didn't sell as well as I'd hoped, and we had a ton extra."

"What's wrong with people these days? I could probably eat a dozen of those babies."

This woman. She was fucking made for him. "Well, that's good, because I think I brought home about two dozen."

To his surprise, Marit wrapped her arm around his and leaned her head against his bicep as they walked. "This is nice. Thank you for inviting me over. I was going to have another frozen meal before wasting at least an hour scrolling through social media and watching stupid videos before probably falling asleep on my couch."

Zach made a mental vow to make sure Marit had fresh food for dinner as often as he could possibly manage. Lord knew he usually had plenty of leftovers from the shack. Some of the things he created for his customers sold very well, and others not so much—like the stuffed mushrooms from today. He was still learning what worked and what didn't. For the most part, people were very receptive to the bougie lobster dishes he came up with. Were open to trying something other than the typical lobster roll.

"Here we are," he said as they approached the house with his apartment. "It's not very fancy," he warned her, as he opened the door.

He gestured for Marit to enter first and watched her carefully as she looked around his place.

He had a studio apartment, with everything in one big room. Thankfully, it was a fairly large room. His queen-size bed—which he slept in diagonally, in order to fit—was on one end of the space, leaving room for two oversize recliners and a modest-size TV.

He supposed most people would prefer a couch, but that would take up a lot more room than the chairs, and he'd wanted a big table, enough to fit his entire family. It wasn't likely all his brothers and his mom would show up at the same time, they'd be more likely to meet up at Lobster Cove if they wanted to have dinner together, but family was important, and he wanted to have enough space to cook for them if they came over.

He'd bought a table with a middle leaf, however, which he currently didn't have in, so it took up less room than it might otherwise. There were two chairs against the wall, currently unused, and four around the table at the moment. He liked to sit while he ate, take his time, enjoy the food.

"It's a lot like mine. Although I have an actual bedroom," she told him. "And I have a tiny little table and a huge couch. I think my TV is bigger than yours."

He chuckled. "I'm not much of a TV watcher. Didn't really get much of a chance when I was working on naval ships."

"Your kitchen is way nicer than mine."

"It's not ideal, but until I get my own place, it'll do."

"You looking to buy something here?"

"Yeah. Linc, my oldest brother, bought an old house on a large piece of property. You know Chad lives on Lobster Cove, and Knox is content with his two-bedroom apartment on the lower level of a house. But I want a house of my own. Not one I have to fix up, like Linc is doing, but a more modern, finished thing. One I don't have to spend a lot of time on. I don't really have the time anyway, not with The Lobster Buoy and helping out around Lobster Cove in my free time."

"I think it's great how connected you are to your mom's place."

"It's our family legacy. And even if I'm not living there, it's where I grew up, where I have so many awesome memories. Besides, it's beautiful as hell. I love visiting."

"I can see why."

"You want to go sit, make yourself comfortable, find something on the TV to watch while I get the chicken ready for the oven again?"

"Can I help?"

"Well . . ."

Marit laughed. "Sorry, let me rephrase that, Mr. I-Don't-Want-Anyone-Touching-My-Chef-Stuff . . . can I keep you company while you do your thing in the kitchen?"

Zach felt himself blushing. She'd pegged him in one. He didn't usually like others "helping" him cook. He was a little type A when it came to food and making it how he preferred. "I'd like that."

The first thing he did was put the stuffed mushrooms into the air fryer on low before he turned his attention to the chicken. It didn't take long to bread the breasts and crisp them up on the stovetop. He put the chicken in a dish and smothered it with the homemade lobster alfredo sauce he had in his fridge for just such an occasion as this. Then he added a couple of large handfuls of mozzarella and parmesan cheese to the top, and some more spices to finish it off.

"That looks delicious," Marit said from his side. She once again leaned into him after he'd shut the oven door. Zach could get used to having her against him, for sure.

"Want to go sit at the table while we dig into the mushrooms?"

"Where are your plates and silverware?"

As Zach plated the mushrooms, Marit set the table. He couldn't help but think they made a great team.

They sat next to each other at the table and dug into the mushrooms, each consuming several before Marit spoke.

"I think I've died and gone to heaven. These are so good, Zach. You're an amazing cook."

"They aren't hard to make," he told her honestly.

"Maybe, maybe not, but whatever spices you used really complement the flavor of the cheese and bring out the delicate taste of the lobster. These could seriously be served in a five-star restaurant."

"When I moved here, that was actually my goal," Zach admitted.

"What, to open a fancy restaurant?"

"Yeah. Like The Lost Kitchen. You know, the one that's so popular that in order to get reservations, you have to send in a postcard and it's a lottery system?"

"Well, I think part of the reason they're so popular is because they had that reality show about them."

"They did?"

Marit chuckled. "Yes. You really *don't* watch much TV, do you?"

"No. Anyway, the last kind of place I wanted to open was another lobster shack. But honestly, it makes sense. People around here love their seafood and lobster, and the tourists kind of expect lobster rolls. But I wanted to put my own spin on it. Make it different."

"Well, you've succeeded. Because these mushroom bites are freaking delicious and like nothing I've had . . . especially not from a lobster shack."

"That means a lot coming from someone who deals with lobsters for a living."

"*Living* is the key word," Marit said with a small laugh. "At least, they're living when I hand them off to someone."

Zach rested his head in his palm and watched her eat another stuffed mushroom.

"What? Do I have cheese on my chin?" she asked, picking up her napkin and wiping her mouth.

"No. I just love watching people enjoy something I've made with my own two hands. And knowing *you're* enjoying them is even more deeply satisfying."

"Why?"

The thing was, Zach wasn't exactly sure. He'd fed a lot of people over the years. But there was something about watching *this* woman eat something he'd prepared. Sitting at his table, in his private space, with him. It was intimate in a way he hadn't expected.

The timer he'd set for the chicken saved him from having to answer. He got up and headed to the oven.

It wasn't long before they were both eating the chicken parmesan he'd whipped up. It was good. Although it could've been better, at least to his taste buds, if he'd had more time. But once again, Marit praised the meal and his cooking skills. And so he felt proud. Happy that he was the one providing her sustenance.

It wasn't until after they'd finished their meals with the donuts he'd purchased earlier, washed the dishes and put everything away, that Zach realized how unfortunate it was that he didn't have a couch. He couldn't sit next to Marit and subtly put his arm on the back of the couch, which would eventually end up around her shoulders. Damn it.

"You want to stay and watch something? I could find a movie or something on Netflix. That's the only app I've got."

"Sure."

They walked into the living area, and Zach gestured to the recliners. "Take your pick."

"Which one are you sitting in?" Marit asked.

Zach shrugged. "I usually sit in that one," he said, pointing to the one on the right.

"Then I'll sit there too . . . if that's okay."

Chapter Five

As soon as the words left her lips, Marit wondered if she'd done the right thing. Tonight had been . . . eye opening. From the time Zach had met her on the dock, when he'd been so upset on her behalf about what Lucas Pearson had said and done, to taking her home, to walking her to his place, to cooking for her, to now . . . she'd never had another date like it.

Despite only knowing him for a week, Marit felt closer to Zach than she had to any other human, other than her late mom and dad. For years she'd felt lonely, alone, even when she'd been living with her brothers, surrounded by lobstermen at her jobs, or even on the occasional date.

Zach made her feel seen. And heard. And cherished. It was a heady feeling. One she wanted to continue.

The last thing she wanted was to sit in one of his huge recliners by herself. Her feet wouldn't come close to hitting the ground. She'd be swamped in the thing. She and Zach could share a recliner and still have room to spare.

But she was probably pushing things faster than he might want. Yes, he'd invited her over, but this was only their second date . . . if the first meal they'd had at Lobster Cove could even be considered a date.

"Sorry, I—"

"Yes," Zach said, interrupting her. He sat so quickly, Marit could only blink in surprise. Then he held out a hand to her, silently.

The second his fingers closed around hers, Marit knew she'd made the right decision. His touch felt like coming home. Gingerly, she lowered so she was sitting on his lap, and Zach didn't hesitate to physically move her around so she was sitting kind of sideways, so her head could rest comfortably against his chest.

"This okay?" he asked softly.

"Perfect," she breathed.

Amazingly, she felt completely at ease in his lap. He was very comfortable, and his warmth soaked into her bones. He'd opened a few windows earlier, and the ocean breeze wafted into the room, keeping things slightly cool and bringing in the fresh air at the same time. She could hear the sounds of downtown Rockville in the distance, but soon that would die down as most businesses closed by eight in the small town.

"Anything in particular you want to watch?" he asked.

"You seen *Stranger Things*?" Marit asked.

"No. Haven't seen anything," he said with a chuckle. The sound reverberated against her back, and it felt intimate and cozy.

"It's pretty good. My favorite season is the first one. It's kind of about aliens and sci-fi and has a bunch of kids as the heroes and heroines. I have to warn you though, it can be confusing at first, until a couple episodes in when they start revealing some of what's actually going on."

"Sounds awesome," Zach told her, as he aimed the remote at his TV and clicked it on. Before long, the eerie sounds of the opening notes of the soundtrack filled the room.

Marit sighed in contentment. Her belly was full, she was relaxed, and she was spending time with a man she trusted implicitly and liked a hell of a lot. Life was good.

The last thing she remembered was seeing the character Eleven on the screen in the first episode.

When she woke up, she was still in Zach's lap. Her head was lying on his shoulder, and he was holding her even closer. One arm was around her back, his hand resting on her hip, and the other hand was lying heavily on her thigh. His thumb gently caressing her, moving back and forth. The light from the TV flickered in the darkness of the room, and his gaze was fixed on the screen.

"What time is it?" she asked quietly.

"No clue," Zach responded. "Shhhh, we're nearing the end of the third episode."

"Holy crap, I've been asleep for almost three hours?" Marit asked, completely shocked.

"You worked hard today. You were tired. I got you. Now . . . hush, I don't want to miss anything. This show is the bomb."

Marit couldn't help but grin as she did as he asked and hushed.

When the episode was over, Zach pushed the pause button and asked, "Will's not really dead . . . right?"

Marit laughed. "Told you it was good."

"It's more than good. It sucks you in. And you're right, I was totally lost at first, but it's all coming together nicely. The writers are amazing."

"I'm sorry I fell asleep."

"Don't be. I'm not. I'm honored that you felt safe and comfortable enough to do so."

"You have to be tired too," she felt obligated to say. "You've been up at the same time I have each morning, and you've been working just as hard. How do your knees feel? Are they okay?"

"They're fine. And I'd give up any amount of sleep to have the privilege of holding you while you rest."

Marit was at a loss for words as to what to say to that. Had any man ever said something so sweet to her before? No. Not even close.

The stress of the day was gone. Melted away, forgotten in a haze of good food, good company, and this man's arms around her. Sitting up, Marit adjusted so she was straddling Zach's lap. Her knees easily fit on either side of his thighs in the big chair. As she'd thought, she more than fit in the recliner with him. Thankful for her small size for once, Marit put her hands on Zach's shoulders.

"I've never felt safe enough to fall asleep in a man's place on one of our first dates. And to fall asleep in his arms? Not a chance. But there's something different about you, Zach Young. You make all my shields evaporate as if they were never there at all. You make me want to be a different person."

"How so?" he asked, his gaze locked on hers.

"More direct about what I want."

"What *do* you want?"

"You."

Silence met her pronouncement.

Just when she thought she'd blown it, that Zach would think she was easy or promiscuous or something, one of his hands grabbed her nape. It felt as if his fingers could almost meet all the way around her neck, his hand was that big. He made her feel even more petite than she usually did.

"I promised you'd be safe with me, and I wasn't just saying what I thought you needed to hear."

"I know."

"I want you too."

Marit smiled at him, loving that she was eye level with him, sitting on his lap as she was. "So what are we going to do about it?"

"Whatever you want. I'll follow your lead."

"And if I want to lead you to your bed?" She felt his dick twitch under her. His reaction made her more confident. Made her want him more.

"Be sure," he said in a serious tone. "I'm not playing around here. There's something about you that's different than anyone I've ever been with, Marit. And I don't want one night. That's not who I am. If we do this, we're doing it because we both want more than a fling."

Nothing he said turned Marit off. It was a relief to hear him admit the same things she'd been feeling about him. "I don't want a fling either," she assured him.

To her surprise, Zach scooted forward on the recliner with her still in his lap and stood. His hands went to her ass to hold her up, and she let out a little screech, then a laugh as he walked the few steps it took to get to his bed. He dropped her on the mattress, then quickly climbed over her.

Marit scooted backward until her head was on one of his pillows, and he followed right along until he was hovering over her on his hands and knees.

"Be sure," he repeated.

"I'm sure," Marit said. And she was. She'd never been as sure of anything in her life as she was that she wanted this man. Right here and now.

Without a word, he straightened and stripped his T-shirt off over his head.

Marit stared up at him, her mouth literally watering. The man was *gorgeous*. He had a smattering of dark chest hair, and every time he moved, his pectorals flexed. He undid the button on his jeans and unzipped them, pushing them down far enough that she could see those muscles inside his hips that most women lusted over, and the happy trail that led between his legs.

But he stopped there, much to her disappointment.

He sat back on his heels, not putting any pressure on her legs but pinning her in place nonetheless. "May I?" he asked, as his hands hovered over her chest.

Marit nodded eagerly, squirming a little under him in anticipation.

His hands went to her belly, over her tank top, and smoothed upward. They went over her breasts, to her shoulders, then he caressed her arms as he made his way down to her hands. He moved to her belly again but this time eased his hands under her tank, so he was caressing bare skin.

She sucked in a breath at the first touch of his calloused hands on her body. The same zing she'd felt when they'd first touched hands coursed through her. But this time it was more intense—and she felt it right between her legs.

Without breaking eye contact, he moved his hands upward, starting on the same path as before, his big hands easily engulfing her breasts when he reached them, but he didn't pull the cups of her bra down.

He simply caressed her through the material. Then he changed course, moving his hands back down to her belly. Up. Down. Up. Down.

"Zach," she whined.

"Yeah?" he asked with a small smile.

"Stop teasing me."

"I want to go slow. There will only be one first time between us, and I want it to last."

This felt so much more intimate than any other time she'd been with a man. In the past, her partners had always wanted to get undressed as soon as possible, maybe suck on her boobs a bit, then have her go down on them before getting inside her and getting off quickly. She'd never seen the reverence in a man's eyes like she saw right now in Zach's gaze.

She huffed out a breath but did her best to relax and let Zach do whatever he wanted with her. On the next pass up her body, he gently pushed both cups of her bra up, so the material rested above her breasts. It wasn't the most comfortable feeling in the world to have the elastic digging into her, but she forgot all about that when his hands closed over both of her boobs.

Her nipples immediately hardened under his touch, and she arched her back instinctively, wanting to get closer to him.

"So responsive," he murmured. "I wonder what you'll do when I suck on them."

"Why don't we find out?" she hinted with a smile.

He grinned at her, but didn't lean down to taste. His hands continued their roaming, up and down under her tank. Long enough that, erotic as it was to see his hands moving under the material, Marit wanted to yell at him to take the damn thing off already.

"Arch," he ordered, sliding his hands under her back.

She gladly did as he asked, sighing in relief when he unhooked her bra. He then proceeded to pull it off her one strap at a time . . . over the shoulders, down each arm, finally dragging the material out from beneath her tank top.

Then he surprised her by moving one hand under her again. She arched to give him room, not sure of his intention.

He gripped the material of her tank tightly in a fist. She was arched a bit awkwardly, her shirt pulled tight enough to display her rock-hard nipples. Then he leaned down—finally—and wrapped his lips around one of her nipples through the thin cotton of her shirt.

The feeling was muted through the material, but nothing had felt as good as his mouth on her.

Marit moaned and brought a hand up to fist the back of his hair. He nipped and sucked, then moved to the other side, giving that nipple the same attention as he had the first. By the time he lifted his head, Marit was more than ready to move on to the part where they took their clothes off. Everything this man did made her want him more.

Except he didn't let go of her shirt, which kept her back arched.

He took his free hand and ran it down her chest once more, his gaze now locked on her boobs. Looking down, Marit again saw how tightly her tank top was stretched . . . and the two wet splotches right over her nipples, making them stand up even more.

"So beautiful," Zach murmured.

"Zach, please," she pleaded. She wasn't sure what she was begging for, but she needed more. Was desperate for it.

"May I take your tank off?" he asked.

His constant need for consent was both annoying and a huge turn-on. "Yes! Please, take it off!" she said in a rush, throwing both arms over her head to make the job easier for him.

She saw his smirk, but she didn't get upset that he was so pleased with himself. She was pleased with him too, and would be more pleased if he touched her without any material between them.

He ever so slowly peeled her shirt up and over her belly, exposing her skin a little at a time. When he got the tank over her chest, he stopped and leaned down. Marit struggled to get her tank the rest of the way over her head as Zach feasted on her breasts. That was the only word she could come up with for what he was doing. He used one hand to plump her boob while he sucked, bit, and devoured the nipple.

"More, Zach. Harder!"

He complied, and electric bolts shot from her chest to between her thighs. But it wasn't enough. She needed to touch him just as he was touching her.

She sat up abruptly, startling Zach enough for him to let go of her nipple. He made a popping noise as he released her, and he chuckled as Marit pushed him onto his back and switched their positions. She ran her hands up and down his chest, much as he'd done to her, loving the feel of the soft hair under her palms. She flicked a nipple as she went by and was pleased to find it just as reactive as her own.

He groaned, and the sound reverberated through his chest into her hands.

"Come up here," he growled, putting a hand on her hip and urging her forward, until she was on her hands and knees and her breasts were over his mouth. His head surged up, and he latched on to one of them, making Marit jerk in pleasure at the feeling of him suckling her. It felt completely different in this position, her breasts more sensitive for some reason.

He opened wider, and he took as much of her breast into his mouth as he could. Marit had always been self-conscious about her boobs. They were big for her frame, so she tended to wear sports bras to make them flatter. The last thing she wanted was to draw any attention to her gender while working on the lobster boats.

But tonight, she'd worn an underwire bra, wanting to feel more feminine for Zach. That was a good thing, considering it allowed him to unhook it and take it off her.

At the moment, her boobs didn't feel too big. Not in the least. Because Zach could more than handle what she had to offer. She felt her underwear getting soaked. She wanted to fuck. But first, she wanted to see what Zach had between his legs.

She once again pulled herself out of Zach's mouth and quickly moved down his body to his pants. He'd already undone the button and zipper, which made her job easier. She didn't hesitate to reach into his boxers and pull out his cock.

Good Lord, he was huge! Marit licked her lips, more than ready to take on the monster he'd been hiding in his pants. She lowered her head and took him deep into her mouth in one fell swoop.

"Holy shit, Marit!" Zach exclaimed, both his hands going to her head. He didn't push her down, simply held on as she began to suck.

She loved blow jobs. Loved the control she felt while giving them. Loved seeing how out of control she could make a man get. Not only that . . . she supposed she was weird, but she loved the taste as well. There was nothing like it in the world, and having the taste of come on her tongue only made her hornier.

She couldn't take all of him down her throat. He was simply too long. Too wide. Which was even more of a turn-on for Marit. One of his hands pulled her hair to the side so he could see what she was doing. Looking up as she sucked and slurped on his monster cock, Marit loved the expression she saw on his face.

Lust. Pure, unadulterated lust. But it was more than that. Respect. Affection. Awe.

"You are fucking perfection," he said, as she continued to do her best to suck him dry. She wanted to swallow his load, fill herself up from the inside out. Then she'd let him do whatever he needed to do to arouse himself again so he could fuck her.

His cock throbbed under her hand and tongue, grew even longer . . . which seemed hard to believe. But right before she thought she was going to get what she wanted—him coming down her throat—he easily pulled her off him.

"Zach!" she complained. "I want more."

"You'll get more, greedy girl. But there's no way I'm coming in that beautiful pouty mouth of yours our first time. I'm gonna come inside your pussy. Feel you explode around my cock. Then we'll sleep, and when we wake up, I'm gonna eat you out, watch you orgasm up close and all over my face . . . then *maybe* I'll let you drink my load."

God. She never would've guessed this man could be such a dirty talker. But she liked it. No, she fucking *loved* it.

Because deep down, Marit was extremely sexual. She didn't let herself go there most of the time because of her trust issues, and never with a man she'd known for as short a time as she'd known Zach. But for some reason, she trusted him already. She trusted him with the real Marit.

"Yes," she moaned.

"Pants off," he ordered, as he stepped off the bed and shoved his jeans and underwear down his legs.

Marit hurried to comply, lifting her ass and shoving her own pants and underwear down and kicking them off her feet. She reached down and peeled off her socks—because sex with socks on . . . *gross*—and watched as Zach walked naked over to the counter where he'd put his keys and wallet earlier. He opened his wallet and pulled out what she assumed was a condom, tearing open the package and rolling it down his cock as he walked back to the bed.

She appreciated that he didn't ask if he should wear one. He simply did what he needed to do in order to protect them both. She was on the pill, but that didn't mean anything in regard to sexually transmitted diseases. She didn't have any, but he didn't know that.

He stood by the bed, letting her take her fill. And if possible, he was even more gorgeous completely naked than he was with just his shirt off. She could see the scars from his knee surgeries, but otherwise his body was flawless. Hairy legs, trimmed pubic hair—which she appreciated; no lady liked hair in her mouth when she was giving head—and a look of complete awe on his face as he took his time admiring her, as well.

Marit opened her legs, inviting him in as he stood there. Her thighs had always been thicker than she'd liked, but since they were muscular, she supposed she'd take that over flab. Her belly had a pooch she'd never been able to lose, but generally she was an average weight for her height.

"I'm not sure how this is gonna work," Zach said, surprising her. Not moving onto the bed with her as she thought he'd do, as soon as he saw her naked.

"What?"

"You're fucking *tiny*. And I'm not. I don't know if we're gonna fit."

"Shut up, Zach. Get on this bed *right now*. I swear I'll hit you if you don't get inside me in the next ten seconds."

He grinned and did as she ordered, although he still looked a little worried. He lay on his back and lifted her effortlessly so she was once again straddling him.

"You do it. You take me so I don't hurt you."

"Zach, women were made to stretch. If billions of them can squeeze babies out their cooters, I think I can take you and your above-average cock into mine."

"Not gonna hurt you," he repeated between clenched teeth.

"All right. But for the record, I'm gonna want you to fuck me missionary style at some point. There's something so sexy about a man being in control and taking what he wants."

"Oh, I want you," he reassured her. "But I refuse to cause you any pain. In fact, come here. Let me make sure you're wet enough to take me." Then he yanked her forward without warning, much as he'd done earlier when he'd sucked on her boobs, forcing her up the bed until she was straddling his face.

Marit wasn't shy about this. She freaking loved being the recipient of oral sex, as much as she loved to give it. Unfortunately, she hadn't found anyone who was particularly good at it. Especially at this angle. But the second Zach shoved a pillow under his head and opened his mouth, she had a feeling he would be the exception.

And he was.

He was an over-freaking-achiever in the oral sex department. He understood that licking her pussy lips wasn't going to make her come. But latching on to her clit and licking rapidly at the same time he sucked would do the trick.

She came almost immediately. But he didn't let up. Simply continued to assault her extremely sensitive bundle of nerves.

Marit squirmed and undulated above him, one second trying to get away from his mouth, and the next, grinding to make him suck and lick harder.

He was grinning by the time he eased her off his face. Marit sat on his upper chest and stared down at him. He was smiling, and his beard was shiny from the copious amount of juice she'd spread all over him while coming.

"*Now* you're ready. You want me? You got me. Take me, Marit."

She didn't need to be told twice.

Scooting down his chest, smearing her wetness all over him, she hovered over his cock, which was still hard. She stroked him once, twice, then notched the mushroomed head between her soaking-wet folds.

She meant to go slow. To enjoy the moment. To tease him a little as she went down on him. But the second the head of his dick popped inside her, she got greedy.

Marit sat down fast, shoving his entire huge dick deep inside her body in one quick thrust.

"Holy fuck!" Zach exclaimed, as he grabbed hold of her hips and halfway sat up.

Marit groaned as he throbbed deep inside her body, filling her up completely. It was a tight fit, there was no doubt about that. And it *had* kind of hurt a bit, taking him all at once, but the pain was fading. All she felt now was desire.

"Told you, you'd fit," she bragged.

"Damn, woman. You're reckless."

In response, she squeezed her inner muscles around him as tightly as she could.

He groaned. "Do that again."

She did.

"Point made. Want me to take over? You're the one who said you thought it would be sexy if I was in control and took what I wanted."

That wasn't *exactly* what she'd said. She'd just been talking in general, but if he wanted to put himself in that role sooner than later, she wasn't going to complain.

"Yes."

Almost before the word had left her lips, Zach had flipped them. Her head was even with his chest, and she had to tilt it back to be able to see his face. He was so much taller than her, it was almost comical, but their sexy bits lined up perfectly, and at the moment, that was all she cared about.

"Hold on," he warned.

"To what?" she asked with an amused chuckle.

"Me."

He waited until she'd curled her hands around his sides, then he began to move. He pulled out of her slowly, then pushed back in just as leisurely.

"Zach, no teasing. I need you. Fuck me. Please!"

"I'm going to. First time, remember? I want to imprint this moment on my brain forever."

That was sweet, but she was past needing or wanting sweet. She needed dick. Hard and fast.

Marit brought both hands up to his chest and pinched his nipples . . . hard.

That seemed to do the trick. He pushed all the way into her in one fast, brutal thrust.

"Yes . . . like that," Marit encouraged.

"I wanted to go slow," Zach complained under his breath, as he began to pump in and out of her body.

Marit was done talking. All she could do was feel. She'd never taken a man as big as Zach, and she was shocked by how much size actually *did* matter. Her nerve endings were tingling, and she felt him from her toes to the top of her head.

He filled her up so completely, and she couldn't think of anything but him. She stared up at him in awe as he rocked his hips faster and faster. At one point, she had to lift her arms and brace herself against the headboard so he didn't push her any farther up the mattress.

Constant moans were coming from her lips now, and she wasn't even self-conscious about it. Every time he pulled out and pushed back in, it stretched the skin around her clit, and when he bottomed out inside her, his pelvis rubbed her just right.

She'd never, not once, come while being fucked . . . but there was a first time for everything.

Before she could warn him, Marit felt herself coming. Her thighs shook, her belly clenched, and every muscle in her body stiffened. And that made her passage tighter, making Zach's cock feel even bigger. Resulting in her climax going on and on and on.

She was still in the middle of her orgasm when Zach shoved himself one more time as far as he could get inside her body, pulling one of her legs up onto his hip, and groaned as he came, as well.

Marit felt as if she'd been turned inside out. She'd never come so hard or so long in her life. Her inner muscles were still twitching around Zach's cock. He made no move to pull out. Nor did he collapse on top of her, for which she was thankful. Instead, he turned onto his back, taking her with him.

Her cheek rested on his chest as she attempted to control her breathing, to recover her equilibrium.

"That was . . ." She literally had no words.

"Yeah," Zach agreed, panting.

She smiled against him. Happy they were on the same wavelength. If he'd wanted to have some long conversation about how great the sex was, she would've been disappointed. Instead, he seemed content to bask in the moment, same as Marit. To enjoy the feeling of fulfillment that coursed through her blood.

All of a sudden, she was exhausted, as if she hadn't taken a three-hour nap earlier. So much so, she could barely keep her eyes open.

She needed to stay awake. Figure out how to say goodbye, then get back to her apartment. She and Zach had had sex—really, really good sex—but that wasn't an invitation to spend the night.

She'd rest here for a second, then get up so he could take care of the condom. Then she'd get dressed, thank him for an amazing evening, and head home.

Yeah, that's what she'd do. In just a moment.

Chapter Six

Zach lay in his bed in shock, with a snoring Marit on his chest. What the hell had just happened? He honestly hadn't planned on having sex with her tonight. So he'd been surprised by her proposition, but not opposed. Definitely not opposed. Christ, he'd been sitting with her on his lap, in his recliner, and trying his damnedest to keep his dick from poking her in the ass.

He'd been completely serious when he'd told her that he didn't do one-night stands. Didn't want a fling. And now that he'd had her? Or rather, she'd had *him*—he still wasn't sure who'd had who here—he never wanted to let her go. She was literally his dream come true.

They were a perfect match sexually. He'd never really let himself go the way he had tonight. Never been with someone who was as open as Marit when it came to sex. And that boded well for a future sexual relationship. He could see them trying all sorts of things . . . and laughing and coming through them all.

The thing was, now he didn't want to move. That alone said a lot about the woman snoring on his chest. In the past, when he was still comfortable with casual, all he'd wanted was to get up and leave, or go to sleep, or clean up. But with this woman, he was content to let her use him as a pillow all night long. In fact, he could definitely get used to that.

It was unexpected, and almost scary, that he felt so at ease with her after such a short period of time. A single week. Love didn't work like that. At least not according to his experience. It kind of freaked him out that he could already envision a life and future with Marit.

She made a snort sound and smacked her lips, shifting on his chest. Zach realized his cock was still buried deep within her body. He'd gone soft, but because of his size, even at rest he hadn't slipped out of her. He could feel their combined juices coating his inner thighs, but he didn't give a damn. He should wake her up, get the condom off, but he was afraid if he did that, she'd leave.

And Zach didn't want her to go. He wanted her right where she was. In his bed. With his dick buried inside her body.

He thought back to the moment she'd taken him. Without caution. It had scared the crap out of him, thinking she'd hurt herself, while also turning him inside out with how good she felt around his dick.

The Marit he'd gotten to know in his bed was nothing like the cautious lobsterwoman he'd first met. But he supposed she could be who she really was here, in the safety of his apartment and behind closed doors. Didn't have to fade into the background so she wasn't noticed by the men in the lobstering industry.

That thought pissed him off . . . which led him to think about that Pearson guy.

He needed to get with his brothers. Figure out who Lucas Pearson was, make sure he understood that he'd better leave Marit alone. But Zach also suspected that if he did that without Marit knowing, he could lose her. She wasn't the type of woman who'd tolerate people going behind her back. She'd see it as a betrayal.

So he'd need to *convince* her to let him and his brothers go to bat for her. To stick up for her in a way her own brothers never had.

Thinking about her worthless brothers made Zach tense up yet again, which made Marit restless on top of him, as if she could sense what he was thinking.

He forced himself to relax. How could anyone who'd ever met this woman just leave her to fend for herself? Not love her to the moon and back? Not do everything in their power to be the best big brothers they could be?

Well, it was their loss. Marit was better off without them.

Eventually the day caught up to Zach, and he drifted off to sleep. The best sleep he'd had in ages, even with Marit draped over him like a living weighted blanket.

He woke up when Marit stirred. Looking over at the clock on his nightstand, he momentarily panicked. He should've been up thirty minutes ago! He needed to get to The Lobster—

Oh yeah. No, he didn't. He was taking the morning off, just as Marit also had the day off.

Sometime in the night, they'd shifted. Marit was now curled up next to him, one leg thrown over his thighs, her arm across his chest, and she was snuggled into him as if he were a body pillow. He could definitely live with that.

What he *couldn't* live with was the disgusting feeling of the condom hanging off his dick like a deflated balloon. Or the damp spot under his ass from his release . . . and hers.

Still, Zach couldn't help but grin at what they must look like.

"Please tell me you aren't this . . . smiley . . . every morning," Marit grumbled from next to him. Turning, he looked at the woman at his side. She hadn't moved. Was still draped over him as if she was attempting to keep him from floating away.

"Nope. This morning's special. How do you feel?"

She shrugged, closing her eyes as she said, "A little sore, a lot embarrassed, rested, grateful I don't have to work this morning."

"What are you embarrassed about?" he asked, not liking that in the least.

"Figures that's what you homed in on," she said with a sigh. "I was pretty forward last night. I'm not usually like that."

"You were. And I've never been so turned on in my life," Zach said simply.

That got her to open her eyes again. "You aren't just saying that because you enjoyed the sex? Sex you weren't planning on having?"

"Absolutely not. It's because I was with you. I told you before, from the moment I met you, something clicked inside me. Last night never would've happened if I hadn't felt that immediate connection, no matter how forward you were. And for the record . . . *enjoyed* is such a lame word for what I felt about last night."

Marit flushed. "Yeah."

"I know I spoke a big game about what I was gonna do to you when we got up, but I think we covered most of those bases before we crashed. What do you say we get up, get showered, and I make us a good old-fashioned American breakfast? With eggs, bacon, biscuits, and French toast."

Marit's stomach growled.

Zach grinned. "I guess that's a yes?"

"I haven't had a breakfast like that in forever. I usually just grab a bagel or something on my way out the door."

Zach had the momentary thought that he wanted to feed this woman a nutritious and filling breakfast every day for the rest of her life. It was way too early for that kind of thought . . . wasn't it? He honestly wasn't sure anymore. He'd never felt this comfortable with someone so early in a relationship.

"How about after we eat, we head down to the festival? It's your first time experiencing it, and I'd love to share it with you. All the good stuff happens this weekend, but we can at least walk around a little bit."

"You just want to check out The Lobster Buoy," Marit teased with a smile.

Zach shrugged. "I do, but that's not the real reason I want to walk around with you. Can't I want to show you off?"

She rolled her eyes. "I'm not exactly a prize, Zach."

Marit went to scoot away from him, but he wasn't having it. Zach rolled until Marit was under him, trapped under his much bigger body. He looked into her eyes as he said, "Wrong. You're hardworking, smart, strong, fucking beautiful, and anyone who sees us will take one look and know that I've hit the jackpot. They'll probably want to know how the hell I caught your attention and why you're with a bum like me."

Marit scowled. "You're not a bum."

"I own a lobster shack. One that has yet to prove itself successful. People around here judge others by how much of a 'Mainer' they are. And my stint in the Navy was probably a strike against me because I spent so much time away from Maine as a result. You? Being a lobsterwoman? You're at the top of the impressive list."

"You don't have to do that," Marit said, staring up at him, still frowning.

"Do what?"

"Pretend I fit in around here. I know that no one is super thrilled that I'm doing a man's job. It was the same in Portland, but since that was a bigger city, I got away with it a lot longer than I have here. I've only been here a short while, and I've already seen the looks people give me around town. I'm petite, yet I work in a male-dominated field. One that's belonged to men for over a century. It's weird, Zach. *I'm* weird. And I'm okay with that."

"Listen to me, Marit. Are you listening?"

She nodded.

"You aren't weird. I think the looks you're getting are ones of respect. Everyone around here knows how tough it is to be in the lobster industry. It's like farming in the Midwest. It's a damn tough job that no one really wants to do, but that everyone relies on. If people want their lobster—and trust me, they do—they have to rely on people like *you* to go out on the water and get them.

"You're new, so yes, you're going to have people curious about you. But you're also friendly, and open, and not an asshole. That goes a long way, especially when the locals deal with tourists day in and day out who aren't so nice."

"I haven't been here that long," Marit protested. "Not long enough for anyone to know that stuff about me. And I can be an asshole." She tacked that last bit on as if daring him to disagree.

"Of course you can. We're all assholes at times. All I'm saying is to give people a chance. A chance to get to know you. I don't really want to go there this early in our relationship . . . but you have some baggage, Marit. Emotional shit related to the way you were treated by the people who were supposed to love you unconditionally and didn't. Just because your brothers were douchebags, doesn't mean you can't be loved by strangers. By people you run into day in and day out. You just have to give them a chance to get to know you."

Zach couldn't read Marit's expression. He had no idea if he'd just fucked up royally, or if maybe he'd gotten through.

After a long moment, she nodded. That was it. A simple nod. But Zach was relieved she hadn't struggled to get out from under him and stormed off.

"So? Breakfast, then walking around? Then we can do whatever else you want to do."

"I thought you were taking just the morning off?"

Zach shrugged. "If I can peek in on The Lobster Buoy and they're doing all right—which I'm sure they will be; Jack will probably be cracking the whip and keeping everyone in line—I thought I'd take the rest of the day off too. Spend it with you. That is . . . if you want."

"I'd like that," Marit said with a shy smile.

The timid woman smiling up at him was so different from the sexually confident and demanding woman from the night before, it made Zach want to uncover all the various facets of her personality.

"But first . . ." she said.

Zach began to get hard just thinking about what she might suggest.

"The wet spot under my ass is getting annoying. Maybe we can get out of bed and get cleaned up?"

He let out a snort of laughter. "You weren't the one sleeping on it all night, woman," Zach told her. "I think my ass is all pruney, like your fingers get when you take an extra-long bath or swim for a long period of time."

Marit giggled. Zach could feel the movement in his body, which turned him on all over again. But this wasn't a time for sex. He really did want to get to know her better outside the bedroom. Spend the day with her.

"If I might be so bold as to offer a suggestion for what we can do later?" he said, after Marit had gotten control of herself.

"Yeah?"

"It's supposed to be nice today. I didn't get to give you the grand tour of Lobster Cove. We have this awesome swing over the water that—"

"Yes!"

"You don't even know what I was going to say," he said with a chuckle.

"You said *swing* and *water*. I'm in. I'm easy, Zach, you should know that by now."

Instead of laughing at the joke she was trying to make, he frowned. "Don't say that about yourself. You aren't."

"I can't believe you're saying that after last night. We've known each other for what . . . a week?"

"Would you have slept with Jonah?"

"What? No! I work with him."

"What about Linc or Knox?"

"Stop it, Zach. They're your brothers."

"Or the guy who works at the coffee shop? Maybe one of the other lobstermen you've met?"

Marit glared up at him.

"You aren't easy. You and I got together because we both felt an amazing connection. You feel it just as much as I do, otherwise you wouldn't have agreed to come to my apartment *or* sleep with me."

"Fine. That's true."

"You aren't easy, Marit," Zach said, his voice gentling. "I have a feeling you're going to be anything *but* easy when it comes to winning your trust. To getting you to open up and see that you're worthy of love, deserving of it.

"One more time, then I swear I'm done—those brothers of yours did a number on your self-confidence, sweetheart. I wish they could see how amazing you are and how you've landed on your feet. They didn't deserve you, and I'm going to do everything in my power to be the kind of man you can rely on. Trust. Lean on when you've had a shit day. I want to be the first person you call both when you catch a fifty-pound lobster, and when life goes to shit. I want to be your safe place, your everything. Just as you'll be the same for me."

"Zach," she whispered, obviously feeling overwhelmed. Tears swam in her eyes, but they didn't fall.

"No crying," he ordered gently. "This is a happy moment. We're naked in my bed, there's a condom stuck to my ass, we need to do laundry because we made a hell of a mess of my sheets . . . which I can't wait to do again, by the way. I'll let you have the bathroom first while I get breakfast prepped. Take your time. The hot water heater in this house rocks."

"I don't take long to shower and change. Remember?"

"That's right. Okay. Are we good?"

"We're good."

"You aren't mad at me for bringing up your asshole brothers?"

She smiled up at him. "No."

"Would you tell me if you were?"

She huffed out a breath. "Of course. I'm not one to let shit slide if I think it needs to be discussed."

"Good. You're really okay with going back out to Lobster Cove this afternoon?"

"Yes. It's beautiful there, and I'd love to get a tour of the grounds . . . and swing, of course."

"One more question before we get up."

Marit rolled her eyes.

"How do you feel about kissing first thing in the morning?"

"It's a hard no," she said with a small grin.

"Damn. Okay. Rain check?"

"Definitely."

Zach leaned down and kissed her lips briefly, nothing at all like how he really wanted to say good morning, then pushed himself up to his hands and knees. He couldn't stop himself from looking down at her body. Goose bumps broke out on his arms as he took in how fucking beautiful she was, and as he recalled all the things they'd done to each other just hours ago.

"Shower. Food," Marit reminded him with a teasing grin.

"Right. At the risk of sounding desperate and way too forward . . . will you stay the night here again tonight?"

"You want me to?" she asked, sounding surprised.

"Hell yes. And for the record, I don't want or expect sex every night. But I have to admit, I really liked having you as a weighted blanket. I always pooh-poohed the very idea of them, but now? I'm a fan. As long as it's *you* holding me down."

"We'll see," Marit hedged.

Zach could respect that. He was very aware he was trying to move this relationship at the speed of light. He simply wanted to be with Marit. The last week, when he hadn't been able to spend time with her, had sucked. And after last night, he wanted to be with her even more.

He pushed off the bed—knowing he could spend hours talking with her while they did nothing but lie around—and headed toward the bathroom to use it quickly before Marit showered.

She let out a burst of laughter so loud, he turned to see what she was laughing at.

"You really *do* have the condom stuck to your ass!" she said between giggles.

Zach twisted, trying to look down at his butt. Then back at Marit. She hadn't covered herself, and it was all he could do not to pounce on her. She looked amazing in his bed. On his sheets. Flushed and mussed from their lovemaking.

"Worth it. Completely worth it," he said with a wink, then walked toward the bathroom without removing the offending condom from his person.

The last thing he heard before he shut the door behind him was more giggles. And because of that, he couldn't keep his own smile from his face.

Chapter Seven

Marit felt better than she had in years. As she strolled hand in hand with Zach through the rows of vendors set up in Rockville's waterfront park, she couldn't help but smile as people greeted Zach over and over.

He may have tried to convince her that she fit in here, but it was more than obvious how much *he* was loved. He'd been gone for many years during his time in the Navy, but people obviously had long memories, and he and the Young family were clearly adored in this town. They were true Mainers, no matter what Zach claimed or how long he and his brothers might've been gone.

Several people offered their condolences for the loss of his father, which Zach accepted with grace. He didn't seem irritated that they were stopped time and time again to chat. Marit could also see that the comments people made to him about The Lobster Buoy, and how much they'd enjoyed whatever dish they'd tried, made Zach beam with pride.

And he *should* be proud. Today, his lobster shack had the longest line of both locals and tourists, eager to eat the delicious concoctions on offer.

They popped their heads into the back of the restaurant and greeted Jack, Zach's cook. The man snarled at his boss and ordered him out, pointing a spatula in their direction. "You're taking the morning off, remember?" he growled.

"I do remember. And if you keep up this insubordination, I'll take the afternoon off too."

Jack's mouth fell open, and he blurted, "Really?"

"Really."

"You're a miracle worker," he told Marit. "You eat free here for life."

"Hey! You can't go around giving away my food," Zach teased.

In response, Jack smacked his shoulder with the spatula this time. "Out!" he ordered with a smirk.

"I hope you're going to wash that thing before you use it again," Zach grumbled.

Jack rolled his eyes, then threw the spatula he'd been threatening his boss with into a bin in the small sink next to the grill, pulling a new one out of a drawer.

"We've got things under control here. Karen is coming in about twenty minutes, and Bill and Casey are keeping the line moving nicely. Now, scat. Skedaddle. Git."

"We're going, we're going," Zach told him. "You need anything, you call, understand?"

"Of course. Got you on speed dial. We got this though."

"Thanks, Jack. You're the best."

"Of course I am. I expect a nice end-of-the-season bonus."

"We'll see," Zach said.

"Fuck off."

"Back atcha."

The banter between employee and boss was funny. And cute. It reminded Marit of how she and Eliot were together, although she wasn't brave enough to be quite as brash as Jack. But the good-natured teasing back and forth had an undercurrent of respect. It was obvious Jack enjoyed the autonomy of being in charge while Zach was gone, and Zach had no problem trusting the other man to oversee his precious lobster shack. It was a great partnership, and Marit loved that for Zach.

Now they were wandering around checking out all the booths and the wares people were selling. Marit had to admit, she was a sucker for lobster paraphernalia. It was cheesy and stereotypical, and crazy since she worked with lobsters day in and day out. But she had to have a lobster charm she saw at one booth, and there was a squishy lobster she couldn't walk past as well. Zach bought both for her, even though she protested that she could afford them on her own.

To pay him back, she bought him a donut from Ruckus Donuts, an espresso crème. They'd eaten a large, delicious breakfast, but he seemed to enjoy the sweet treat . . . as much as Marit liked the taste of the coffee-flavored whipped cream on his tongue when he kissed her in thanks.

So far, Marit hadn't discovered anything about Zach Young that she *didn't* like. It was still very early in their relationship, they were still in the honeymoon stage, but seriously . . . the man could cook like a dream, he did laundry, he slept in the wet spot, he didn't make her feel left out when he was talking to people he knew, and he went out of his way to introduce her to everyone they met as "my girlfriend, Marit, who's one of the hardest-working lobsterwomen I know."

Of course, she was the *only* lobsterwoman he knew, but he didn't tell anyone that.

While in the shower that morning, Marit had taken to heart some of the things he'd said. He was right, she wasn't super happy that he kept bringing up her brothers, but he wasn't wrong in that they'd made her feel unlovable. If her own brothers hadn't found anything within her to love and cherish, how could a stranger?

But Zach was doing an amazing job so far of proving that she *was* worthy. That her brothers were the ones in the wrong. It would take more than one night of good sex and a public date for her to completely change the way she'd thought for so long . . . but some of the things Zach had said were making her reevaluate parts of her life.

After a couple of hours at the festival, she was feeling mellow, and happy, and relaxed . . . which ended when she saw Lucas Pearson walking toward them.

He was tall—which was why she saw him right away—and muscular, as many lobstermen were. He had closely cropped hair and a scowl on his face. She fully planned on ignoring him, but as they approached the man, he saw her . . . and loudly grumbled something about not being able to go anywhere without running into "fucking bitches."

"Excuse me?" Zach asked, obviously hearing the snide comment as well. It could've been directed at anyone, but since Lucas was glaring at her when he'd said it, it wasn't hard to miss who he was referring to.

When Marit herself didn't respond, Lucas raised his voice and said, "Why don't you just go back to whatever rock you climbed out from under? No one wants you here. We don't need you defiling our fleet with your tits and ass."

Marit could only stare at the man spitting such vicious words at her. She'd been minding her own business, on her time off, and yet he still felt the need to spew his nasty thoughts loud enough for everyone around them to hear.

In the past, she would've turned around and walked away, not giving any bully the satisfaction of getting a rise out of her. It was how she'd learned to survive around her brothers. To ignore, rather than confront them. To just take what they dished out, then walk away.

But Zach wasn't like that. He was more than ready to stand up for her. He subtly—or not so subtly—pushed her behind him and crossed his arms over his chest as he glared at Lucas.

"What the absolute *fuck*?" he bit out. His voice wasn't raised, probably because they were surrounded by people, kids included. "Lucas Pearson, I presume."

"You know me? I don't know *you*."

"Then you obviously aren't from around here," someone from the growing crowd said. They were standing on the main street of Rockville and were attracting quite a lot of lookie-loos. People who were curious as to what was happening. "Zach owns The Lobster Buoy. The Young family has lived in the area for more than fifty years."

"Whoop-de-do," Lucas taunted. "You think owning a shitty food trailer means you're a big man?"

"No. But I think being a decent person who pays my taxes, doesn't overcharge customers, and who served his country for years makes me a bigger man than *you* for sure."

That didn't make Lucas happy. Marit could see in his eyes that he was absolutely furious. Which wouldn't bode well for her.

Though honestly, she had no idea why he'd decided to suddenly target her in the first place. What had she ever done to him? She didn't even know the man, not really. She knew he'd been friends with Thorne Deaton back in Portland, had probably seen him at the docks a time or two, but she'd never really paid attention, as she kept to herself as much as possible.

"I know all about *you*," Lucas said, turning his attention back to her. Obviously, he understood that he couldn't beat Zach in a war of words, so he was targeting her once more. "Thorne made sure to warn me and his other captain friends about you. He knew you moved here after he ran you out of Portland. Wanted to make sure none of us hired you, since you're damn lazy and can't do half the amount of work the rest of us can."

"By 'the rest of us,' you mean *men*, right?" Zach asked.

Marit wanted to stick up for herself, she really did . . . but she was tired. Tired of the discrimination. The misogyny from men who didn't even know her. She thought women had the right to do whatever job they wanted, *if* they were qualified. She didn't want a handout. She didn't want to be treated differently. She simply loved being on the water, loved hauling lobster pots, loved the thrill of bringing up a pot and finding a rare blue lobster inside. That had only happened once in her career, and of course, the creature had been thrown back into the ocean, but not before she'd taken a shit ton of pictures.

She worked damn hard, and she knew it. This Lucas guy was making presumptions based on shit he knew nothing about. But then again, he was obviously a part of Thorne's inner circle; it was no wonder he had such a poor impression of who she was as a person, what kind of lobsterwoman she was.

"Of course I mean men!" Lucas said pompously. "It's called the Lobster*men*'s Association for a reason. Women shouldn't be allowed.

You're bad luck not only to the boat you're on, but to everyone you come in contact with. Everyone knows women shouldn't be aboard."

"That man needs a donut," someone muttered from the crowd.

Marit wanted to laugh, but she didn't dare do anything that might push Lucas over the edge. It was scary that someone who didn't even know her seemed to hate her so much. It was an unsettling feeling.

"You have no idea what you're talking about. You're living in the past, Pearson. Marit works *harder* than most men, simply because she has to prove to dumb assholes like you that she's just as capable as anyone else at the job. Besides, she isn't on *your* boat, so what do you care?"

"Because!"

Marit waited for him to say more, but when he didn't, she realized he literally had no other reason for not liking her other than because she was a woman . . . and because Thorne Deaton *told* him not to like her. It was pathetic, really.

"Let's go, Zach," she said quietly. "He's not worth our time or effort."

"Fuck you!" Lucas shouted.

There were loud grumblings around them now, about there being kids present.

"I'm sorry you don't like me," Marit said, keeping her voice calm and even as she stepped around Zach. He didn't stand in her way, but remained one step ahead of her, as if he was more than ready to stop Lucas if he did something stupid like take a swing at her.

Marit could handle him. She'd taken plenty of self-defense classes for situations just like this, but she appreciated Zach's willingness to protect her. She hadn't had many people, if any, who were willing to stand between her and danger.

"But I've done nothing to you, or Thorne Deaton, for that matter. I keep to myself, do my job, and that's it. None of the captains I've worked for have had any issues with me, because I'm good at what I do, Lucas."

"I know for a *fact* that's a lie. They just never said anything to your face. Besides, they only hired you because they wanted to look good to the association. But it's bullshit. There's no way you're as good as a man at hauling pots. Look at you! You're not even five feet tall! Anyone who works with you would have to take up the slack for your lack of strength and height."

"I'm five-two, thank you very much, and no one has *ever* had to work extra because I can't do something. I make it work. Period. Again, talk to Eliot and Jonah if you want. They'll tell you that I carry my own weight. *More* than carry my own weight, actually."

Lucas snorted. "You're probably sleeping with Jonah. Maybe even Eliot too. That's the only way you could've gotten hired in the first place."

Marit was done. She wasn't surprised sex came into the conversation. It seemed that anytime a woman rose in the ranks of any male-dominated profession, some guy was convinced it was only because she'd slept her way to the top. It was offensive and ridiculous. And she was *done.*

But before she could say another word, Zach moved. It seemed he was even *more* done with Lucas than she was.

Lucas wasn't a small man, but Zach was taller, and he had righteous anger on his side. He lunged forward and fisted the guy's shirt, pulling him in close until they were nose to nose. He said something in a tone so low, Marit couldn't hear. Then he pushed Lucas away with an abrupt shove, making him stumble back several steps, straight into a man with two kids and a wife.

That guy didn't take kindly to Lucas almost pushing his kids into the street, and he shoved Lucas so hard, he hit the brick building next to the sidewalk they were standing on.

"Watch it!" the guy with the kids growled.

"*You* watch it," Lucas countered lamely. Then he turned to glare at Marit with a look so full of hatred, she internally flinched.

No. This encounter hadn't done her any favors at all. It was only a matter of time before lobstering here became just as oppressive and dangerous as it eventually became in Portland. She thought she'd gotten away from Thorne Deaton by moving to Rockville. She should've known his reach was long . . . and that he wouldn't give up making her life miserable so easily.

Lucas turned his back on them and stomped off down the sidewalk.

"Hey, don't listen to him," a woman standing nearby said. "I know Eliot Sullivan, and he doesn't put up with incompetent workers. In fact, his oldest son worked with him for a while, and he actually fired him because he was constantly late and not pulling his own weight. If you're working for Eliot, you must be doing a great job."

"That guy's clearly an asshole."

"If you're with Zach Young, that's enough of an endorsement for you."

"Stay strong, girl!"

The encouragement from strangers was surprising. Marit couldn't remember a time when she'd had so much support from people she didn't know. When she turned to look at Zach, a muscle in his jaw was ticking, as if he was gritting his teeth, and his hands were in fists.

She stepped to his side and put her hand on his back. "You okay?" she asked quietly.

"No," he said sharply. "I need to walk."

Marit nodded. Unfortunately, she was used to being on the receiving end of blatant discrimination and hatred. She didn't like it, but figured she was better able to deal with it after so many years of similar treatment.

The crowd parted as Zach took her hand in his and started in the direction of the waterfront park, where they'd started their day.

Hating that such a great day had turned so bad because of her . . . well, not directly because of her, but because of a bigoted asshole like Lucas Pearson . . . Marit kept quiet while they walked. She smiled at people who said hi to them as they passed, but Zach didn't stop to talk to anyone, as he had earlier. He was truly lost in his head as they walked, and Marit was worried about him.

They walked all the way to the end of the park, where there were fewer people. They had a clear view of Rockville Harbor, and the lighthouse at the end of the breakwater path was visible from where they were standing. Marit made a mental note to walk out to visit the lighthouse at some point.

How long they stood there, staring out at the water, she wasn't sure. Just when she was about to suggest that maybe she should head back to her apartment, Zach said, "I'm sorry."

She looked up at him in surprise. "For what?"

"I hate that there are people out there like Pearson. Who think you can't do your job because of your gender. What the hell does gender have to do with it, anyway? If you can do the backbreaking work of hauling pots out of the ocean for hours on end, and you *want* to, who's to say you shouldn't? The only reason there aren't more women in the lobstering field is because it's damn hard work."

There were quite a few compliments in there somewhere, but Marit was stuck on the fact that he was apologizing for something he had no need to apologize for. "Honestly, I don't give a crap that people don't think I should be a lobsterwoman. If I did, I would have stopped years ago. I know that I'm damn good at what I do. What I don't like is *you* thinking you have to apologize for every asshole out there who isn't like you. I'm thinking you're one of a kind, Zach Young. You don't judge, and you're—"

"Oh, I judge," he interrupted bitterly. "Anyone who thinks they're better than someone else. Anyone who thinks his or her rank makes them better than others. Anyone who thinks it's okay to bully someone on a public street. They're no better than the gum on the bottom of my shoe."

"You don't have gum on your shoe," Marit said, trying desperately to lighten the mood.

Zach looked down at her, and without so much as a twitch of his lips said, "Fine. No better than the nasty fry oil I've been using all day, and haven't had time to change, and is full of bits and pieces of various food that's sitting on the bottom, all soggy and clumped together."

"Right, that's pretty gross," Marit agreed.

Zach took a deep breath, then turned to her and pulled her into his embrace.

Marit went willingly and held on tightly, resting her cheek on his chest. She needed this hug as much as she thought Zach did.

"What did you say to him there at the end? I couldn't hear you."

"I told him that if he so much as said one word to you ever again, I'd rip his balls out and fry them up and shove them up his ass."

Marit blinked in surprise, then her lips twitched. She couldn't help the chuckle that escaped.

"You're laughing?" Zach asked in surprise, pulling back and trying to catch her gaze.

"I'm sorry, I can't help it. Only *you* would intimidate someone by threatening to fry his balls before shoving them up his ass."

Zach closed his eyes for a moment, and when he opened them, he was smiling. "I don't know how, but somehow you've made me feel better."

"Good. Because I don't want to waste any more time thinking or talking about Lucas. Do you still want to go swing at Lobster Cove? I understand if you don't."

"Yes. Absolutely. I think we both need to forget about this morning and have some fun."

"As long as we don't forget about *everything*. That kiss you gave me after I showered was pretty darn nice."

"Yeah, it was, wasn't it? We could forget the swing and go back to my place," Zach said with one brow raised.

Marit laughed. "You were the one who brought up the swing. You can't go back on that now."

"You like swinging that much?"

"Yup. And it's Maine. We don't have that much longer to play in the water until it gets too cold."

"True. All right. Lobster Cove it is."

But instead of taking her hand and leading the way back to his apartment and his SUV, Zach put his hands on either side of her face and tilted her head back. "I'm proud of you. I think you're amazing. And anyone who doesn't see it must be blind, drunk, and have an IQ of four."

Pleasure bloomed inside Marit. He was being ridiculous, but she didn't even care. She went up on tiptoe, trying to reach his lips. Thankfully he leaned down, giving her access. The kiss started out chaste and heartfelt, but quickly morphed into pure passion. If they weren't in a public place, she was pretty sure they would've ended up naked, having sex.

As it was, they were both panting by the time Zach straightened. "Swing," he muttered, as if reminding himself more than her.

"Swing," she agreed.

Even though she really wanted to go back to Lobster Cove and see the entire property, and she really did want to see this swing and experience it for herself, she also looked forward to that evening, when she and Zach would go back to his apartment and could pick up where they'd just left off.

Chapter Eight

Zach was doing his best to put the incident with Pearson behind him. It was more than obvious Marit had. And even *that* pissed him off. That she was so used to people being assholes to her because of her gender and profession that she could so easily forget about what happened.

Then again, he figured she hadn't forgotten about it—how could she?—so much as intentionally put it to the back of her mind. They hadn't talked much about why she'd left Portland, but it was obvious to Zach now. This Thorne Deaton guy had driven her out, and she'd had no one to stick up for her. To help her fight back.

Rockville was different from Portland. Small towns were notorious for their tight-knit locals . . . and for being not so welcoming to newcomers. But Marit had something not every newcomer had—a boyfriend who'd grown up local, and who now owned a business in the town.

He'd seen it today when he'd introduced her to people he'd known for ages, and again during the interaction with Pearson. The locals were clearly on Marit's side. That loyalty would only continue to grow. If anyone was going to be chased out of town, he had a feeling it would be Lucas Pearson.

The question was how fast it would happen. Zach didn't want her to face any other confrontations like the one she'd had today. But he knew it was probably inevitable. He didn't think Pearson was smart enough to heed the threat he'd made against him.

For now, he did his best to put the incident behind him so it didn't ruin their rare day off. They'd stopped at her place so she could change into her suit before heading to Lobster Cove, and now had just pulled onto the property. He was looking forward to showing her around. Last time, she'd only gotten to see the house and the beach behind it. He wanted to introduce her to Walt and Barry, and show her the boat storage facility, which would soon start filling up as the weather turned colder. Show off his and his brothers' old fort in the woods, which Chad had named Fort Bad Assery after meeting their twelve-year-old neighbor, who'd commandeered it.

And of course, the lobster swing.

As he cleared the long drive, Zach saw Linc's SUV parked in front of the house. He was always glad to see his brothers, but he had a soft spot for his oldest. Linc was a decade older than Zach, and he'd been off in the Air Force flying jets when Zach was in middle and high school, but he'd always looked up to him.

Linc was a badass former fighter pilot . . . and even though he didn't talk about his missions, Zach had used his connections in the Navy to find out more details about the crash behind enemy lines that had ended his brother's career because of an injured shoulder. He'd evaded the enemy by walking ten miles a day until he'd simply walked across the border, back into safer territory.

Yes, Linc was a total badass, even if he never bragged about the things he'd seen and done.

Zach felt no awkwardness at all walking into his family home holding Marit's hand. He had no doubt his mother wouldn't even blink at how fast things were developing between them. In fact, she'd most likely be delighted.

"Mom! It's me. Zach. Are you here?"

No one answered, and the house had an empty feel to it. So she was probably out back or at the beach. It was a beautiful July day; the sun was shining and the breeze was light. Everyone around these parts knew to enjoy the warm days of summer while they had them, because all too soon the cold and clouds would descend on their little corner of the world for the winter.

"Come on, let's see if we can find everyone," Zach told Marit, still holding her hand and walking to the door in the living room that led out to the back deck.

The second they went outside, they could see and hear people down at the beach. His mom was cheering loudly from the shore as Linc high-fived a boy with bright-red hair, who'd just stood up after falling off a row of wooden crates floating in the water.

"What the heck?" Marit asked in confusion.

Zach grinned. "Come on." He led the way down the steps of the deck and headed for the beach to join the fun.

His mom noticed them as they got closer—and when she saw Marit's hand in his, her grin grew exponentially. She didn't comment on it, though, instead just said, "Look! Kash is rockin' the crates!"

The boy had gone back to shore, then taken a running start toward the crates strung together in the water. He ran across the crates bobbing in the water as if he was running on dry land.

"Um . . . someone want to explain why that kid is running across lobster crates?" Marit asked, the confusion easy to hear in her voice.

"He's training for the annual crate race," Linc answered. His eyes were glued to the boy as he ran back and forth across the fifteen or so crates that had been strung together in the shallow waters close to shore. "It takes place at Lobster Fest, on Saturday, and when he heard that some of us had won it, he came over asking for tips. So I found some old crates in storage and got them fixed up . . . and now he's practicing." Linc turned and grinned at Zach. "He's better than you were. Than *all* of us were. He's light on his feet and has extraordinary balance."

"I see that," Zach said with a small smile.

They all watched as Kash, the boy who lived next door with his mom and his grandfather, crabby Victor Rogers, ran across the crates Linc had set up for him.

"So . . . he's been coming over to Lobster Cove a lot?" Zach asked.

Linc shrugged. "He and Britt have become pretty good friends. She visits him out at the old fort and bribes him—I mean, brings him Mom's cookies and lets him babble on about astronomy. I guess he mentioned entering the crate race, because he wanted to do something to make his grandfather respect him, and she told the kid about us winning a couple of times. That was apparently all it took for him to overcome his reticence to visit the house. And now here we are. Watch it, Kash!"

The last three words were shouted, but it was no use. Kash tripped over one of the ropes holding the crates together and fell into the water.

Marit inhaled sharply, but the boy popped right back up, looking worriedly over at Linc and the rest of the adults.

"It's okay. You're doing amazing! I have no doubt you're going to be one of the top finishers!" Linc called. "The key is to move your feet as fast as you can. Spending as little time as possible on each crate. You'll get to rest a few seconds between laps. Once you get to the other side, you can regroup, breathe, then go again. You've got what it takes, Bud!"

The pride on the boy's face transformed him. Zach could almost see his little chest puff up and his shoulders go back a bit more. The small bit of encouragement Linc was giving him was doing wonders for his self-esteem.

Then the boy noticed Marit. "Who's that?" he asked, in that way kids had. Unabashedly curious and not afraid to say what they were thinking.

"I'm Marit," she told him.

"You're short."

Zach frowned, but Marit simply laughed.

"I realize that." She tilted her head and looked from the boy to the crates floating on the water, then back at him. "I've never seen one of these crate races, but you're definitely light enough that they don't sink too far when you step on them. And you're so quick on your feet! Nimble. I don't know who you might be going up against, but I have a feeling you're going to kick everyone's butts."

Her words also had a visible effect on Kash. "You think?"

"Oh yeah. I spend my life around these crates . . . well, plastic ones, not wooden like the ones you're running across, and I know how unstable they can be in the water. Seeing you run across them, and they're barely moving at all? You've totally got this."

"You work with the crates?" Kash asked, sounding confused.

"Yeah. I'm a lobsterwoman."

At that, Kash's eyes widened. "You are? I thought only boys could do that."

"Well, most people who work on the lobster boats are men, but the job isn't reserved just for guys. Anyone can do it if they have the strength and stamina, and if they want to."

"Cool," Kash breathed.

"You think that's something you might want to do?" Marit asked.

Kash wrinkled his nose in disgust. "No way!" he said without hesitation. "I'm going to be an astronomer. I wanna discover a new planet and maybe find evidence of intelligent life out there somewhere."

"That's pretty neat," Marit told him.

"Yeah. My granddad doesn't think so though. He thinks I should be a football player. I'm not big enough for that, but maybe if I win the crate race, he'll be impressed. At least a little. Running is athletic. He always tells me I should be more athletic. Like he was."

"Well, I think you should be whatever you want to be. And whether he's impressed or not with your ability to run across those crates, *you* should be proud of yourself. I don't think I could stay up on even three of those things."

"You want to try?" Kash asked with a smile.

"I don't think so."

"Actually, I think that's a great idea," Zach said.

"Oh sure, says the crate race winner," Marit mumbled. But she was smiling, so Zach didn't think she was all that disgruntled about this change in plans.

"Ms. Evelyn said *she's* even participated before," Kash said. "And she's old."

"Well, I wasn't *that* old when I did it," Evelyn protested with a laugh.

As Marit began to strip down to her bathing suit, Zach gave her a little info about the crate race to take his mind off the body she was slowly revealing. It was difficult to keep his *own* body from reacting to the sight of the woman he'd thoroughly taken the night before, but since he was in the company of his mother, brother, and a kid, he had no choice.

"The participants in the race are given socks to wear, so everyone is on an even footing, so to speak."

"Let me guess, lobster socks?" Marit asked with a laugh.

"Of course. There are fifty wooden crates strung together across the harbor. Each crate is filled with seaweed to make them more buoyant. If they make it across all fifty, they turn around on the connecting platform and go back. They do that again and again until they fall into the water. The first record ever was a thousand crates. That was in the eighties. The all-time record is sixty-five hundred."

"Holy crap . . . that's a lot of running back and forth!" Marit said.

"A hundred and thirty times," Linc said with a nod. "It was a tie that year, and neither Scarlett nor Harrison ever fell in. They finally just called it because it didn't look like either kid was going to ever falter."

"They were like . . . little," Kash said with a small frown.

"Seven and nine," Zach confirmed.

"I'm twelve. And taller than them." Then he perked up. "But I'm not that much heavier than they were. That's what Linc says."

"That's right. So forget about your age or weight. Concentrate on your foot placement and getting across. That's all you need to do," Zach assured him.

"What if I get tired?" Kash asked Linc.

Zach noticed for the first time that the boy looked at Linc as if he hung the moon. He drank in every word of encouragement that left Linc's lips. It was obvious the boy had a bit of hero worship going on. Something that Zach had himself when it came to his brother. He was one of the most humble and brave men he'd ever had the pleasure of knowing.

"Then when you get to the platform, you ham it up. Play to the crowd. Make a stupid heart out of your hands. Smile and wave to the spectators. Lean over and pull up your socks. Stretch. Anything that will give you a moment to take a breath."

Kash nodded solemnly, taking in every word Linc told him as if it was gospel. Then he turned to Marit. "Your turn!" he said excitedly.

"Oh joy," she mumbled, but she smiled at the boy. "No laughing when I fall," she told him.

Zach was doing his best not to stare at Marit. She had on a perfectly modest one-piece suit. Well, he thought it was one piece. It was possible it was a tank top with a bottom thing. He didn't know what women called them. All he knew was that she was just as sexy with all her private bits covered as she'd been naked as the day she was born in his bed last night.

But his attraction to her was more than just because of her looks. It was the way she spoke to Kash. How she seemed to understand that he had low self-esteem and did her best to lift him up. How she didn't talk down to him.

"All right, what tips do you have for me?" she asked the boy as she walked toward the shore.

As she and Kash talked strategy, Zach's mom sidled up next to him.

"She's pretty," she said with a little grin.

Zach rolled his eyes. "Don't start, Mom."

"What? I'm just saying."

"Just because Chad and Britt got engaged, and she's pregnant, doesn't mean I'm going to follow suit."

"I know. But . . . son, I've never seen you look at a woman the way you're looking at Marit right now."

For a second Zach was appalled, thinking his mom could see the lust in his eyes. Then she went on.

"You like her. I mean, *really* like her. You aren't just with her for sex."

"Mom! Stop!" Zach pleaded. He couldn't talk about sex with his mom. He learned all about the birds and the bees from his brothers. Although, there was that one time when his mom had come home with a box of condoms and handed it to him before dinner, as if she was giving him a can of shaving cream. It had been horrifying and mortifying.

All she'd said was, "Make sure you use those if you feel the need to have sexual relations."

His dad had simply chuckled, enjoying his son's discomfort.

"All right, all right. But . . . for the record . . . I like her."

Zach simply shook his head. His mom. He loved her more than anything, but she was as transparent as a piece of glass. She wasn't satisfied with Chad and Britt giving her a grandbaby. She wanted more.

"All right, I'm going for it!" Marit called out, looking back to where Zach was standing on the pebbled shore with his mom.

"You got this!" he encouraged. "Be careful though, it's pretty shallow here near the shore."

"Are you hinting that I'm going to fall after the first crate?" she asked a little grumpily, putting her hands on her hips.

Zach held up his hands in capitulation. "No, no, no. Just sayin'."

"Whatever," Marit muttered. She looked at Kash. "Ready?"

"Ready!" the boy said eagerly, with a huge smile on his face.

Zach saw Marit take a deep breath before counting down.

"Three, two, *one*!" She dashed toward the crates. She stepped on the first . . .

And it sank under her weight.

She almost went down right then and there. Instead, she managed to regain her balance and was able to step on two more, before she finally fell with a loud screech.

Zach stepped toward the water, hoping she wasn't hurt, but she popped up immediately, laughing hysterically.

"Okay, that was terrible. I want another shot!"

And thus began the start of an hour full of laughing, falling into the water, and cheering for Kash when he ran all the way to the end of the crates and dove into the cove time after time. Zach even took a turn at running the crates. But he was much heavier than when he'd won as a kid, and he wasn't able to make it past more than five or six before falling into the water.

Marit improved enough that she eventually made it to the end of the fifteen crates Linc had scrounged up, and she and Kash whooped and hollered enough that someone would've thought they'd just won the Olympics or something.

His mom got hot in the sun, so she wandered back up to the deck to sit in the shade and drink some water while she watched . . . but not before putting a hand on Kash's shoulder and saying, "You've got what it takes to win, Kash. Mark my words."

Even more confidence bloomed across the young boy's face.

When Kash finally got bored—or probably more accurately, tired—he asked Marit if she wanted to see Fort Bad Assery in the woods. She said of course she wanted to see this amazing fort. Zach and Linc both tagged along, content to let Marit and Kash talk among themselves.

When Kash started talking about asterisms, binary stars, and nebulas, Zach tuned him out. Honestly, the information was over his head. But it didn't matter whether or not Marit understood a word the boy was saying. She nodded and listened carefully, encouraging him to keep talking. It seemed as if the kid didn't get nearly enough chances to talk about his greatest passions. Space and stars.

He proudly showed Marit the fort he'd fixed up in the woods, near the property line between Lobster Cove and his granddad's place. Zach and Linc stayed outside, because there wasn't nearly enough room for either of them inside the tiny little structure made out of sticks and random pieces of lumber Kash had used to strengthen the old fort.

"He's a good kid," Linc said softly.

"Yeah. You really think he has a chance at the crate race?" Zach asked his brother.

"I do. You saw him, he's good. Better than we were."

"True."

"I don't like that Victor seems to be as much a judgmental asshole toward his grandson as he is toward everyone else, though," Linc said with a frown. "Why can't he accept Kash the way he is? And why isn't Harper sticking up for her son?"

Harper was Kash's mom . . . and someone Linc had a not-so-great history with. They were in the same grade in school growing up, and apparently she was a typical "mean girl," especially toward Linc. And he'd never forgotten.

Harper moved away right after high school, vowing never to return to the "hick town" of Rockville . . . but now here she was. Living back next door with her grump of a father, with a twelve-year-old kid in tow. No one knew her current story, or even saw much of her at all, for that matter.

Kash continued to babble on and on to Marit about his books and how dark it was out here at night and how well he could see the stars through his telescope.

"Maybe because she's not around much. You know, because she's working," Zach suggested with a shrug.

"Maybe. But it sucks that Kash doesn't think his grandfather approves of anything he does."

Zach couldn't disagree.

"Kash? Are you out here?"

The sound of a woman's voice calling for the boy rang out through the trees.

Kash reacted immediately. His head popped out of the fort, and he had a panicked look on his face. His red hair was sticking up all over the place, still damp from swimming in the cove.

"Oh no! That's my mom! She doesn't know about Fort Bad Assery. If she knows I'm playing on Lobster Cove, she'll be upset!" he fretted.

"I'll pack everything up for you nice and tight. You go on home," Marit told him calmly from inside the fort.

Kash didn't hesitate. He nodded, then scrambled out of the fort on his hands and knees before standing and turning to run toward the property line.

"Hang on, Bud. I'll go with you," Linc told him, catching him before he could bolt by latching on to his arm.

The relief that crossed Kash's face was easy to see. "You will? Thanks! You'll tell Mom that you invited me over and we were practicing for the crate race, right? You won't tell her about my fort or what I do here, will you?"

"Yes, and no. The fort can still be our secret. But do you really think she'll be mad?"

"No. But she'll worry. And she has enough to worry about."

That was an extremely telling statement, and Zach saw that his brother realized it as well.

"All right. Well, let's go make sure she's not worried about you."

They started walking toward Victor Rogers's place, and Zach heard Linc ask Kash, "Did you know your mom and I knew each other when we were kids?"

"You did?"

That was the last thing Zach heard before they walked out of earshot. He would've *loved* to witness the reunion between the mean girl and the boy she used to torment, but Marit took that moment to stick her head out of the fort and smile at him.

"This is really a cool fort. Bad Assery, indeed."

"That wasn't what we called it growing up," Zach admitted. "Chad made that name up the first time he found Kash out here."

"Well, it's appropriate. And have you seen all the stuff Kash has lugged out here? Books galore and a telescope that looks pretty expensive."

"Yeah. He's a pretty special kid," Zach said . . . and he found that he meant it. He hadn't spent a lot of time around children, but Kash was easily smarter than any other kid he'd ever met, and Zach enjoyed spending time with him.

"You get everything secured?" he asked Marit.

"Yup."

"Good. You want to see the rest of Lobster Cove?"

"Absolutely!"

The next hour was spent with Zach showing Marit around the land he grew up on. He showed her the boat storage facility, then they walked through the smaller of the two rental houses, as the scheduled guests hadn't arrived yet. They went down to the auto shop, and she was able to meet Walt and Barry. They'd been extremely busy ever since Camden, their part-time help, was thrown in jail for kidnapping Zach's mom and Britt. But they still took a moment to meet Marit, both of the men extremely friendly and welcoming.

Zach wasn't ready to share Marit with his mom again yet, so he suggested they walk along the shoreline. "I haven't shown you the lobster swing," he said with a smile.

"That's right! The whole reason we came over," Marit said with a laugh. "Lead on."

They walked in comfortable silence toward where the rope swing was attached to a large tree. Zach expected Marit to want to immediately take a turn when they arrived, but she surprised him by asking if they could simply sit on the nearby bench instead.

"I needed today," she said softly after a moment.

Marit had her hand in his as they sat and stared out at the water. "You okay?"

"Just tired. I mean, I'm usually *always* tired, but seeing Lucas today, and hearing his awful taunts . . . it reminded me so much of how miserable I was in Portland. I truly don't understand people, Zach. Why are they so mean? Why can't they leave me alone?"

"I don't have any answers for you, Marit. But I agree. Mom always taught us to mind our own business. As long as we're taking care of our own issues and being good human beings, we shouldn't care what others are doing. We can't control them anyway. All we can control is ourselves.

There are so many issues in today's world that could be solved if people simply minded their own damn business."

"So true," Marit agreed. "I'm not hurting anyone by working on a lobster boat. I work hard, do the best I can. If I was ever a liability, I'd totally quit. I'd never put anyone I worked with in danger because of my shortcomings. I honestly don't know why Thorne Deaton hates me. So much so, he'd actually go out of his way to tell people in Rockville not to employ me! The same with Lucas. I mean, he doesn't even *know* me, and yet he felt perfectly justified in spewing all that hateful stuff to me in public. So, yeah . . . that's why I'm tired. Tired of fighting so hard to do something I love."

"Don't let them get to you," he ordered a little gruffly, turning toward Marit on the bench. "I think it's awesome that you're doing what you enjoy. Don't let them take it away from you."

"I don't want to. But it's really hard to do my job day after day, knowing there are people like Lucas and Thorne out there who would love to see me fail."

"I've always liked to cook. From a young age, my favorite thing to do was be in the kitchen with Mom. I'd put an apron on just like her, and we'd be in there for hours, baking, mixing, cooking. As I got older, I was a lot like Kash. I worried that I wasn't manly enough. My dad took me aside and told me that as long as I enjoyed what I was doing, to hell with what others thought. Of course, it was easier said than done. When I joined the Navy, I had thoughts of becoming a Navy SEAL. With my brothers being badasses in their own right, in their branches of the military, I kind of felt like I needed to go that route.

"That time, it was Linc who sat me down and had a heart-to-heart with me. He asked what would make me happiest if there was anything in the world I could do. And I told him be a chef. He said I was an idiot for even *thinking* about suffering through what prospective SEALs did, if my heart wasn't truly in it. He urged me to talk to my recruiter and go a different route. To be a CS. A culinary specialist. It wasn't as impressive as a jet fighter, but I took his advice to heart, and I'm so glad I did.

"My point is . . . you gotta do what's right for you. What *you* want. You can't spend your life trying to please others. You're great at what you do, Marit. Don't let those assholes tear you down."

"You've never seen me work," Marit protested. "You have no idea if I'm good or not."

"You are," Zach said with conviction. "If you weren't, Pearson and Deaton wouldn't feel so damn threatened by you." Zach put his hand on Marit's cheek and gently urged her head around so she had no choice but to meet his gaze.

"You're funny, sexy, smart, strong, sensual, kind, willing to try new things . . . and I'm falling hard for you. I've never met anyone like you before, and I have a feeling I never will again. My brothers like you, Kash is halfway in love with you, my mom is *all the way* in love with you already, and you won Walt and Barry over after being in their presence for five minutes . . . and trust me, after the shit they've gone through with Mom and Dad's former best friend and his son, that's impressive. Screw what those assholes think, Marit. They aren't worth your time or energy."

Her muscles had gradually relaxed as he talked, and she rested her head in his palm. "Thanks," she whispered.

Zach leaned in and gave her a kiss. "You're welcome," he said against her lips.

"I can try to ignore them, but they aren't going to stop," she said with a sigh.

"It'll get old eventually," he said, although he wasn't entirely sure he believed that.

It was obvious Marit didn't either. "Yeah."

That one word was filled with doubt, but Zach didn't know what else he could say to make her feel better, or even what he could do besides threaten Pearson to stay away from her.

"For the record . . . I'm very glad you went the cooking route. Because I definitely don't like it myself."

Zach chuckled, glad for the change of topic. He didn't like to see Marit emotionally or mentally tired. Or frustrated. Or scared of someone. And it was obvious there was a bit of fear behind her words. He renewed his mental vow to make Pearson back off for good. Somehow. Someway.

"You want to try out the dish I'm thinking about making for Saturday? It's one of the busiest days of Lobster Fest, and I need something that's easy for people to carry and eat."

"Um . . . *duh*," Marit said with a grin. "What're you making?"

"You said yes before you knew what I was planning on serving," Zach pointed out.

"Of course I did. Whatever you make will be delicious. I have no doubt."

"Lobster pot pie with a buttery biscuit topping. I thought I could make them miniature size and put them in little aluminum cupcake-size tins."

Marit's stomach growled. Loudly.

She giggled and put a hand over her belly. "Sorry. I swear my stomach is constantly growling around you."

"Because I've done a crap job of making sure you're fed," Zach said. "Come on, let's go say our goodbyes to Mom. Then I'll take you back to town and make you pot pie for dinner. Unless you want to take a crack at the lobster swing."

"After all the crate running, I think I'm done being in the water today. Rain check on the swing though. Lobster pot pie sounds perfect right about now."

Zach went to stand, but Marit stopped him by putting a hand on his arm. He sank back to the bench beside her.

"Thank you. For sharing your home with me and for your words of encouragement. And for just being you. I think you're pretty amazing yourself."

This time when Zach kissed her, it wasn't a short peck of affection. It was deep, carnal, and it was all he could do to pull back and not take her right there on the bench. The only thing stopping him was the fact he'd never be able to spend another nice family day at the swing. Not if he was constantly reminded of having sex with Marit on the very bench where everyone sat while watching the swingers.

"You gonna stay the night again?" Zach couldn't help but ask as he stared into her eyes.

"If you want me to."

"I want you to," he confirmed.

"I have to get up early," she warned.

"Me too," he said easily as he stood, taking her hand in his once more. "We fit, Marit. Our schedules, our personalities, our love of lobsters." He grinned at that. "I really want this to work."

"Me too," she said a little shyly.

He liked how she could be shy one moment, and describing just what she wanted to do to him the next. The dichotomy was a turn-on. Made him feel as if he, and only he, got to know the real Marit.

When they reached the house, Chad and Britt were back from the store. They were unloading groceries, and while Zach normally would've happily stayed to chat, he really did want to get Marit back to his place so he could feed her. He didn't like knowing she was hungry. The donut from Ruckus Donuts was quite a while ago, and she'd burned a lot of calories trying to cross the crates in the water.

"It's so good to see you again," Britt told her. "I'm sorry we didn't have more time to chat the other night."

"Congrats again on your engagement and pregnancy," Marit said.

"Thanks! I'd love to get together sometime. I want to talk about lobstering. I know so little about it, since I'm from the South. Are you going to the Lobster Festival?"

"We went today," Marit said.

"Oh, but you have to go on Saturday. Or maybe Sunday. Chad says those are the best days."

"I'm pretty sure I'll have to work. At least on Saturday. Someone has to catch all those lobsters everyone is eating," Marit said with a grin.

Of course, Marit and the *Wave Rider* weren't catching *all* the lobsters served throughout the event. It was impossible for any one boat to provide the number of lobsters consumed at the festival. But they all knew what she meant. Lobstering was a year-round job, but even more important in the summer months, when the weather was better and there was a greater demand from tourists.

"Kash would love for you to be there when he runs the crate race," his mom added. Her head was inside a cabinet as she worked to put away the groceries Chad and Britt had brought home.

Zach opened his mouth to scold everyone for pressuring Marit. If she had to work, she had to work. Coming from military backgrounds, everyone knew how that went.

But Marit spoke for herself first.

"I'll talk to Eliot. I might not be able to get the whole day off, but maybe we can work our schedule around the crate race. I'd love to see what it's all about, and of course, support Kash."

"Awesome. I have your number—I hope you don't mind, I got it from Chad, who got it from Zach. I'll text you, and maybe we can meet up before or after."

"I'd like that," she told Britt with a smile.

"Me too. There's a lot of testosterone around here. I kidded with Chad once that this place should be called Alpha Cove instead of Lobster Cove."

Marit chuckled. "I can see why."

"What am I, chopped liver?" Zach's mom asked with a small pout. But she ruined it by laughing right after. "I begged their dad to give me a girl, but his sperm insisted on producing boys."

"Mom!" Chad complained, at the same time Zach stuck his fingers in his ears and hummed.

Both Britt and Marit laughed along with Evelyn.

"Alphas indeed. They can't even talk about babies," his mom said, smirking.

"It's not babies we have an issue with," Chad protested. "It's you talking about sex with Dad. Yuck!"

The mood in the house was jovial. Zach looked over at Marit, and saw she was smiling and relaxed. He loved that for her. Especially compared to their first visit to the house, when she'd been so stressed after meeting his brothers.

"We need to get going. I need to work on what I want to serve on Saturday at The Lobster Buoy, and Marit said she'd be my taste tester," Zach announced.

"Why can't *we* be your taste testers?" Chad complained.

"You can. Saturday. Lobster pot pie. Ten ninety-nine for a cupcake-size serving," Zach returned.

"Wow, that's steep. Good for you!" Chad said, giving Zach a high five.

Getting praise from his family never got old. "Thanks. And now we're really heading out. Say bye to Linc for us."

"Where is he?" Evelyn asked.

"He walked Kash back to his place. Not sure what kind of mood he'll be in when he gets back though. Harper was calling for her son, so I'm sure they probably had words. We all know they've never gotten along."

"People change," his mom said easily. "I'll tell him you were sorry you didn't get to see him before you left, though."

"Thanks."

Zach led Marit outside and back to his Explorer. Once they were inside and on their way, she asked, "Do Linc and this Harper woman really hate each other?"

"No clue. They haven't seen each other since they were in high school. But I know she wasn't nice to him back then. At all. Not sure why. I don't think *Linc* even knows why she was so hateful toward him all those years ago."

"It'll be interesting to see how things go between them, in that case. Because it's obvious Kash likes him a lot, and he clearly enjoys spending time on Lobster Cove."

"Yeah. Hopefully neither Harper nor her dad will be assholes about Kash spending time with us."

"Hopefully."

"Are you really going to ask Eliot if you can get some time on Saturday to go to the crate race?"

"Yeah. That is . . . if you think Kash would really want me there?"

"I'm sure he would. But more importantly, I'd love to spend more time with you. Saturday at Lobster Fest is fun, like Britt said. There's the five- and ten-K races in the morning, the Codfish Carry right before lunch, the lobster-eating contest at lunchtime, then the crate race starts at two-ish."

"I think if Eliot and Jonah are okay with it, if we go out early, we could be back by one. In time for me to run home, change, and meet you somewhere for the race."

"Sounds perfect. I'll bring you something to eat so you aren't hungry while we're watching. How about that?"

"Oh, I can just grab something when I run home."

"Nonsense. You'd probably nuke something not very nutritious. And if you've been out working for hours, you'll need something more filling."

"How do you know me so well after such a short time?" she asked with a tilt of her head.

Zach simply smiled over at her.

The rest of the drive back to Rockville was spent talking about their favorite foods—other than lobster—and Zach telling Marit stories about growing up on Lobster Cove. She didn't share a lot about her childhood, but Zach understood that her memories weren't the best.

They'd spent the entire day together, but it felt like he'd gotten to know her so much better in just the last couple of hours. And the more he was around Marit, the more he *wanted* to be around her. He could only hope he didn't screw things up between them.

He could envision a future with this woman, he just prayed she felt the same.

Chapter Nine

On Saturday, as Marit stood on the deck of the *Wave Rider* and hoisted pots from the depths of the ocean, pulling out lobsters that fit the criteria for keeping and throwing back oversize ones and females with eggs, she contemplated the last few days.

She could lobster in her sleep and had no problem doing her job while lost in her thoughts.

Zach was . . . almost too good to be true. She kept waiting for the other shoe to drop. For him to turn out to be an asshole to kids or dogs. To talk smack about his employees. To not wash his hands after using the bathroom. But he'd done none of those things. The more time she spent with him, the more she talked with or texted him on the phone, the better and better he seemed.

Which was kind of freaking her out. Since losing her parents, the run of bad luck in her life really did extend to everything. Family, jobs, friends. Despite fighting to retain her optimism, it was still hard to wrap her mind around how well things were going with Zach.

Today, Eliot and Jonah had agreed to get a head start on the water so they could come in and watch the crate race and enjoy the afternoon at Lobster Fest. It meant Marit would be exhausted by the end of the night, because three a.m. was an *extremely* early start to the day, but it would be worth it.

She'd spent the night at Zach's place after their day at Lobster Cove, and the sex had somehow been even better than the first time. She'd been almost feral with lust for the man, and he'd met her needs and then some.

They were *so* compatible, it actually worried Marit. So much so, she'd put the brakes on and made up excuses as to why she hadn't been able to stay at his place the couple of nights since.

Zach was a great guy. Why she wasn't grabbing him with both hands and refusing to let go, she had no idea.

Probably because, since she couldn't find any flaws in the man, she expected something to happen that would make him come to his senses and question why *he* was with *her*.

Sighing, Marit notched the tail of another female with eggs before throwing her back into the ocean to have her babies and live another day. That was kind of how she felt sometimes, as if she was thrown back time and time again, when all she really wanted was to settle down with a few kids of her own and live a peaceful life. Free from harassment. From men trying to tell her what she could and couldn't do. Convincing her that she wasn't enough . . .

In the back of her head, she heard Zach's voice on that beautiful bench at the lobster swing. *You're funny, sexy, smart, strong, sensual, kind, willing to try new things . . . and I'm falling hard for you.*

She remembered his words exactly. Something had melted inside her at hearing such praise. She'd drunk in the words she'd never heard anyone else say about or to her. And that was honestly sad. She was almost thirty, and she felt as if she'd missed out on so much. She went to work, came home, sat on her couch, and repeated that routine over and over. She was afraid to go outside her comfort zone. To risk being rejected.

Case in point, Marit was avoiding spending time with a man who liked her exactly as she was.

And Zach wasn't the only one who'd accepted her.

Britt had been texting nonstop. Sending memes, saying hello, giving her updates on what was going on at Lobster Cove, even asking for her opinions on baby names. Marit was thrilled to be included, to have a female friend, and she'd stayed up way too late the other night, looking for memes to send back that she thought Britt might find amusing.

She'd also stopped into Ruckus Donuts so many times this week, the owners, Todd and his wife Lee, were now on a first-name basis with her. And, shockingly, she'd even gotten a couple of polite nods from lobstermen on neighboring boats when arriving at the *Wave Rider* the last few mornings.

She was making friends and acquaintances, opening herself up to the people she saw every day around her, and they were responding positively.

Of course, things weren't all sunshine and roses. Lucas was still around. It was as if he was purposely trying to cross paths with her. He hadn't said anything, not since Zach had threatened him, but if looks could kill, she would've been six feet under by now. He hadn't given up his grudge against her, that much was obvious. Not in the least. It was disconcerting, wondering when and where he might make a move against her.

She liked the Lobsterites, all the people who lived and worked on Lobster Cove. Liked the locals, who were getting friendlier by the day. Enjoyed the thought of being part of a community for once in her life. And she wanted to go all in with Zach . . . but she was still afraid. Scared of losing everything she felt she'd gained in such a short period of time.

"You okay, Marit?" Jonah asked.

She glanced at her coworker. The guy had had a crush on her when they'd first met, but ever since she'd started seeing Zach, Jonah seemed to have come to his senses, no longer making moon eyes at her throughout every shift. Now she felt much more of a camaraderie with the man. She liked that a lot.

"Yeah, just thinking. And tired."

"I get it. I had a date last night and didn't get home until midnight."

Marit whistled. "Seriously? Only three hours of sleep?"

"Try two. Called to make sure she got home all right, then had to get up in time to be at the dock by three."

"Jeez, Jonah. I hope you're going home after we get back to the dock to get some sleep."

The man grinned. "Nope. Have a date with a different woman tonight."

Marit rolled her eyes.

Jonah simply laughed. "After you broke my heart, I figured I'd better get out there and find the next best thing."

"Whatever. You and I were never going to work out. We're too much alike. Can you imagine working side by side with your partner day in and day out? No thank you. I prefer some non-together time."

"She's got a point," Eliot said from his spot next to the wheel. Far from simply standing there, watching the work going on, the captain of a lobster boat had an active role in the harvesting. He was responsible for hooking the pots, and Marit would help bring them on board. Then she took out the lobsters, and Jonah would rebait and push them back overboard. It was a smooth operation, and the three of them worked together as if they'd been doing it for years, rather than just a few short weeks.

"Your mom and I were complete opposites, and it worked for us. I think she would've murdered me in my sleep if she had to spend every waking hour with me," Eliot went on.

"I admit I was upset at first that you wouldn't even give us a shot, but Zach's good for you. Anyone can see that. You're different since you two started dating."

"In what way?" Marit asked, genuinely curious.

"I don't know. Happier? Not that you weren't friendly before or anything," he was quick to say. "You just exude, like . . . an inner happiness you didn't have before. That sounds corny. Sorry."

"No, it's okay," Marit said. She thought about Jonah's comment and realized he was right. She felt more content deep down, knowing she had the respect and attention of a man like Zach. And the amazing sex didn't hurt either. She was probably still glowing from the intense orgasms Zach had given her, and the pleasure of knowing he'd enjoyed the things she'd done to *him* in bed, as well.

"What is that idiot doing now?" Eliot growled. It was such a change from the easygoing tone he'd had a moment before, Marit whipped her head up in alarm.

The *Men At Work*, Lucas Pearson's boat, was placing lobster pots almost on top of the *Wave Rider*'s. It was an unspoken rule for lobstermen to respect others' pot placement and not lay theirs too close. It was as if the man was trying to sabotage their catch.

Which was probably exactly what he was doing.

Instead of getting on the radio, Eliot turned the wheel and aimed his boat at Lucas's.

"What are you doing?" Marit asked with a frown.

"Finding out what that asshole thinks *he's* doing," Eliot answered as he piloted quickly, straight toward the other lobster boat.

He turned just in the nick of time, sending a huge wave toward the *Men At Work*. Lucas stumbled on the deck, and probably would've fallen if he hadn't grabbed the wheel. There wasn't anyone else on the boat with him that Marit could see, which was unusual.

"What's the matter, your latest deckhand quit again?" Eliot taunted.

Everyone knew the turnover on Lucas's boat was extremely high. For someone who'd only been in town a short while, that was saying something—and that *something* wasn't good.

"At least I'm not desperate enough to hire a chick," Lucas retorted.

Marit refrained from rolling her eyes. Barely.

"Seems the *chick* I hired is out-lobstering the most seasoned deckhands in the area," Eliot boasted. "We're ahead by forty pots today. Our hold is full. We'll be done in another hour or so. How many have *you* caught?"

"Fuck off," Lucas spat.

"Stop placing your pots on top of mine, Pearson. You know full well that's not cool. If you so much as touch one of the *Wave Rider* pots, I'll turn you in faster than you can say 'Expensive fine.' Understand me?"

"I was here first," Lucas protested.

"You were not, and you know it. Knock it off. *Now.* You don't have to like my employees, but you have no right to harass me *or* her. Just mind your own business. Catch lobsters your way, and I'll catch them mine."

Marit did her best to hide the smile at hearing Eliot say "Mind your own business." She recalled the conversation she'd had with Zach about that exact thing. It was a relief to know her boss felt the same way she did about what others did with their lives.

Lucas glared at Eliot but didn't say another word. Nor did he make any move to pull up the pot he'd just dropped.

Apparently deciding he was done dealing with Lucas, Eliot put his boat in reverse and gunned it, sending another wave into Lucas's boat. It rocked back and forth once again, and Marit loved that Lucas had to grab the oh-shit bar above the wheel to avoid falling.

"Asshole," Eliot muttered. "Jonah, can you get out your phone and take pics of his pots on top of ours? If we come back out here and his aren't moved, I'm reporting him for sure."

"Of course, Pop." Jonah took off his rubber gloves and headed to the dry bag where he'd stashed his phone before they'd headed out.

"I'm sorry," Marit felt obligated to say to Eliot.

"For what?"

"For causing Lucas to be such a jerk."

"You didn't cause that. He was always an ass. As was his father. Knew the man when I worked over in Portland, years and years ago. Always wanting to take shortcuts. Always breaking the rules. Wanting money, but not willing to put in the work to get it. *Not* your fault."

"I worked for someone like that in Portland, when I first started in the industry. I actually reported him for unsafe conditions and ignoring the laws, and for harvesting breeding females. He was heavily fined, but I didn't care. He was going to end up killing someone, and I quit before it could be me. Lucas reminds me of him, thinking he's above the rules." She sighed. "Still, he's only messing with you because of me. He's definitely mad I'm here," Marit said unnecessarily.

"He can be as angry as he wants, that doesn't give him the right to insult you, or me, or to break lobstering rules. I may not have said something when he first started harassing you, but I'm done letting him walk all over both of us. I've got your back, Marit. Don't worry. And for the record, I've done a little askin' around on the docks. No one else around here cares that you're lobstering. They're intrigued, and maybe confused about why you *want* to do a job like this, but they certainly aren't upset about it. So just ignore Pearson. He'll get over himself sooner or later."

Marit wanted to cry. Of course, lobsterwomen didn't cry. They were tougher than that. But the fact that Eliot had gone out of his way to talk to his friends in the industry, and they didn't care that she was working on his boat, meant more than he could ever know. She might never be actual friends with the other lobstermen in the area, but as long as they tolerated her presence and didn't actively try to drive her away, she was okay with that.

Looking at his watch, Eliot shrugged. "I told Pearson we had another hour, but I think we're done for now. We have a great haul, and I know you want to get back to watch the crate race. I remember seeing my first one, and how in awe I was. Of course, the lightweights, the kids mostly, have the upper hand as the crates don't sink when they step on them, but it's just as fun to watch them scamper across as it is to see the adults fail spectacularly. Assuming you're meeting Zach to watch?"

"Yeah. The boy who lives next to Lobster Cove is competing."

"Kash Bates. Good kid. Shame about the situation with his mom. Anyway, after Jonah gets his pictures, let's get you back to shore so you can have some time with your man."

Marit wanted to ask what he meant about Kash's mom, Harper, but she got busy helping to clean up the deck and get the boat ready to dock and get their daily haul off-loaded.

When they docked, Eliot shooed both Marit and his son off, insisting that he might be old, but he'd been taking care of the *Wave Rider* longer than either of them had been alive . . . which wasn't exactly accurate, but Marit wasn't going to argue.

She walked home as quickly as she could, which wasn't as fast as she would've liked, since the streets of Rockville were packed. The shower she took was quick, and, after throwing her hair up while it was still damp and changing into shorts and a T-shirt, she headed out to meet Zach. They'd made arrangements via text to meet at The Lobster Buoy.

When Marit arrived, she grinned at seeing the line at Zach's lobster shack. It was at least fifteen people deep. The employees working the window were in constant motion, one taking money, one calling out the name of each person as their order was ready, and another preparing the orders, moving the food from the grill into the small paper baskets they used for serving.

Everyone was smiling, and Marit heard more than one person raving about the little pot pies.

The small buoys Zach had also made to sell were disappearing almost as quickly as the food. They weren't anything super special, just simple PVC buoys with "The Lobster Buoy" printed on the sides, but people seemed to love them. Now that she was paying attention, everywhere she looked, Marit saw one hanging on someone's backpack or purse.

They were quintessential Maine, since they were tiny replicas of an actual lobster buoy, but including the name of the shack on them was pretty darn smart, as far as she was concerned.

"Hey, Zach! Marit's here!" Casey called out.

"Be out in a sec!" Marit heard him yell from the back of the shack.

She waved at Casey to let her know she'd heard, then stood off to the side to study the crowd. Despite being so busy, everyone seemed to be in a good mood. Kids were running around, parents were doing their best to keep an eye on them, and everyone had some kind of food or drink in their hands. Ice cream, Zach's pot pie, beer.

The weather was perfect, lower eighties, and the sound of people chatting and laughing was constant all around her.

This was what Marit had been looking for. A place where people could relax, enjoy hanging out with their neighbors, slow down and take a breath now and then. Yes, many of the people here were tourists, but the fact that they could appreciate a small-town festival like this one and didn't need to head to a huge city to be happy was heartening. It even felt good that she had a hand in the joy people were feeling by catching some of the very lobsters they were eating.

"Hey," a deep voice said in her ear.

Marit didn't jump in surprise; she immediately recognized Zach's voice. And the feel of his arm going around her waist and pulling her back into his chest was like coming home.

"Hey," she said softly, turning her head to look up at him.

"How was work?"

"It was work," she replied.

Zach frowned as he stared at her. "What's wrong? What happened?"

So much for her hiding what happened with Lucas. Marit shrugged. "Lucas decided to put his pots basically on top of ours."

"He can't do that, can he?"

"Well, there's no law against it in Maine, but it's severely frowned on. And if he touches our gear, there can be huge fines. No one is allowed to haul anyone's pots but their own. But it's definitely a douchebag thing to do. His catch will be less, and ours too. But I suppose at this point, he's more concerned about screwing me over than worrying about how many lobsters he's catching."

"Did he say anything to you?" Zach asked, turning her in his arms so she was facing him.

"Not really. He and Eliot mostly had words. He was awesome. Eliot, that is. I think Lucas was kind of humiliated. And it seems as if he's working solo again."

"Again?"

"Yeah. He can't keep a deckhand to save his life. I haven't been here long, neither has Lucas, but even I've heard the stories about what a dick he is to work for. How he cuts corners on safety, and more than once, he's kept lobsters that are too large. Or breeding females with eggs. Just like Thorne did back in Portland. Rumor has it that Lucas even has a hidden compartment on his boat to store them, so if he gets inspected at the dock, no one will find any illegal lobsters he's kept."

"What an asshole."

"Yeah," Marit agreed.

"I'm sorry he's still being a pain," Zach told her. "You want me to talk to him again?"

"No!" she answered quickly. Then she gave Zach a weary smile. "I appreciate it, but it won't do any good. Lucas is convinced I'm bad luck, and having Thorne encouraging him from Portland, and possibly even egging him on to harass me, Eliot, and Jonah, doesn't help. Winter's coming soon enough, and by then, hopefully things will cool off, literally and figuratively."

"I'm struggling to let you deal with this on your own, or not put any pressure on you to let me and my brothers help," Zach admitted. "I know you left Portland because of that Thorne guy, and the last thing I want is for you to think the best way to deal with Pearson's bullying is by leaving Rockville as well. I don't want that. I just found you. Losing you because of some bigoted asshole would suck."

"I don't want to leave," Marit reassured him, feeling all warm and fuzzy inside from his words. It wasn't a declaration of love, but knowing he felt that way about her, about their relationship, felt really good. "And I love that you want to help, but you already are. By doing *this*. Being with me. Showing me the things that are important to you, like this festival. By sharing your family with me and taking me to the crate race. Being with you makes me forget that there are people out there who hate me simply because I have boobs instead of a dick."

In response, Zach hugged Marit hard.

She held on just as fiercely while she blinked back tears. Moving to Rockville was one of the best decisions she'd ever made. Of course, she'd come here because she'd basically been driven out of Portland because of Thorne and his viciousness toward her, but she could see herself making Rockville her forever home. She loved this little town.

"How was today at the shack?" she asked, tilting her head back but not letting go of Zach.

He grinned. Huge. "Good."

"Good?" she questioned. "Just *good*?"

"Great. Fantastic. Better than I could've imagined. I'm going to have to make those lobster pot pies a regular menu item. I could jack up the price simply because they have lobster in them, but in reality, they're mostly bread, which is fairly cheap. People are happy about the lobster, though. When in Maine . . ."

"They're happy because they're damn tasty," Marit corrected.

"That too," Zach said.

She studied him for a moment. "You really love what you do." It wasn't a question. He'd told her that he'd wanted to be a chef from the time he was young, but standing here, with Zach smelling like fried food and grease, sweating from being in the back of his shack, smiling from ear to ear because he wasn't just making people happy with his food, he was making money while doing it . . . all that made him more attractive to her.

"I definitely do. You want to head out, get a good spot to watch the race?"

"Yes!"

He handed her a paper bag with The Lobster Buoy's logo on the side. "I bet you thought I forgot. Lunch for you," he said, nodding toward the bag as she took it from him. "It's a lobster roll. I know, I know, it's cliché, but I really loaded the lobster on. So it's more lobster than roll. Just don't go spreading tales about how my lobster rolls have twice the amount of lobster as everyone else's, because I made it that way special just for you. I'd go broke if I stuffed every roll I sold with that much meat."

Of course, Marit's mind immediately went into the gutter. "That's what he said," she muttered, as she reached into the bag.

Zach roared with laughter. His hand rested on the small of her back as they made their way toward the harbor, and as she ate the delicious sandwich. He was right, it was literally overflowing with buttery lobster. And it tasted delicious. She was ruined for any other lobster roll for sure.

As she ate and they walked, Zach asked, "You have tomorrow off, right? Because in the summer, no pots can be hauled on Sunday, yeah?"

"Uh-huh."

"You want to spend it with me? At least the afternoon, after I spend the morning at The Lobster Buoy?"

It was just that morning that Marit had been thinking about slowing things down with Zach. It was why she hadn't seen him for the last couple of days. But him asking if she'd spend the afternoon with him, and not just assuming, made all her reservations disappear in a puff of smoke.

Growing up, her brothers had preferred she remain out of their sight as much as possible. They didn't like the constant reminder that they were responsible for her. They saw her as a huge burden. As a result, she'd taken it for granted that people didn't want her around. That they'd prefer she do her own thing.

Having Zach insist he *wanted* to spend time with her felt nice. Heady.

"Marit?"

"Sorry, yes, I'd like that."

"Anything in particular you want to do? It's supposed to rain all day, so doing much of anything outdoors is probably out."

Amazingly, Marit didn't get any sexual vibes from his statement. He wasn't suggesting she come over and have sex with him all afternoon—although she probably could be convinced to do so—he simply wanted to spend time with her. There went those butterflies in her belly again.

"Britt said things were crazy at Lobster Cove. Cleaning the rental houses and baking in preparation for the next guests. Chad and the guys are swamped at the auto body shop, and she mentioned something about helping with their inventory? Said she loves living there, and helping out wherever and however she can. Sounds like she works a lot," Marit said. "Maybe . . . we can go over and help them out?"

"When did you talk to Britt?" Zach asked.

Marit shrugged. "She texts me all the time. And she called last night."

Zach was beaming.

"What? What are you smiling all freakishly like that for?" she asked.

"I'm just thrilled she's reached out. Chad's been worried about her. She *does* work a lot, hardly takes any time off. And she hasn't really made any friends here yet, because she's always out at Lobster Cove. I'm just happy you two are hitting it off."

It said a lot about Zach that he was happy for his sister-in-law-to-be. Some people couldn't stand their siblings' significant others. Marit liked that Zach seemed to honestly care about Britt the way he would a sister.

"I like her. She's nice." That was probably an understatement. The other woman had made Marit feel so welcome. And it felt great to have a friend. Even if they'd just met, they'd clicked. "Anyway, since it's going to be rainy, maybe we could go over to Lobster Cove and lend a hand.

Maybe even help decide what they need to do to the rental house after the season's over, before they move in. She mentioned ripping up carpets and gutting the kitchen. Said they wanted all-new appliances, but she has no idea where to start trying to figure out what to buy to replace them."

"Is that really what you want to do on your day off? We could hang out at your place, or mine, and watch a movie. Or go out for dinner. We could get some donuts from Ruckus and eat them in bed," Zach hinted, with a teasing glint in his eye.

"Or, we could get some donuts for *everyone* before we head to your mom's place. Maybe watch a movie with your mom and Britt and Chad after a hard day's work."

Zach laughed. "It's a date."

Marit had never had such unique dates with a guy before, and was happy Zach had agreed. Not that she'd had all that many dates to begin with, but she liked their twist on them. A lot. Enjoyed knowing they'd be helping out his family, and she was excited to go back to Lobster Cove. There was such a welcoming, homey feel to the place. Something she'd been missing for a long time.

That wasn't to say she wanted to live there. She liked Evelyn, but she didn't think she'd want to live with Zach's mother. Besides, Lobster Cove was too far away from the boat docks. She'd have to get up even earlier than she already did to get to work, which didn't appeal.

Of course, once winter hit, while the lobster industry was no longer prohibited by law from working on Sundays, the amount of time they'd spend on the water would be reduced. As would her salary. But Marit didn't mind. While she loved lobstering, she *didn't* love being on the water in subzero temperatures.

Marit felt Zach watching her, and she tilted her head to meet his gaze. "What?" she asked, wondering why he was staring at her so intently.

"I'm just wondering what I did right in my life to deserve you. Having a girlfriend who willingly wants to go to my family home and work, or shop for a house she won't be living in, or hang out with my mother, and who seems happy about all of it."

"Funny, I was wondering how *I* got so lucky to have a boyfriend who's willing to share his family with me, and who doesn't mind spending his day off with them."

"Who said I had the day off?" Zach asked with a grin. "I need to go by in the morning and do some cooking, then set the menu for next week. We won't get nearly as much business as we are now, during the festival, but I want to make sure I have some new stuff for anyone who might be sticking around. And for the locals. I thought maybe I could experiment while we watch that movie."

"Can I help?"

"Sure."

She loved that he agreed so quickly, despite knowing she wasn't much of a cook . . . and given he wouldn't let her near the food during that first dinner in his apartment. She grinned at the thought. "What are you thinking about making?"

"Lobster and truffle macaroni cups. The cupcake tins went over so well with the lobster pot pie, so I figured we could use them again, charge the same price for mac and cheese cups. I also thought I'd experiment with some breakfast food, and see if people might be willing to buy it for lunch or dinner. Lobster and cornbread waffles with maple butter—from right here in Maine, of course.

"For those who might not want carbs, or who're watching their weight, I want to try out a lobster and blueberry salad with citrus vinaigrette. Again, with the blueberries coming from a farm not too far from Rockville. I've already talked to the owner, and she said she'd bring a bushel of blueberries down to the shack this week. Oh hey, before summer's over, maybe we can go blueberry picking together? I used to love to do that when I was little. Maine has the best blueberries. They're smaller than what you get in the stores, but so much sweeter."

Marit grinned even wider at hearing Zach's passion. About the meals he wanted to create and the possibility of spending more time with her, showing her things he'd loved while growing up around here.

She'd finished her lobster roll by the time they got to the area around the harbor that had been set up for spectators. It was already getting crowded, and Marit was glad they'd gotten here early. Zach texted his brothers and let them know approximately where they were standing. It wasn't long before Knox, Evelyn, Chad, and Britt joined them.

"Where's Linc?" Zach asked.

"He's with Kash, over near the starting platform. His mom couldn't come, and of course, Victor refused to watch 'something so ridiculous,'" Evelyn said.

Marit frowned. That sucked. The kid had been so anxious about proving to his grandfather that he could do something athletic, just to make him proud.

"So Linc took it upon himself to watch over Kash and be his coach. To keep him company and try to keep his nerves settled," Evelyn finished.

"Harper's not here to watch her son?" Knox asked, slight derision in his tone.

"She had to work," Britt said, defending their neighbor. "She tried to get the day off, but her boss said no. I told her that I'd record Kash's run for her, so she can watch it with him when she gets home."

"You've been talking to her?" Zach asked in surprise.

"Yeah. She came over the other day because she couldn't find Kash, and she was worried. I broke down and told her about the fort, then I swore her to secrecy. We got to talking a bit. She's nice. I like her," Britt said firmly.

"Easy, Peach. No one's saying they *don't* like her," Chad soothed.

"Coulda fooled me. I know Linc has a history with her, but Kash is a good kid. He wouldn't be that way if she was a *complete* bitch. She works all the time, and her dad isn't the easiest person to live with. I don't know her entire story, but she's obviously had a rough go of it, from the little things Kash has let slip. She's doing her best to raise her kid, save enough money for a place of their own, and to make amends for the person she used to be when she lived here. So, I decided she could use a friend. Like I did when *I* first got here."

"Where does she work?" Zach asked.

"The big-box store on the outskirts of town."

"She can't be making too much there," Knox mused.

"I don't think she does. But as I said, she's working as much as possible to save up some money."

"You sure know a lot about her for just meeting with her once," Knox observed.

"That's just who she is," Chad explained. "I swear if the Russian president came over, she'd convince him to give up his power-hungry ways and be a decent person."

Everyone chuckled.

"If you want to give her my number, I'd be happy to text her," Marit blurted. "I mean, I'm new here too, and I wouldn't mind making another friend."

"I'll do that," Britt said with a grin.

Talk turned to the upcoming race, and Zach took that opportunity to lean down and whisper into Marit's ear, "You're a good person. Thank you."

"You don't have to thank me for befriending your mom's neighbor. I like Kash, and like Britt said, Harper can't be *all* bad if her kid is anything to go on. Besides, I wasn't lying. I *could* use more friends. Other than you and your family, that is."

"She'd be crazy to turn down your offer of friendship," Zach replied.

Just then, the public address system let out a loud and ear-piercing squeal. Everyone moaned, and some people covered their ears.

"Sorry about that, folks! Welcome to this year's world-famous Lobster Festival Great Crate Race. Are you ready to cheer on our contestants?"

The crowd roared in response. Marit tried to find Kash among the crush of people down at the docks, near the floating platform. The crates were strung across the water all the way to another floating platform, ready for those brave enough to attempt to race across them.

She crossed her fingers, hoping Kash would do well. It was obviously important to the boy, and she wanted him to be proud of his performance.

Chapter Ten

"It's tradition for members of the Coast Guard to go first. Even if one of them does manage to put in an impressive performance, they're ineligible to win. But because they help out with the crates and safety during the competition, anyone who's involved is allowed to give the crates a go."

Zach was standing behind Marit, his arms around her waist, his hands resting on her belly as she leaned into him and they watched from the edge of the harbor. He loved standing like this with her. He was tall enough to easily see over her head, and the feel of her against him was intimate and cozy. He bent slightly to speak into her ear, explaining what was going on as it happened.

"When does Kash go? That's what I want to see," Marit said impatiently.

Apparently she didn't care about the exhibition competitors.

"Wait," she said, looking over at Knox. "Why aren't *you* out there? You're in the Coast Guard."

"I was," Knox said with a laugh. "I'm not anymore. Besides, I've wised up in my old age. I don't need to humiliate myself by only getting across two or three crates before falling into the water."

"Whatever," Zach told him. "You'd show everyone up, and you know it."

Knox patted his belly. "I'm in the super category now, no showing anyone up no matter *how* much skill I might still have."

"There are four classes of participants," Evelyn told Marit. "Featherweight is up to seventy-five pounds, lightweight is seventy-six to a hundred and twenty-five pounds, medium is one twenty-six to one seventy-five, and super is anything over a hundred and seventy-six pounds."

"The overall winners in the past have mostly been in the featherweight class," Chad said.

"Which makes sense, considering the crates don't sink as much when they step on them," Marit said with a nod. She was watching the Guardsmen with interest as they all tried, and failed, to even get across to the other platform one time.

"Next up will be a representative from the local police department. They also usually have some sort of local celebrity, as well. They all ham it up before the actual contestants start," Evelyn continued. She had a spark in her eye that Zach loved to see. It was only a few months ago that she'd lost her husband, so it made him happy to see her out and about and having a good time.

"How many people actually compete?" Marit asked, tilting her head back to look at Zach.

"Generally under a hundred. Of all ages and all weights. We'd be here all night otherwise."

She nodded and turned her attention back to the water.

"Kash is in the middle of the pack. He's number thirty-nine," Chad said, as he looked at his phone. "Just got a text from Linc."

"Cool. He'll have time to hopefully lose some of the nerves by watching everyone else. And seeing others fall will show him that this is all in good fun. Hopefully," Knox muttered.

Zach loved how everyone was all in for Team Kash. He just hoped and prayed the boy did well.

The field was mostly kids or teenagers, but there was the occasional mom or dad who decided to take a shot at the crates. Most people fell before getting even ten feet from the starting platform. But they all came up from the water smiling. Everyone was having a good time, even when they fell.

There was one man in the super class who made it halfway across the crates before falling, earning him a huge cheer from the crowd. Many of the smaller competitors went much farther, but everyone understood that the people competing in the super class had a major handicap . . . of weight.

Marit fidgeted against him as it got closer and closer to the time for Kash to go.

"I'm so nervous," she said, looking back up at Zach.

"Me too!" Evelyn chimed in.

"Me three!" Britt agreed.

Zach was too, but he didn't say anything, simply squeezed Marit's waist.

Then it was time. A little girl who was contestant number thirty-eight was preparing to have a go at the crates.

Zach saw Linc next to Kash. He was kneeling down, saying something to the boy, most likely encouraging him. Or giving him last-minute tips. Kash looked nervous. *Really* nervous. He was shifting from foot to foot. His gaze locked on the crates as if mesmerized.

"Oh man, he's too nervous," Knox said softly.

"We were the same way our first time," Chad reminded his brother.

"Yeah, and we all crashed and burned as a result. It wasn't until we learned to have fun, to take it in stride, that we actually did well."

"He'll be fine," Marit said sternly. "Just watch. He'll get past those nerves. I know it."

Zach loved her optimism . . . but secretly, he agreed with his brothers.

Everyone in the crowd gasped when the little girl finally fell. She hit her head on one of the crates on her way down, and there was an immediate hush in the crowd. But a member of the Coast Guard was right there with his boat, helping her into the vessel. After about thirty seconds, she sat up in the boat and smiled. She waved, letting everyone know she was all right. The crowd cheered and yelled in relief.

She'd crossed five hundred and thirty-nine crates. It was an incredible run. Of course, the record was sixty-five hundred, but over five hundred wasn't anything to sneeze at.

Now it was Kash's turn.

"Please, please, please," Britt whispered.

"He's got this," Marit said, as she shifted her weight from foot to foot, much as Kash had done earlier. She looked extremely excited and nervous as they all waited for their neighbor to take his turn.

"Next up is Kash Bates. He's twelve years old and just squeaking into the featherweight limit, one of our most competitive categories. It's his first time at Lobster Fest, and his first time facing the crates. Let's give him a big ol' Lobster Fest greeting!" The announcer was hamming it up for each contestant, and the crowd loved it, giving him what he asked for by cheering and clapping loudly.

Kash looked back at Linc once he was standing on the platform. He really was a scrawny kid. All bones and angles. He leaned over and pulled up the white socks with lobsters on them that every contestant was given to wear to make the field more even, as far as footwear went.

After Linc gave him a thumbs-up, Kash turned back to face the line of crates bobbing on the water in front of him.

"You've got this, Kash! Kill it!" Marit yelled at the top of her lungs.

Kash heard her, and his head turned in their direction, causing everyone in their little group to cheer loudly, encouraging him as much as they could.

To Zach's amazement, Kash's shoulders went back as he straightened. He could almost see the confidence spreading through his body. Seeing for himself how many people were there to support him, even if his mom and grandfather couldn't be there, obviously made him feel good.

Then his brows furrowed, and he took a deep breath.

"All right, Kash, show us what you've got," the announcer said. "Go ahead whenever you're ready."

Before the last word was out of his mouth, Kash was off. He took a few running steps—and then he was crossing the crates.

Zach watched in awe as it seemed as if the boy flew over the water. He could barely see his feet touching the crates, and they hardly seemed to even bobble under him.

Before he knew it, Kash had made it across the first fifty crates and was safe on the platform on the other side.

When the boy turned around, Zach saw a look of surprise on his face, as if he couldn't believe he'd actually done it. The surprise quickly morphed into determination. It was as if all it took was making it across that first time, to prove that he could do it, and Kash's entire attitude shifted.

As the kid ran back across, Zach could see that he was really going to do it. He might not win, but he was going to give whoever else went after him a serious run for their money.

Their little group lost their collective minds as Kash continued to run back and forth over the crates. Two hundred. Five hundred. A thousand.

And he just kept going.

He was like the Energizer Bunny. There were a few times when he stopped on one of the platforms, hamming it up for the crowd, just as Linc had suggested back at Lobster Cove. Giving himself a break without making it seem like he was stalling.

Britt was filming it all, screaming along with the rest of the crowd, who were now clueing into the fact that they were watching an extraordinary performance. As much as everyone laughed and liked seeing people wipe out, they loved it even more when someone crossed the crates thousands of times.

Of course, every time Kash wobbled or almost slipped, a huge gasp would go up from the spectators, and then they'd cheer even louder when he regained his balance and continued onward.

"He's doing awesome!" Marit gushed, turning toward Zach, tugging on his shirtsleeve as if that would make her words more impactful. Then she immediately spun back around so she wouldn't miss a second of Kash's performance, not waiting for him to respond.

He *was* doing awesome. But the kid was getting tired. His steps weren't quite as nimble. He wasn't running as fast as he did in the beginning. He looked a little more wobbly as he ran. It was only a matter of time before he took a misstep and lost his balance. But Zach was more than impressed with how many crates he'd been able to cross already.

It was on his thirty-eighth time crossing the crates when he slipped. Kash went down hard, face-first. He was halfway across when he fell, his face hitting a wooden crate, and he literally bounced into the water.

Everyone around them gasped.

Every muscle in Marit's body stiffened as they all waited for him to pop up from the water. It only took a second or two, but they felt like the longest moments of Zach's life.

When Kash's head finally appeared from the water, he was actually grinning from ear to ear. Upon seeing that, the crowd lost their minds. A roar went up all around them, with everyone cheering at the top of their lungs.

The safety/rescue boat picked up Kash and quickly brought him to the starting platform. Zach, and everyone else, watched as Linc plucked the boy from the boat and hugged him, spinning him in circles as he did.

The cheering was still going on when Linc put Kash back on his feet and urged him forward. Kash shyly took a step toward the end of the dock and raised his hand in a wave to acknowledge the crowd.

Once again, everyone lost it, screaming and yelling for Kash and his extraordinary performance.

Making it across one thousand, eight hundred, and seventy-ish crates wasn't close to the record of sixty-five hundred, but it was still impressive as hell and seriously awe inspiring, especially when the next best number so far was just over five hundred.

The crowd was amped up, and the cheering for the next contestant was loud and boisterous, even when he didn't make it across the crates one time.

"Come on, let's go find them," Knox said.

He didn't need to ask twice. Everyone in their group was more than ready to find Kash and congratulate him.

"Told you he was gonna win," Zach's mom said smugly as they headed toward the crowded area around the starting platform.

Zach found Linc and Kash first; it helped that he had the height to see over most of the crowd. Kash had a towel wrapped around himself, and he was beaming as a man wearing an EMT shirt stood after putting a bandage on his face.

"That was amazing!" Britt exclaimed as they got close.

"Britt! Did you see?"

"Of *course* I saw, Bud! I filmed it all to show your mom, although you should probably watch the video without sound because we were all screaming our heads off."

Kash looked extremely proud of himself, as he should be. Zach could remember how he'd felt when he'd been in the boy's shoes. He'd been on top of the world. It was a heady feeling.

"The competition isn't over yet," Evelyn warned. "Someone could still beat his score, doubtful, but it could still happen."

"Maybe," Linc said, putting his hand on Kash's shoulder. "But it wouldn't take away from how awesome Kash did. Especially since that was his first time running the crates."

Zach stood back and let everyone fawn over the boy. Marit leaned against his side, and he put his arm around her shoulders, enjoying her closeness and the fact she had no problem showing affection toward him in this very public place. Everyone was looking at them, since they were huddled around the current leader in the crate race.

She looked up at him, and even though he could see her pride for Kash, her excitement over the moment, he could also see exhaustion behind her eyes. She'd gotten up extremely early this morning to get to the boat, so she could put in a full day of work and still get back in time to see Kash's race. Her desire to support a kid she'd just met hit Zach hard . . . in a good way. She was unselfish, supportive, and so incredibly kind.

"You okay?" he asked.

"I'm great. Thank you for encouraging me to be here today. I would've been so sad if I'd missed this."

In response, Zach leaned down and kissed her.

It took every ounce of strength he had not to deepen the kiss, as he longed to do. He was keenly aware that Marit had pulled back in the last couple of days. He didn't really blame her, as they'd been moving very fast in this relationship. He'd had a few misgivings himself. But it wasn't as if they were getting married in the next week or anything.

He just loved being around her. She made him happy. He looked forward to talking to her, seeing a text from her when he got up, seeing the look on her face when she tried one of the concoctions he made for his shack.

The bottom line was, he wasn't going to think too much about things. Either he and Marit would work out or they wouldn't, but he refused to put any roadblocks in their way simply because most relationships didn't play out the way theirs was.

She stared up at him as she licked her lips, and he could practically see her thoughts in her gaze. She was feeling the same thing he was—the need to be alone.

"We'll stay to see if Kash does win, then we'll go to my place, where I can feed you."

"I'm not a dog," she said softly with a chuckle.

"I know. But I feel the need to take care of you. I know you're tired, and you burned a lot of calories working today. How does grilled chicken, asparagus, and peanut butter pie for dessert sound?"

"Not lobster?" she asked, the smile still on her face.

"I can mix it up every now and then," he said with a shrug.

"That sounds awesome. Thank you."

"You'll stay?" Zach found himself asking. He wouldn't take it for granted that she'd spend the night with him, especially after the last couple of days, when he'd felt her pulling back.

"If you want me to," she told him.

"I definitely want you to," Zach reassured her. "Always. And for the record, you have an open invitation. You don't have to wait for me to invite you over. There will be some evenings I need to work late, but for the most part, after the festival, I'll have more time. And when the cold weather hits, I'll have to decide what to do with the shack. It's not as if people will be coming to grab something to stand around and eat in the cold."

"You could offer takeout," Marit suggested.

Zach blinked. Duh. Of course he could. He'd been so fixated on the fact that no one would come to a lobster shack in the winter that he'd been considering closing down, the way most businesses like his did. But if he could keep his customers throughout the winter, it was likely they'd continue to come by when the weather warmed up.

"Yeah. I could even offer delivery. At least maybe during the dinner hours. As long as the weather isn't bad and the streets are safe, Casey, Karen, and Bill might even be willing to deliver for me after school hours," Zach mused.

"I know if I could get lobster mac and cheese and those pot pies delivered to my door when it's freezing cold outside, I would do so in a heartbeat," Marit told him.

"You're going to offer delivery? That's an awesome idea!" Knox said, obviously overhearing the conversation between Zach and Marit.

"There aren't enough places that deliver around here," Britt agreed.

"You're going to have to set boundaries, though. You don't want to be driving all the way to Waldoboro or Camden. That'll eat into your profits because of the cost of gas," Chad chimed in.

"If you deliver to Lobster Cove, I'd definitely order," their mom said.

"Mom, you know if you ever want anything, all you have to do is ask," Zach told her wryly.

"Do you have pizza? We haven't had pizza delivered in forever," Kash piped in.

Everyone laughed.

"You like lobster, Bud?" Zach asked.

In response, Kash wrinkled his nose.

"Right," Zach said with a smile. "I bet I could whip up a pretty decent pepperoni with extra cheese for you one night."

Kash grinned—but then his smile immediately dimmed. "Oh, well, that's cool. But never mind. Mom can't really afford for us to eat out."

It took everything within Zach not to ask why Victor couldn't pay for it. The man had money. He might not be a millionaire, but he definitely had enough to buy his daughter and grandson a fucking pizza now and then.

Linc was obviously thinking the same thing, because he was frowning ferociously.

Just then, a cheer went up around them, and everyone turned to look at the crates. A girl, probably around nine, was running back and forth over the course like a gazelle.

Kash's brow furrowed as he watched her intently, waiting to see how many trips she'd make over the crates.

Linc squatted down next to Kash and said, "Even if she beats your score, that doesn't take away from how awesome you did."

"I know."

Zach supposed he *did* know, but he was probably still wishing the girl would fall. He'd been in his shoes once upon a time. Trying not to be a bad sport but still wanting to win.

The girl had just passed the fifteen-hundred mark, and the crowd was cheering wildly, when she stepped off the platform for another lap. Unfortunately, she misjudged where the crate was, or she just landed wrong, because she lost her balance and her arms windmilled as she desperately tried to stay upright.

It was no use. She fell sideways into the water, all but securing Kash's first-place position.

"Is it wrong that I feel bad for her, but also good for myself?" Kash asked Linc.

"It's normal," Linc reassured him. "It feels good to win."

"I've never won anything. Except a science show when I was in the fourth grade, but that doesn't count."

"Why doesn't it count?" Evelyn asked. "Seems to me a win is a win."

Kash shrugged.

Marit straightened from where she'd been leaning against Zach, breaking body contact with him, but immediately reached for his hand, which Zach eagerly took. He used to think people who held hands all the time were . . . strange. But now he couldn't get enough of touching this woman. Having some sort of connection with her all the time.

The line for contestants got shorter and shorter as people took their shot at running across the crates. There were a couple of other kids who did well but didn't make it above a thousand crates.

It looked more and more like Kash really *was* going to be this year's winner. Zach was thrilled for him.

When the last person stood on the platform, hamming it up for the excited crowd, Zach couldn't stop smiling. Kash had done it. He'd won. The last contestant was in the heaviest weight category. There was no way he'd be able to cross more than a dozen or so crates before wiping out.

And Zach was right. The man did his best, but he fell into the harbor after only eight crates.

Linc picked up Kash and hugged him tightly. "You did it! You won!"

Kash was grinning when Linc put him down. The award ceremony would take place in half an hour. The minutes until then were spent with locals and tourists alike all crowding around, wanting to congratulate Kash on his extraordinary performance. The local TV station even did a short interview with the boy.

Throughout it all, Zach and Marit stood off to the side, taking in the excitement of the moment.

"I'm so happy for him," Marit said at one point. "Look how proud he is. Overwhelmed, but I don't think he's ever been the center of attention like this before. Please tell me some of these kids are in his school. That they're seeing he's more than the nerd they probably believed him to be."

"I'm sure they are. He's gonna be the stud of his class now," Zach teased.

Marit chuckled. "I'm not so sure about that. He's still the same skinny, height-challenged, and nerdy kid he always was. But maybe, just maybe, this will gain him enough cool points to not be picked on as much."

"How do you know he's been picked on?" Zach asked. He wasn't doubting her. He wasn't an idiot, and he'd been Kash's age once. He was well aware that the neighbor boy didn't have the superficial attributes that were important to kids in middle school.

"Britt told me. She's spent the most time with him, and he's confided in her a lot."

That made sense, and Zach couldn't help but love that his family was embracing Marit as quickly as they had. They probably sensed the same thing he did . . . that she was different. Special.

"It's time," Linc said, turning to Kash. "You ready to get your medal?"

The boy nodded. Everyone headed over to the main stage, which was in the park where the heart of Lobster Fest was held.

Kash ended up winning with one thousand, eight hundred, and sixty-eight crates. He had an ear-to-ear grin, and the black eye from that last face-plant into the crate was only getting darker by the minute. But he was apparently feeling no pain as everyone applauded wildly when he stepped onto the stage.

Zach took the time after Kash rejoined them—once again fielding congratulations from locals and tourists alike—to check on The Lobster Buoy. Everything was good, and it looked as if they'd have just enough food to last until the close of festival that day. There was one more day to the fest, and Zach would need to get to work early in the morning to start cooking, but he was pleased with the revenue his little shack had brought in for its first few months of operation.

He wished he could stay at home with Marit all day tomorrow, since she had the day off, but the reality of owning a restaurant was that he almost *never* had a day off. He was always on call. There was always something to do, something to make.

"You ready to go?" he asked Marit, when he rejoined his family. Kash was finally looking as if he was feeling the effects of the adrenaline rush he'd been riding for the last couple of hours. Evelyn had already left with Chad and Britt, and Linc was going to bring Kash back to Victor's.

"Yeah," she said with a nod.

Zach held up his hand to Kash for a high five. "Good job again, Bud. You did all of us Youngs proud. And yourself too. I think now you're an honorary Lobsterite. That's what we call those of us who live and work at Lobster Cove. I think you qualify, since you've taken over Fort Bad Assery, and you've won the crate race just like some of us have done."

"Cool!" Kash breathed, as he smacked his palm against Zach's.

"I'm sure Britt has probably already sent the videos she took today to your mom. How about we head home so you can watch them with her?" Linc asked.

"Sweet! Thanks for coming to watch me today," Kash told Marit and Zach.

"Wouldn't have missed it," she said.

Linc and Kash had started walking toward wherever Linc had parked, when Kash turned around. "Marit?"

"Yeah?"

"Do you think maybe, one day, I could go out on your lobster boat with you? I don't think I want to be a lobsterman, but a lot of the kids at school have dads who own boats. And I thought it would be good if I knew a little about it. You know . . . so I wouldn't seem so dumb when they talk about it."

Zach's heart swelled that the kid wanted to learn more about the industry that was so popular around here, and it simultaneously broke because he thought he was the slightest bit dumb. He was so smart it was almost scary.

"It would be my honor. I'll talk to my boss, Eliot. I'm sure he'd be delighted to take us out sometime and show you the ropes."

"Awesome! Thanks again for coming today." With that, he waved once more, then turned back around and jogged a little to catch up to Linc, who'd stopped to wait for him.

Kash still had his medal around his neck, and Zach wondered if he would sleep with it tonight. He certainly had when *he'd* won.

"He's such a good kid," Marit said.

"He is," Zach agreed. He was more than ready to have Marit to himself, and he could see she was exhausted. "Come on, let's get you off your feet."

"Yes, please," she said quietly, as she looked up at him.

Thankful that his apartment was so close to town, Zach held her hand as they walked. Neither spoke as they made their way through all the people still milling around, and each time he glanced at Marit, he could see she was deep in thought.

The moment the door to his apartment closed behind them, she began to pace the small space. Zach frowned, praying he hadn't done anything to agitate her. He leaned against the kitchen counter and waited for her to tell him what was on her mind.

It didn't take long. She stopped about eight feet from him—and he was alarmed to see tears in her eyes. He straightened, intent on going to her, but she held up a hand to stop him.

"I didn't get it at first. How could I? I mean, it wasn't as if I've had any experience."

"Get what, honey?" Zach asked gently, hating the amount of space she'd put between them.

"What it meant to have a true family. You already know the fact that you have brothers was tough for me, because of my own history. You'd think I would've at least felt a camaraderie with the men I've worked with on boats. But I didn't. They only tolerated me, much as Mav and Max did. And I like Eliot and Jonah, they're great . . . but they're still just coworkers.

"Today? Cheering on Kash, and seeing your family come together to be there for an awkward little boy who's struggling to figure out who he is and how he fits into the world . . . I felt as if I was part of a family for the first time since my parents died. Don't take that for granted, Zach. *Ever.*"

He was done keeping his distance. Zach quickly stepped toward Marit, pulling her into a heartfelt and tight hug. She didn't resist, snuggling into him as if she was born to be there. "I won't," he whispered into her hair.

Then he pulled back, because he wanted to look into her eyes as he said this next bit. He waited until she met his gaze. "You *are* a part of our family. Even if things between us don't work out, you're *still* a part of us. If you think my mother is gonna let you go, you're wrong. And Kash thinks you walk on water. He's officially a Lobsterite, just like you've been dubbed. Everyone you meet loves you, honey. Hell, you haven't even known Britt that long, and you two text as if you've been friends forever.

"Family isn't just about blood. It's about choosing to be with those you love, who love you back. My family is your family, Marit. It might've taken you a while to find us, but now that you have, you're stuck with us."

She chuckled, and the tears she'd been holding back dripped down her cheeks.

Zach gently wiped them away. "I'll warn you, though. They can be annoying. All up in your business. Nagging. Irritating. You might not *want* to be a part of our family at times."

"Will they hurt me?"

"No!" Zach told her with a fierce shake of his head. "Never."

"Then I'll never *not* want to be a part of your family."

Zach closed his eyes, wishing that they'd known each other longer. That their relationship had started months ago, rather than the couple of weeks that had passed.

Because like a bolt of lightning, it hit him that he wanted to *officially* make her a Young.

It was way too soon for that, but the seed was planted. She fit in perfectly. She was made for them. For *him.*

"You're tired," he said gently. "Why don't you nap in one of the chairs until dinner's ready?"

"I can help," she protested.

"I know you can, but you can also nap. Besides, I'm gonna keep you up past your bedtime tonight," he said suggestively.

She smiled. "Yeah?"

"Yeah," he confirmed with a nod. "So you need to get a nap in now, so you don't fall asleep when I've got my face between your legs."

She snort-laughed. "Don't think that would ever happen."

"You never know. You've been up for a long time today. And you've worked hard."

"Zach?" she asked, as she used her shoulders to dry the rest of the tears on her cheeks.

"Yeah?"

"Thanks. For everything."

He leaned down and kissed her. "You're welcome. Now, come on. I'll get you a blanket and you can snuggle up until everything's done."

She nodded and let Zach lead her to his favorite of the two recliners. He got her settled and turned on some music.

By the time he'd prepped the chicken and was ready to grill it on the stovetop, he saw that she was fast asleep. He stared at her for a beat, more thankful than he knew how to put into words that she'd come into his life. That he'd been smart enough to recognize something special when he'd seen it.

Then he got to work cooking. He had big plans for both of them tonight. Plans that involved lots of naked time and quite a few orgasms, and ended with his cock buried as deep inside her as he could go as she fell asleep on top of him. That was his favorite way to sleep now, and if the last couple of restless nights without her were any indication, he wasn't sure he could sleep any other way. Not a deep, soul-healing sleep, that was.

He grinned as he concentrated on the chicken and thanked his lucky stars for all he had in his life. His health, his mom, his brothers, his business, a hometown that had embraced his and his brothers' return . . . and his woman.

Life wouldn't always be easy, but he hoped with Marit by his side, they'd be able to weather whatever storm might arise.

Chapter Eleven

Marit couldn't believe how fast time was flying. It seemed as if it was just yesterday when they'd all watched Kash crush the competition in the crate race. The Lobster Festival was far behind them, and it was now October. The last couple of months had flown by. The end of tourist season was officially here, and while the weather was still moderate, it wouldn't be long before temperatures began to really drop.

Lobstering had slowed but never really stopped. That was one thing Marit enjoyed about her job—there was a break in the winter but she still earned a paycheck. She saved up in the summer, when she was working six days a week, and enjoyed the bit of down time she had in the winter.

Then there was Zach.

He was everything she'd ever dreamed of in a boyfriend. Attentive but not smothering. Just as hardworking as she was. He didn't see his work as being more important than hers, and he treated her as if she was the best thing that had ever happened to him. She wasn't so sure about that, but it was amazing to feel as cherished as she did when she was around him.

They hadn't spent much time at her apartment; most of the time, she stayed at Zach's place. She'd brought over quite a few of her things, and seeing her shampoo, conditioner, and lotion in his bathroom, her clothes mixed in with his in his closet, and their dirty laundry together in the same hamper made her heart do funny things.

She loved him.

And that terrified her.

Because he could so easily break her.

They hadn't said the words yet, but she was pretty sure he returned her feelings. Could a man be as sweet as he was and spend as much time with her as he did and *not* love her? She wasn't sure. After all, she hadn't had good role models growing up. It was tough to believe she was lovable in the first place. If her own brothers hadn't cared for her at all, how could someone as amazing as Zach?

But she was working hard to change her thinking. She'd spent a lot of time out at Lobster Cove with Zach's mom, and it was easy to see why he'd turned out to be as good a man as he was.

Evelyn Young was one of those people who rekindled your belief that humans were basically good. For every person who cut Marit off in traffic, who wrinkled their nose at how she smelled after spending the day on the water, who looked down at her, literally, because of her short stature, there was Evelyn, who welcomed her with open arms. Who laughed at her silly jokes. Who constantly told her how happy she was that Marit was in her life.

Yes, Marit now viewed Evelyn as her own mother, and she'd do whatever it took to protect the woman.

Then there was the rest of Zach's family. His brothers, who'd seemed so scary to her at the beginning, were now some of her best friends. She saw Chad the most, as he was always at Lobster Cove when she was there, but Knox and Linc were around a lot as well. They laughed and joked with her as if they'd known her forever. They gave no indication that they thought she and Zach were moving too fast, or that they resented her for any reason. And sure, they were annoying at times, as Zach had warned they could be, but not in any way that ever made Marit uncomfortable or doubt her relationship with their brother.

In fact, the only thing that wasn't going well in her life was Lucas Pearson.

The man hadn't let up on her. Not even now, with lobstering season slowing significantly. If anything, he'd doubled down on harassing her. He'd somehow gotten her phone number, and for weeks, not a day went by when he didn't text her some nasty note or slur. He didn't even try to hide that he was the one sending the messages. He was either conceited enough to believe he wouldn't get in trouble, or convinced that she wouldn't go to the cops about the harassment.

And he was right about the latter. Marit didn't feel as if he was enough of a threat to involve the police. In his messages, he pushed her to quit, to leave town, to leave lobstering to the men, who he claimed could do the job twice as well as she ever could.

It was annoying, but she didn't really feel threatened, per se. She actually hadn't seen the man in person for weeks, but she knew he was always there. In the background. Lurking.

She hadn't mentioned the texts to Zach, because at first she wasn't sure who was sending them. She had an excellent idea, but she had no proof. Until Lucas mentioned his boat, *Men At Work*, in one of the messages. Until that point, she had to admit it could've been Thorne Deaton, resuming his harassment from Portland.

Even then, she didn't tell Zach, figuring it was best to just ignore the texts. And when *that* didn't encourage Lucas to stop, she blocked his number.

Of course, that didn't make the harassment disappear. It gave her a reprieve for a few days, then the texts started up again from a different number, and that pattern had continued again and again. She supposed he was using a computer to generate different numbers for sending texts. Or maybe one of those free phone number programs or something. He certainly wasn't rich enough to be buying new phones over and over, that was for sure.

Now, the texts had gone on long enough that Marit actually felt weird telling Zach about them. He'd want to know how long the harassment had been going on . . . and she'd have to admit that it had been weeks. Then he'd be mad that she'd kept such a thing from him, and she'd feel awful. It was easier to just keep on ignoring them.

However, the guilt she felt over keeping such a big problem from Zach was eating at her. She was going to have to tell him at some point. Soon. Because the texts were finally starting to worry her.

She'd honestly thought Lucas would've quit harassing her by now, but no such luck. And his nastiness had gone on long enough. It was time to report him to the police, in case he felt the need to escalate, now that the main lobster season was over and he had more time on his hands.

But today wasn't the day, because she and Zach were heading to Lobster Cove to help Britt and Chad move into their new house. Evelyn had stopped renting the two-bedroom house on the family property in late August, and Chad and Britt—with help from Chad's brothers, Marit, and even Walt and Barry on occasion—had been working hard to renovate the space. Now it was finally done. It had a brand-new kitchen, new floors, a new roof, paint, and while they hadn't been able to afford all-new furniture yet, Chad had insisted on buying a bed.

Marit agreed with that purchase; she wouldn't want to sleep on a mattress that countless strangers had slept on over the years. Of course, that's exactly what people did every day when they slept in a hotel, but she didn't want to even think about that.

Zach was driving. When they went somewhere, he almost always drove. Not that she couldn't drive or didn't have a car, she simply had no problem with Zach chauffeuring her around.

"What's on your plate for tomorrow?" he asked, as they headed out of Rockville.

"Lobster pot maintenance," Marit said with a wrinkle of her nose. It wasn't her favorite thing to do, but it was one of those things that if not done, and not done correctly, all their hard work to catch the lobsters would be for naught. If the creatures could get out of the traps because there was a hole somewhere, the boat owner and deckhands could lose a lot of money.

"Down at the docks?"

"No. Eliot and Jonah brought the traps to their place. We'll swap them out this winter. We've got about a third of the pots in the water that we do in the summer, so we'll work on this batch, then switch them with the ones that are currently on the bottom of the ocean. We also have to repaint some of the buoys."

"Tedious work," Zach commented.

He wasn't wrong. "Yeah. But necessary. What about you? You mentioned yesterday the delivery business is going okay?"

"Uh-huh. Slower than I'd like though. My main issue is getting word out about the weekly specials. I've been using social media, but not everyone is online all the time. I have a newsletter list, but it seems that only about forty percent of the people who signed up for updates even open the emails. And even if I put a big sign outside the shack, only the people who happen to drive by will see it. It's frustrating."

"You have a phone number for The Lobster Buoy, right?" Marit asked.

"Of course. It's how people call in to order. They can also submit an order online."

"What if you put a recording on the phone? Like, push one to hear the weekly specials, push two to place an order . . . that kind of thing. That way, you can print flyers and stuff with the phone number on it and tell people to call to hear the special of the week . . . making sure they know it will always involve lobster in some way. Or you can set up an automatic message, where people can get texts with the specials. A lot of people would probably prefer that option."

"That's not a bad idea, actually."

"I know back in the old days, the eighties, that's how people found out the movie schedules. They'd have to call and listen to the recording for the times of each show. Did you know there was even a number people could call to get the time and temperature? It seems crazy today, but that's how it was back then."

Zach chuckled. "You make it sound as if it was a million years ago."

"It feels like it was. Oh, what about an app?" Marit asked.

"An app?"

"Yeah! Everyone has one these days. You can hire someone to keep it updated. Maybe the girl you're using to update social media. Or you can see if you can find someone from one of the universities in the area. Aren't they always looking for internships or something?"

"Maybe. What would this app do though?"

"Well, it wouldn't actually *do* anything. It's not like it's a game. It would be for information. But wait . . . what if it *was* a game? Or at least a section of it was? One part could be for pictures of the dishes you've created, another for the weekly special, hours of operation, where you're located, things like that. Then another part could be a lobster trap game! Something simple but entertaining. People would have to click on lobsters swimming in the ocean, or click on a lobster and drag it into a pot . . . I don't know. But it might be a way to get people to download the app and *keep* them on it."

"I wouldn't know where to start with something like that," he admitted.

"Me either, but you know *everyone*, Zach. Someone around here has to know someone *else* who can help you."

Zach was splitting his attention between her and the road. And he was smiling like a goof.

"What?" Marit demanded. "We're brainstorming here."

"I know. And you're very good at it. I'm just wondering how in the hell I got so lucky to have you in my corner."

"It's one thing to come up with ideas. It's another to actually get them implemented," Marit couldn't help but caution.

"I understand that. But they're very good ideas. Changing the subject here . . . Are you sure you wouldn't rather hang out at your place today? It's cold outside, and it's not exactly going to be fun lugging Chad and Britt's stuff to their new place. Not to mention the fights that will most certainly break out when we start putting together the baby's furniture."

Marit smiled. "There's nowhere I'd rather be than with you and your family. They're awesome . . . even if you guys all fight over who gets to do what in regards to that baby and his or her furniture. I still can't believe they already have practically everything they need for the baby's room."

"Are you kidding? That was the first thing my mom did. I swear, she's been preparing for grandkids for years. She probably had that furniture bookmarked on her computer, or already in her cart, and the second she heard Britt and Chad say they were pregnant, she just went in and clicked on the purchase button."

Marit giggled. She could definitely see Evelyn doing something like that. She was so excited for spring and the arrival of her first grandchild. "Harper said she was going to come over with Kash for a bit today. She has the evening shift at work but said she has some time this morning to come help. How are things going with her and Linc?"

"No clue. He doesn't talk about her, and it's not as if I'm texting Harper every day like you and Britt," Zach said in a teasing tone.

"I like them. I really do. I know Harper was . . . difficult when she was a kid, but I'm guessing she's nothing like she used to be back then. Life has a way of kicking you in the teeth, then stomping on you to make sure you stay down."

Zach frowned. "Do you really feel that way?"

Marit thought about his question for a second, then shrugged. "I used to. I mean, with everything I'd been through with my family. Moving all the way to Maine and struggling to find a job when I first arrived. Then finding lobstering, and not being welcomed by some of the people I worked with day in and day out. It was a lot."

"And now?"

"I'm cautiously optimistic," she said diplomatically, thoughts of Lucas lurking in the back of her mind. The man could seriously derail everything she'd come to love about Rockville. He could turn people against her. Make her life so miserable, she'd eventually feel as if she had no choice *but* to leave.

She couldn't figure out why Lucas was so hell bent on destroying her career and making her life miserable. It was one thing to believe that women shouldn't be working on lobster boats, she'd met plenty of people who thought that way, but *none* had gone to the lengths Lucas had to run her off. Not even Thorne. She'd racked her brain to come up with some reason why he was taking things so far, other than gender. Something she could've done to upset him without even realizing.

But no. Nothing came to mind. She really didn't know him at all in Portland. And she couldn't come up with anything she'd done since arriving in Rockville that would make him so . . . *unhinged* when it came to her.

She loved being a lobsterwoman. Loved the area. And she absolutely *did not* want to leave. But if things got so bad that she thought Zach's livelihood was in danger because of his association with her, she'd leave in a heartbeat. He'd worked too hard to fail because of her. Because Lucas couldn't seem to stomach working in the same industry as a woman.

"Well, I'm looking forward to spending more than two seconds around Harper. But don't expect me to be very friendly if Victor shows up."

"You think he will?" Marit asked, surprised.

"No. He's a grouchy old man who can't seem to understand that Lobster Cove will never be his. He needs to give it up already and spend more time and energy on his own property."

"Kash said he was proud that he'd won the crate race. That he'd even given Harper money to bring home a cake from her workplace to celebrate," Marit reminded Zach.

"I know, but he should've gone out and gotten that cake himself. Not made his daughter do it. And he can totally afford something more extravagant than a crummy ol' cake from Walmart."

Marit secretly agreed, but Kash had been thrilled when his granddad acknowledged his accomplishment in winning the race. Even if he hadn't been there, even if he still wanted his grandson to play football or baseball instead of being in the science club at school. He was trying, and Marit had to give him points for that.

"Well, if he does show up, can you please try to be civil? For Kash's sake?"

She didn't understand why Zach was grinning so huge at her question.

"What?"

"I love that this is where we are."

"Huh?"

"That you feel comfortable enough scolding me for the way I speak to our asshole neighbor. You sound like my mom . . . and I mean that in a good way. Being with you makes me a better person, Marit. I just want you to know that."

His words made her feel warm and fuzzy inside. He complimented her all the time. But something about hearing those words today, when she was worrying about what Lucas might be planning, made her feel extra special . . .

And extra guilty.

They were driving along the road toward Lobster Cove, the same stretch where his mom and Britt had gone over the edge because a former employee had tampered with both the brakes *and* steering in his mom's car, when she blurted, "Lucas has been texting me."

The smile on Zach's face immediately disappeared. "*What?*"

Marit sighed. This wasn't exactly the best time or place for this conversation, but now that she'd said the words, there was no taking them back.

"Lucas has been texting me," she repeated softly. "Telling me to leave. That no one wants me here. That I'm stupid for trying to do a man's job."

"Are you fucking kidding me!? How long? How long has he been sending you these texts?"

Zach sounded *really* mad—which made memories of her brothers yelling at her surge into Marit's consciousness. She'd worked hard to put everything they'd done and said to her into the deepest corners of her mind. But hearing Zach sound so angry made her feel as if she were a teenager all over again.

"Awhile," she finally said.

"Awhile," he repeated.

She didn't think it was a good sign that his only response was to repeat what she'd said. They rode in silence as Zach turned onto the driveway that led to Lobster Cove. Marit mentally kicked herself for bringing up the texts now. She should've kept her mouth shut. Things were going so well between them, and now she felt as if she'd ruined what should've been a happy day.

Zach parked his SUV, then turned toward her. "Look at me, Marit."

She didn't want to. Was worried about what she'd see in his face. He'd think she didn't trust him, but that wasn't the case. Yes, she'd been afraid to tell him after all this time, but more than that, she was protecting him the best way she knew how. She didn't want Lucas to turn his negative attention to Zach or The Lobster Buoy. He had a lot more to lose than she did.

Taking a deep breath, Marit raised her gaze from her lap to look at Zach. She was surprised that he didn't look angry, which was a relief. But she hated the disappointment she saw in his eyes.

"Why didn't you tell me before?" he asked.

"I figured he'd get bored when I didn't respond. That he'd stop."

"But he hasn't," Zach said.

Marit shook her head. "I've blocked him, but the texts always start up again from a different number."

Zach raised his hand, and Marit flinched.

The stricken look on his face made her instantly ashamed of her reaction. When he started to drop his hand, she grabbed it and placed it on her face, where she assumed he was about to touch her.

"I'm sorry!" she said. "I don't know why I flinched. I trust you, Zach. I've never trusted anyone as much as I trust you. I didn't want you to know because I was worried about what you might do. I don't want you to get in trouble because of me."

"How would I get in trouble?" Zach asked.

Marit frowned. "I didn't want you to confront him. Have him call the cops on you or something. That last time, during the festival . . . you were so angry. Lucas seems like the kind of guy who'd call the cops if you even looked at him wrong."

"A coward, you mean," Zach said in disgust. "Someone who has no problem harassing a woman over the phone, but isn't man enough to stand up to her boyfriend who's defending her. Typical. You've been worrying about this for a while now, haven't you?" he asked.

Marit gave him a small nod. "I can handle whatever he throws at me. But I *can't* handle the first man who supports me unconditionally, the first man who doesn't constantly joke about my height, the first guy to defend my choice of career, suffering because of some asshole's misogyny. I'm used to people thinking I can't do my job and underestimating my abilities. Or thinking I'm an easy mark because of my gender and size. But if someone hurts *you* because of me?" She shook her head. "I couldn't handle that, Zach."

"Look over at the house, sweetheart."

Confused, Marit took her gaze off the man she loved and swung it toward the main house. Standing there were all three of Zach's brothers, his mom, and Britt. They all looked worried and confused about why she and Zach were still sitting in his car. But more than that, the men looked . . . tense. On edge. As if they were two seconds away from pulling swords out of scabbards on their backs and jumping onto their trusty steeds to gallop into battle.

It was a fantastical thought, but Marit had been reading some pretty intense and cool alien romances lately about macho, alpha alien males who were more like Vikings of old instead of the short, green, big-eyed aliens most people associated with the word. So that's the first image that came to mind when she saw Zach's brothers.

"Supporting my girlfriend will *not* get me into trouble. I'm smart enough to know what I can and can't say or do to someone to avoid getting the cops called on me. And if Pearson is stupid enough to call the police anyway, they aren't going to do anything, because I wouldn't have done anything wrong.

"But more important is this—the Young family sticks together. No matter what. No one fucks with one of our own, and that includes *you*. You're in our inner circle, sweetheart. I know you're afraid Pearson will do something that'll hurt me, but we've been in this town for way longer than he has. Our friends aren't going to believe or take to heart anything he says.

"Besides . . . you're like a local celebrity around here. The only woman working the lobster boats? That's enough for people to be curious and to take notice of you. I think *that's* what has Pearson so bent out of shape. People like you. The lobstermen have no beef with you. No one has rushed to join his campaign to run you out of town. You do your job, don't mess with anyone else's gear, and you work hard. You're a great ambassador for the industry. If they had to pick between you and Pearson, they'd pick you one hundred percent of the time. Never doubt that."

Marit looked back at Zach. She wasn't quite ready to believe him. Although, thinking back to the presentation she'd given at the elementary school about lobstering, the two men from another boat who were presenting with her didn't seem to care that she was a woman. They didn't bring up her gender. They were very nice to her, actually.

"We can talk about this more later. I'll want to see the texts if you still have them. But for now, everyone's waiting. They're going to want to make sure you're okay, then we've got a metric crap ton of stuff to move from the big house to Britt and Chad's new place. I know Britt just moved here recently, but somehow she's accumulated a roomful of knickknacks, doodads, and clothes."

Marit smiled. "Okay."

"Okay," Zach agreed. Then he leaned over and kissed her, lingering on her lips for a moment but not deepening the kiss. "Lucas Pearson is an idiot," he whispered. "If he got his head out of his ass, he could learn a lot from you. But instead, he's acting like a five-year-old and throwing a temper tantrum for no good reason. There's room enough on the water for anyone who wants to be there. We'll figure out a way together to get him to leave you alone. Okay?"

"Yeah." Marit felt much better, and she couldn't believe she'd been afraid to tell Zach about the texts in the first place.

"And for the record, you do know that I'd never hurt you, right?"

Marit hated the concern and disappointment she heard in his voice. "I'm sorry," she told Zach. "It was instinctive. I was afraid that you were upset with me, and it reminded me of how I felt when my brothers yelled at me, and they'd usually end up slapping me. So when your hand came up . . ." Her voice trailed off.

She *hated* the look of horror on Zach's face right now.

"I'm not upset with you, Marit. Do I wish you'd told me earlier? Yes. But I do understand the reasons why you didn't, even if they were unfounded. And I'll repeat, I will never, ever raise my hand to you in anger, frustration, or anything other than love. If my hand is coming toward your face, it's to wipe away your tears or to touch you tenderly. Okay?"

Marit nodded quickly, then surged toward him, doing her best to wrap her arms around Zach. It was awkward, as they were both still strapped into the seats in his Explorer, but she did her best. "I'm sorry! I know you won't hurt me. I promise."

"Good. Now . . . my brothers are really freaking out. Shall we go reassure them that we're good and see what kind of snacks my mom has made for the day?"

Marit eased back into her seat and gave Zach a wobbly smile. "Is that all you think about? Food?"

"No. I think about you naked a lot too."

She burst out laughing. "Zach!"

"What? I do," he said with a smile. "Because you're so damn beautiful. This morning? On the table? Eating you for breakfast? Combination of two of my most favorite things in the world."

Marit blushed. Her boyfriend was very sexual, easily her match, and she certainly wasn't complaining. Because he always made sure she was thoroughly satisfied before he took his own pleasure.

He winked at her, then unbuckled and finally opened his door. Marit took a deep breath before following suit. She'd experienced a full range of emotions already this morning. She was ready for the attention to be on someone else for a change, namely Britt and Chad and the move to their house.

She was reminded of just how lucky she was to be in this family's inner circle when she got huge hugs from everyone once she and Zach reached the porch. And when Linc asked in a soft voice in her ear as he hugged her, "Who do I have to kill?" she laughed.

Looking at his face, she figured he was only half kidding.

"Come on, before we start the hard work, I've got biscuits and gravy, bacon, waffles with blueberries and authentic Maine maple syrup, and some mimosas for anyone who might want one . . . except for you, Britt. No alcohol for you and our little one," Evelyn said happily.

Zach took Marit's hand and squeezed it as they all made their way inside. She'd hit the life lottery when she'd hooked up with this family, and Marit vowed to make the most of it.

Chapter Twelve

Zach was pissed. Not at Marit, but at Lucas Pearson. How *dare* he harass Marit like he was? What was the point? What did he hope to gain? Zach had no idea, but the fact that the man was acting like a grade school bully didn't sit well with him. Not at all.

Marit had been through hell at the hands of her brothers. And apparently down in Portland, as well. She didn't talk much about Thorne Deaton, but she'd said enough for Zach to know she'd felt as if she had to leave for her own safety. The last thing he wanted was for her to feel that same way here in Rockville because of Pearson.

He needed to do something about it, but he wasn't sure what. He hated that Marit hadn't told him about the texts, but he hadn't lied. He really did understand. Being part of a true family was new to her. Having people in your life who would support you no matter what, who'd have your back . . . it wasn't something she'd experienced before.

And he could even understand her fear that he'd find himself in trouble if he stepped into the situation with Pearson. But Zach wasn't dumb enough to do or say anything that might get him thrown into jail.

No, there were ways of dealing with Marit's tormentor that would guarantee the man would slide back under whatever rock he'd crawled out from under. Zach and his family knew everyone in Rockville. Without doing anything illegal, they could get *others* in town to make Pearson's life as miserable as he was making Marit's.

"You okay?" Linc asked, as they took a break from moving boxes from their mom's to the rental house . . . which was no longer a rental.

"No," Zach said honestly. He briefly explained Marit's situation, and what had been going on for months, and the fact that he'd just learned about the text harassment when they'd pulled into the driveway earlier.

"You want me to talk to him?" Linc asked.

That right there was something Zach vowed to never take for granted. The fact that he had people who would take on his burdens with no questions asked.

"Not yet. I'm thinking I'd like first crack at him. The man has got to understand that Marit is off limits. I don't even understand why he's continuing this asinine line of harassment. If Marit wasn't good at what she did, no one would hire her. But the fact that Eliot has not only kept her on, but given her more and more responsibility, and even let her take his boat out a couple of times to do pot and buoy maintenance when he couldn't be there, tells me everything I need to know. And it should tell all the *other* lobstermen around here the same thing. She's a damn good fisherman. Why can't he just leave her alone?"

"Because that's how bullies are. But you're right, there has to be another reason. Something more than just her gender. Does she have any idea why he hates her so much?"

"No."

"Huh," Linc said. "I mean, I could be wrong. Sometimes people just take an exception to others. There might not be a reason. Like how people bullied me when I was in high school, and they thought it was okay to treat me like shit just because I was different than them."

"Speaking of which . . . how are things between you and Harper?"

Linc shrugged. "Don't see her much. Don't really talk to her either. Just in passing when I drop Kash off after spending some time with him."

"You're doing that more and more, aren't you?" Zach asked.

"He craves male one-on-one time, and it's not as if Victor will give that to him. The man just enjoys pointing out all his supposed weaknesses. He's gonna lose his grandson if he continues to be such an ass to him."

Zach didn't disagree with his brother. But he did wonder why Linc was taking it upon himself to become Kash's mentor. Deciding a change of topic was in order, he asked, "How are things with you? How's your shoulder?"

"How're your knees?" Linc countered.

Zach snorted. "About as good as they *can* be."

"There's your answer for me too then."

Linc. He was stubborn as hell. The man's shoulder had almost been ripped from his body in the crash behind enemy lines, but Zach supposed the very stubbornness that was driving him crazy at the moment had helped Linc put one foot in front of the other for a week as he evaded the enemy forces trying to track him down.

"She's different," Linc said after a moment.

For a second, Zach thought he was talking about Marit. Then he realized Linc was talking about Harper. That he'd circled back around to their previous topic.

Linc went on. "She's struggling. Did you know she's paying her father *rent*? That bastard is charging his own daughter to stay at his house. She's working her ass off to make enough to pay her dad, while trying to give Kash the kind of Christmas she's never been able to give him before. It sucks."

Zach was a little surprised Linc cared so much. Especially after the way Harper had treated him when they were teenagers. But that had been a long time ago, and as Britt and Marit both pointed out, people changed. It seemed as if maybe Harper *had* learned a hard life lesson . . . and was still learning it.

A loud peal of laughter rang out from the other room, where their mom had been storing all the baby stuff she'd been accumulating.

Something occurred to Zach. He looked over at his brother. "What about the other rental house?"

"What about it?" Linc asked.

"It's empty. Mom isn't planning on doing any more rentals. You think she might be open to letting Harper and Kash move in? Having one bedroom isn't ideal, but we might be able to put up a curtain or something to give Harper some privacy, because we both know she'd give the room to her son. It would give them both space away from Victor, and it'll be up to Mom how much she wants to charge, of course . . . but I'm guessing she'd barely charge them anything, considering how much she enjoys having Kash around."

Linc's head whipped around to stare at Zach. "I hadn't thought of that."

Zach grinned. "See? I might be the baby, but I've got a good idea now and then."

Linc chuckled and leaned sideways, knocking into Zach's shoulder. "Naw, you're only good for the food you can make. That's the only reason we tolerate having you around."

"Asshole," Zach said.

"Pecker head," Linc retorted.

"Lickspittle."

"Mumpsimus."

"Pettifogger." Zach grinned. This was just like old times. Growing up, they'd had to look up words that were insults that didn't sound like curses so their mom wouldn't make them do extra chores as punishment for saying them.

Linc smiled at his little brother. "It's good to be home. I'll talk to Mom. Thanks for the suggestion."

"Shouldn't you talk to Harper first?" Linc asked.

"Nope. She'd probably refuse out of pride. Which would be stupid. And if *I* ask if she wants to move into the house, she'd almost certainly say no simply because it's me asking. If Mom brings it up, and makes her think it was her idea . . ." Linc's voice trailed off.

"Right. Smart. But won't Harper be pissed when she learns that it was you who first brought it up? You know she'll figure it out eventually. Love Mom to pieces, but she's not exactly Fort Knox when it comes to keeping secrets."

Linc shrugged. "Probably. But technically, you suggested it. Not me." He winked. "Either way, since it's for Kash, she'll deal."

Zach figured his brother was probably right.

"If you need me—or Knox or Chad—you know we've got your back, right? With this Pearson asshole? No one fucks with a Lobsterite," Linc said fervently.

"I know. Thanks. I'd already decided that it might be necessary to bring in the local Rockville network . . . you know, get people to subtly do things to make Pearson's life here . . . difficult. I'll keep you updated as to what's going on."

"I'd appreciate it."

"Hey! You guys gonna stand there holding up that wall or come and help us carry some of this stuff to the other house?" Chad called out.

"Keep your pants on, we're coming!" Zach yelled back.

Linc clapped his hand on Zach's shoulder, then they headed toward the room where everyone else had gathered. It would be a tight fit in the new house with everyone there, trying to help get things set up how Chad and Britt wanted them, but since everyone was family, it could never be too crowded.

~

Later that evening, Zach sat in his favorite recliner with Marit on his lap. He was surprisingly exhausted after a long day out at Lobster Cove. A lot of it was emotional exhaustion. Many people didn't believe men could be emotional, but with the surprise of hearing about the texts Marit was getting, the excitement he felt for his brother and Britt, the talk with Linc, seeing how happy his mom was about the upcoming grandchild . . . he was more than ready to sit and simply "be" with Marit.

Which was a new thing for Zach. In the past when he'd had girlfriends, he'd always felt as if he had to entertain them every second they were together. Make sure they were happy. That they didn't need or want anything. With Marit, that was rarely the case. She didn't need entertaining every moment of the day. She seemed just as content to sit in a quiet room, like they were doing now, as she was to go out and do something.

The bottom line was, it felt like Marit was a perfect match for him. It had been almost three months since they'd been dating, and he loved that she'd spent most of her nights here at his place. She had clothes here, toiletries next to his in the bathroom, and he got such a kick out of seeing her boots and fishing gear taking up most of the room in his front closet. He'd clear out *all* his drawers and closets for her stuff if it meant she spent more time here with him.

"What are you thinking about so hard?" Marit asked quietly. Her head was resting on his shoulder as she snuggled into him. She fit perfectly in his arms. She really was tiny compared to his six-six height. It amused a lot of people how disproportionate they were, but he didn't even notice anymore. She was just Marit. Her larger-than-life personality made her seem as if she were ten feet tall.

"How happy I am that you're here," Zach said quietly. "How well we fit together. Both physically and with our lives in general. How I've never been with anyone who fits me like you do. How I could spend the rest of my life enjoying evenings like this . . . you using me as a body pillow as we relax after a long day."

Marit's head came up, and she stared at him, but Zach couldn't read her expression.

"Too cheesy?" he asked without even a hint of a smile.

"No," she whispered.

"Good. Because that's how I feel. This morning, I almost tripped over one of your boots. It had tipped over and was partially blocking the hallway. I'd gone to the front closet for something, no clue why now, but I wasn't paying attention and almost face-planted into the wall."

"Oh my gosh, I'm so sorry!" Marit exclaimed, sounding embarrassed.

But Zach simply smiled. "No, you don't understand . . . having you here, your things, it makes me feel less lonely. Even when I was in the Navy, on a ship full of people, working with the other sailors in the galley, I felt alone. Everyone was doing their own thing, in their own world. Having your stuff in my place, mixed with mine, tripping over your boots . . . it reminds me that I'm not alone. That you're here."

Marit's head dropped back to his shoulder. "That's sweet. But I'm still going to be more careful about where I leave my boots from now on. The last thing I want is you bashing your head into the wall because of my crap."

"How are you feeling?" Zach asked.

Marit looked up at him again. "Um . . . fine?"

"No, I mean, after spending all day with my crazy family. After our talk. After Linc taking you aside and telling you that he has no problem 'dealing' with Pearson if you want him to."

"Honestly?"

"Of course. Always. My family can be a little intense, and I can tell them to back off if I need to."

"I told you that I've never understood the concept of family. You know how mine was. But being around your brothers, and mom, and even Britt and Kash, it makes me feel incredibly lucky . . . and sad at the same time."

"Sad?"

"That I missed out on what you have."

"But you have it now."

"Yeah, I do," Marit said in a faraway tone, putting her head back on his chest.

"Look at me, Marit."

She did as he said.

"I told you this before, and I'll say it as many times as you need to hear it to make it stick. You'll always have a place with the Youngs. I don't care what happens with us, relationship-wise, you're stuck with us now. If you think my mom will ever let you just quietly slip away, you don't know her nearly as well as you should. And Linc, Knox, and Chad already see you as the little sister we never had. They're more than willing to fix this issue with Pearson, but I told them to back off until we need their help. And Britt's so happy you're around. Chad said she's really missed having someone closer to her age to talk to."

"She's awesome," Marit agreed.

"I can see us sitting just like this when we're old and gray, exhausted after sending our grandkids home with our kids, happy with how our life has turned out."

"Zach," Marit whispered, her eyes wide.

"I just want you to know that this, us together, feels right. As if I've finally found my person. The other half of my soul. The person I want to spend the rest of my life with. I'm going to do everything in my power to not screw it up. To make sure you never regret being with me."

"I won't. I . . . I feel the same," Marit told him almost shyly.

So many feelings welled up inside Zach. Gratitude. Relief. Love.

"I love you, Marit. Some people would probably tell me it's way too soon to say the words. That I should wait until you say them first. That we haven't been together long enough for me to know if what I'm feeling is really love or not. But they're wrong. I know down to my very bones that you're it for me.

"And I'm not telling you how I feel to pressure you to say the words back, or even to say anything at all. I just wanted you to know that I'm in this for the long haul. That I like being around you. Spending time with you. Hearing about your day when we both get home. Bouncing marketing ideas off of you. Watching you interact with my family. Seeing how happy you get when we're at Lobster Cove. Sleeping with you in my arms. It's all stuff I've never experienced with anyone else. It feels like I've finally come home, literally and figuratively."

Marit opened her mouth to respond, but Zach quickly covered her lips with his, stopping whatever it was she was going to say.

When he broke the kiss, he ran the backs of his fingers over her cheek tenderly. "I just wanted you to know."

Marit reached up and took his hand in hers and pressed a kiss to the palm before moving so she was straddling him. She then took his face in her hands and stared into his eyes. "You're braver than I am—"

Zach snorted. He couldn't help it. This woman, she had no idea how amazing she was. How much he admired her.

"You are!" she insisted. "It scares the shit out of me to say this, but I love you too, Zach Young. I don't know how it happened. I wasn't in the market for a boyfriend. I was simply doing my job, keeping my head above water. Trying to stay under everyone's radar. Trying not to draw any attention to myself. And then you entered my life, asked me out . . . and here we are. Your family intimidates me, but not in a bad way. They all seem so put together. They know what they want, and they don't take shit from anyone."

"We're all a little broken inside, for different reasons. But we're stronger together than apart. I think that's what has made our move back to Maine work out so well," Zach admitted.

"Well, whatever it is, it's definitely working."

They smiled at each other.

Then Marit chuckled. "Now what? Now that we've admitted our feelings for each other . . ."

"Sex. Definitely," Zach said with a straight face. "Lots and lots of sex."

Marit burst out laughing. "I need to get up early and go work on lobster traps out at Eliot's place tomorrow," she reminded him.

"I know. And I have a bunch of orders to make first thing. So maybe just a *little* sex," he conceded.

Marit smiled, then collapsed against him. Zach ran his hands up and down her back, loving that he could feel her breaths against the bare skin of his neck. He was half hard thinking about the sex he was going to have with her in the very near future, but for the moment, he was content to simply hold her and bask in the aftermath of them sharing their love for each other for the first time.

"Speaking of your family and everyone being a little broken. Did you see Harper and Linc when she dropped off Kash? I think they like each other."

It was an abrupt change of topic, but Zach was used to that kind of thing, growing up in a big family. Everyone took the chance to talk whenever possible, even if it wasn't exactly on topic.

"Are you crazy? There's no way. Harper bullied Linc all through high school."

But then he recalled the conversation he'd had with his brother earlier that day. How he'd thought it . . . interesting . . . that Linc kept talking about Harper.

"Maybe she did. But she's not fifteen anymore, Zach. It's like they're pretending they don't like each other, but they actually do."

Zach shook his head slightly. "I don't know."

"Mark my words," Marit said firmly. "Harper's been through some shit, and so has Linc. Different shit, but shit all the same. That can bring people together. But more than that . . . *Kash* is gonna bring those two together. Linc already has a soft spot in his heart for the kid, and Harper would do anything for her son. From what I understand, she already has. She's suffered, Zach. Even lived in her car with him for a while. And she's working hard now, trying to give him the life he deserves."

"Well, if you're right, it makes what I suggested today all the more interesting," Zach mused.

"What did you suggest?"

"That Harper and Kash move into the other rental house on Lobster Cove. It's just sitting there unused now."

"Oh! That's a great idea! Your mom would be over the moon if she accepted. Having Kash so close would be the next best thing to her having a grandbaby already."

Zach chuckled. Marit wasn't wrong.

"Speaking of babies . . . you want them?" It was another awkward transition, but he didn't really care.

"Yes."

One simple word. It made Zach's lips move up into a huge grin. "How about we go practice making them?" he suggested.

Marit sat up again and stared at him. They were eye to eye in this position, and Zach couldn't help thinking about how much he loved when she took him like this, and he could look her in the eyes as he exploded deep inside her body.

In response to his suggestion, she sat even straighter and peeled the T-shirt she was wearing up and off her body. "How about we don't bother going over to the bed?" she asked instead.

Clothes went flying, and Zach was almost elbowed in the face as they raced to get their pants off without losing contact with each other or getting up from the chair. It seemed that Marit was just as ready as he was, because Zach slid his cock into her with hardly any resistance. Her inner muscles gripped him like a vise and his eyes almost rolled back into his head.

"Damn, woman. You feel amazing. I love you. So much."

"I love you too," Marit replied, as she began to move up and down.

It wasn't enough for Zach. He wanted her hard and fast. He felt as if he was two seconds away from exploding as it was. He needed her to get there too. One hand went to her clit, and he roughly stimulated her as she rode him. Her hips rocked as she bobbed up and down, her tits bouncing in his face. Any other time, Zach would've taken one into his mouth and feasted, but he could feel his come building up in his balls. He was way too close.

His fingers dug into her hip as he helped her take him. Marit's back arched, her upper chest flushed, and thankfully she seemed just as on edge as he was.

"I'm going to come," he warned.

"Me too," she agreed, reaching between her legs and pushing his hand away from her clit, taking over stimulating the small bundle of nerves herself.

That left Zach's hand free to grip her hips more firmly. He held her still and began to fuck her from below, able to go faster and harder with him doing the work. Her pussy gripped him even tighter as her orgasm neared.

She was the most beautiful woman he'd ever seen . . . and she was *his*. Just as he was hers. It was a dream come true, and Zach felt like the luckiest son of a bitch in the world.

Her muscles began to shake, and he knew she was coming. That was his signal to let himself go as well. Grunting, Zach felt the come burst out of the tip of his cock, deep into her channel. Each burst made Marit even more slippery, as he continued to fuck her through their orgasms.

It wasn't until she sighed in contentment that he pulled her all the way down onto his dick and enjoyed the aftershocks of both his orgasm and hers.

"Um . . . Zach?"

"Hmmmm?" he asked, lost in the pleasure of the moment.

"You didn't use a condom."

He froze in shock. "*Fuck.* I'm so sorry!"

"It's okay. I'm still on the pill."

He knew that, as the little pack of pills sat on the counter next to her toothbrush and toothpaste in his bathroom. "I swear I didn't mean for that to happen."

"I know. And other than it being messy . . . I actually prefer it."

Her words made his cock, which was still inside her, twitch with interest.

She laughed, and the movements of her internal muscles around his still-sensitive dick signaled that he wasn't done showing this woman how much she meant to him.

Scooting forward on the chair, he stood with Marit still in his arms.

She laughed, hooking her ankles together at his back as he kneaded her ass cheeks while making his way over to the bed.

"Just to be clear . . . we're done with condoms?" Zach asked.

"If it's okay with you. We're exclusive, and I haven't been with anyone other than you in . . . well . . . a long time," she said.

"Same. And yes, we're damn sure exclusive. For the rest of our lives. I know we both need to work early, but it might take me a while to tire out tonight. I've never had sex without a condom, and it wasn't until you pointed it out that I realized why you felt so different tonight."

"Men," Marit said with a roll of her eyes.

"*Your* man," Zach corrected.

"My man," Marit agreed.

It was indeed several more hours before either of them got any sleep. Right before Zach drifted off, his ass in the giant wet spot on the bed—and not giving one little shit about it—Marit deadweight on his chest, his cock finally sated but still embedded inside her soaking-wet pussy, he couldn't help but think about how blessed he was.

He had a job he loved, lived in a supportive community, had his family nearby, and a woman he wanted to spend the rest of his life with, and who felt the same about him. He never thought moving back home could have this kind of outcome.

With any luck, they'd both continue to be blessed with nothing but goodness in their lives and future.

Chapter Thirteen

Marit couldn't be happier with the way her personal life was going. She was still pinching herself that Zach had said he loved her. She kind of half expected things between them would get a little stale, now that the blush of first romance was behind them. But with every week that passed, Marit only felt herself loving Zach more.

He was truly a wonderful man. She was guilty of thinking *All the good ones are taken* more than once over the years, and yet, here she was, with one of the good ones, who amazingly seemed to love her as much as she loved him.

They had disagreements, but nothing that made her feel scared of what Zach would do, not like she used to feel around her brothers when they got angry or irritated with her. Their biggest argument to date was actually caused by something kind of stupid on her part. Zach had wanted to walk her to work in the morning, and she'd refused.

He couldn't understand why she was irritated, and Marit didn't know why he thought she needed an escort everywhere she went. She'd been walking to work since moving to Rockville with no issues whatsoever, and even when she'd lived in Portland—which, in her opinion, was far more dangerous because of the homeless camp she had to pass every morning to get to the docks, filled with men and women desperate for money so they could get their next fix.

In Rockville, passing anyone at *all* in the very early hours was an anomaly. So when Zach insisted he'd be escorting her to work every morning, Marit got irritated. She'd told him she was perfectly capable of getting to work on her own, thank you very much. Then Zach's feelings got hurt, and he lashed out, telling her she was a walking robbery statistic with her gender and size, and the fact that she usually wore her fishing gear, which made it more difficult to run if necessary.

Marit had stormed out of the apartment, and he'd let her go. She'd thought about their fight that entire day—and hated how she'd felt as a result. A little sick to her stomach, and not because the waters around Rockville had been choppier than usual due to an incoming storm. By the time she got home that afternoon, she was more than ready to talk about their disagreement.

When she'd opened the door to Zach's place, they'd both blurted "I'm sorry" at the same time, and the relief that swam through Marit's veins made her almost dizzy. They'd talked it out, and Zach explained that he was simply worried about her. That his dad had taught him to protect his loved ones at all costs. He'd spent his life looking out for his mom—moving home was proof of that—and even while in the Navy, he'd spent a lot of his time making sure everyone who worked under him was safe and had everything they needed.

Marit admitted that she was sensitive about her size, and she explained once more that she'd taken quite a few self-defense classes so that if someone *did* decide to harass her, she could handle them. They'd ended up making slow, tender love that night, and they'd both promised to try to be more open with their feelings so they wouldn't have a misunderstanding like that one again.

It was closing in on the middle of November, and Zach's mom was in a tizzy planning a huge Thanksgiving dinner for everyone. Marit wished she could be more help, but Britt was doing a very good job of both assisting and keeping the woman reined in. In a text Marit had gotten the night before, Britt said that Evelyn wanted to make *four* turkeys, which seemed like extreme overkill to Marit. But then again, she supposed four adult men could probably eat a lot of food.

She was looking forward to what would essentially be her first traditional Thanksgiving. Most of the time she spent the holiday in her apartment, eating a frozen meal and watching movies. Growing up, before her parents died, they'd had turkey and all the trimmings, but after, celebrating Thanksgiving, birthdays, and Christmas simply wasn't something her brothers bothered themselves with.

"It's going to be a nice day," Zach said, as they sat at his table together in the morning, before she headed off to the docks. He always got up at the same time she did, and while she showered and got ready for work, he made coffee and breakfast for her. Sometimes it was eggs, sometimes it was waffles, other times it was something she could eat on the go, like a bacon, egg, and cheese bagel.

He always seemed to know exactly what she was in the mood for. Although, it wasn't like eating *anything* Zach made was any kind of hardship. And the man spoiled her, to the point Marit had recently noticed her pants were becoming a bit snug, and she told herself she'd stop eating so much. But living with a fantastic cook like Zach, who appreciated her trying out his concoctions, was hell on her good intentions.

"Yeah," she answered, after she swallowed the bite she'd just taken of the chocolate-zucchini bran muffin Zach had made that morning. "These are amazing," she told him.

"Thanks. Saw them in an article I found online. Thought you might like them."

"They have chocolate in them, of course I like them," she told him with a chuckle.

"My girl does like her chocolate," he agreed.

His girl. She liked the sound of that so much. Almost as much as she loved how bossy the man was in bed. Over the last several weeks, they'd been experimenting a lot, and they'd both found that they got off on him being a little more alpha and her being a little more submissive. She'd never be a true submissive, she liked being in control a little too much for that, but she did like when Zach literally picked her up and moved her around, putting her in the positions he wanted.

She took a big bite of the double-apple baked oatmeal casserole he'd made earlier in the week, which they were still munching on. It had a ton of spices, plus eggs, syrup, pecans, and of course, lots of apples and oatmeal. It was freaking delicious, and Marit had to control herself not to eat half the dish at one time.

Dragging her thoughts away from the food, she continued their conversation. "It's supposed to be in the lower fifties today, and sunny. Which is great, considering the storm that's coming later in the week. Eliot wants to pull as many pots as he can today, so they can soak for a few days during the storm."

"Which means you'll have some time off, yeah?" Zach asked.

He was getting used to her unpredictable schedule. In the summer, she nearly always worked six days a week, but in the winter they might work three days in a row, then take a week off. It all depended on the weather.

"Most likely."

"You have Thanksgiving off though, right?"

"Yes. Eliot and Jonah are spending it with family up in Bangor, so I have at least four days off in a row. I thought maybe I could go over and help Britt and your mom. Not sure exactly what help I'll be, but I'm guessing I can do *something*."

"Or you could just go over there and relax," Zach suggested. "Something you don't do very often."

"Pot, meet kettle," Marit deadpanned.

Zach chuckled. "I know. I work just as hard. But I have to admit, I'm freaking out a little since business has slowed to a point that it's almost nonexistent."

"Have you thought any more about closing The Lobster Buoy from Thanksgiving to Easter?"

"I'm thinking I almost have to. Which sucks, because I really wanted to be a year-round restaurant."

Marit put her hand on Zach's forearm. "Cut yourself some slack, Zach. This is your first year. I have a feeling the longer you're around, the more people are going to want your food."

"I'm going to expand into a more permanent space," Zach said, and it sounded like a vow. "I'll always keep the shack, because it's in a primo spot downtown, but if I get an actual restaurant, then people can come in and eat no matter what the weather."

"And it'll be awesome," Marit said from the heart. He was going to succeed because anything else simply wasn't an option for him. But not only that, his food was damn good.

Looking at his watch, Zach said, "It's getting late. You need to go if you're going to beat Eliot and Jonah to the boat."

"Damn," Marit said. "You're right." She'd gotten into the habit of getting to the dock before her boss and Jonah to prep the boat. It technically wasn't her job to do so, but she took pride in having things ready to go when the others got there. She could also admit she was a bit of a perfectionist, and she liked things the way *she* liked them when it came to her workspace. She could check the ropes and the safety equipment, and make sure the radio was working properly.

Safety was important to her. Not that Eliot didn't insist on proper protocols, but Marit simply liked to see for herself that everything was in its place and ready to go . . . just in case.

They stood, and while she climbed into the oilskin overalls that would protect her from the icy spray, and made sure her tool belt was secure and she had her insulated waterproof gloves, Zach got down on one knee and helped her put on her rubber boots. Somedays she felt like the little brother in *A Christmas Story*, waddling around in all her gear, but especially in the winter, when it was important to have everything zipped and buttoned up tight.

"All good?" Zach asked when he stood.

"Yeah, thanks."

"Here's your lunch," he told her, handing her a bag with the meal he always prepared for her the night before. She didn't always get to eat it, especially if the lobstering was especially good, but he hated to think of her going all day without anything to fuel herself.

"You're too good to me," Marit said, as she smiled up at him.

She used to find their height difference a touch startling, but she was used to it now. Loved it. She always felt more feminine when she was around him . . . which was particularly useful when she had on all her bulky fishing gear. He also made her feel protected and safe, always tucking her under his arm, putting himself between her and the street.

All in all, this man had quickly become her everything. She couldn't imagine life here in Rockville without him in it.

"No such thing," Zach said, before he leaned down and kissed her long and deep. When he finally pulled back, they were both breathing harder.

"Damn, woman. Suddenly I'm thinking about that evening when you were so worked up, you didn't even let me get your overalls or boots off completely after work before you insisted I get inside you."

Marit giggled. She remembered that day clearly. She was irritated and tired, but horny as hell. The second she'd walked in, she'd gone to her knees and given Zach one hell of a blow job. Then he'd picked her up, slammed her onto the table, and removed just enough of her clothes to get inside her. The experience was hot as hell. And thinking about that fast and dirty sex made Marit want him right now.

"No time," he said, reading her mind.

He was right. Damn it. "All right, but for the record . . . tonight . . . when I get home . . ." She let her thought trail off.

"Yeah?"

She sighed. "I'm gonna be tired, cold, hungry, and probably grumpy."

Zach chuckled. "Noted. I'll have a snack ready for you. Maybe a glass of wine. You can run a bath, and while you're soaking, I'll get the lobster ravioli going."

"Ooooh, sexy," Marit said with a huge grin.

"Anything for my girl. Now . . . stop stalling and git."

"I'm going, I'm going." Marit usually loved what she did for a living. But today she felt a little out of sorts, and she wasn't sure why. The weather was supposed to be good for lobstering, and she and the Sullivans worked together as if they'd done it their whole lives. Maybe it was the holidays approaching, maybe it was nearing her time of the month . . . which, now that she thought about it, was late in arriving.

Or maybe it was some kind of sixth sense. Whatever was making her feel out of sorts, she had the sudden thought that she should just climb back into bed and hibernate until spring.

She went up on her tiptoes and Zach met her halfway, kissing her more sedately this time before she headed for the door.

It was still dark as Marit headed for the docks. Late fall in Maine meant it got dark around four-thirty in the afternoon and stayed that way until around seven in the morning. But that was fine. It wasn't a long walk, just enough for her to have a bit of time alone with her thoughts. Normally, they focused on the coming workday and the tasks that needed to be done. And thinking of the job inevitably led to thinking of Lucas Pearson . . .

Surprisingly, in the last few weeks the texts from Lucas had all but stopped. Well . . . surprising until Zach admitted that he'd found out where the man lived, and he'd paid him a visit. Actually, he and *all three* of his brothers had shown up on Lucas's doorstep, and they'd basically told him that if he ever communicated with her again, it had better be respectful . . . except they'd used harsher words.

Britt had told her the whole story. About how Lucas had acted all brash and cocky at first, but then Zach had leaned in and told him that he'd gone to school with the police chief, and their moms were really good friends. That if he thought he could continue getting away with harassing Marit like he'd been, he was dead wrong.

Which didn't seem like much of a threat to Marit, but apparently Lucas thought differently. She supposed it was the delivery of the message that mattered most. She could see Zach in her mind, scowling and delivering the threat, backed up by his three brothers, maybe all standing with their arms crossed and similar scowls on their faces.

It was one thing to bully a five-foot-two woman, quite another to come up against four grown-ass men who'd done time in the military and who were hometown heroes.

Lucas had to know he was outmatched and outnumbered. Still, she was a *little* surprised she hadn't seen much of the man since then. He'd proved he wasn't the type to give up easily. But that confrontation with Zach and his brothers had been a little over a month ago, and while she and the Sullivans saw Lucas at the docks, he didn't say much to any of them . . . which was perfectly all right with Marit.

She didn't let down her guard though. In the back of her mind, she couldn't help but suspect he might be planning something. If Lucas was anything like Thorne Deaton, he definitely wouldn't take kindly to being threatened. It was only a matter of time before he was back to his old tricks, of that Marit had no doubt.

Doing her best to shake off the funk of a mood she was in, despite the amazing previous evening she'd had with Zach and the delicious breakfast he'd prepared, Marit continued through the quiet, dark streets of Rockville toward the docks.

As she walked through the harbor parking lot next, she frowned. The lights in the lot were on, but the one on the tall pole at the end of the dock, which led down to where several boats were moored, was out. She hadn't been working here for long, so it was possible it was normal for a light to go out occasionally . . . but the odd feeling she'd had all morning increased.

Marit looked around but saw no one lurking in the shadows. There were a few vehicles in the lot, but those were empty too. She had no reason to feel on edge, and yet she did all the same.

Picking up the pace, she hurried toward the *Wave Rider*, knowing she'd feel better once she was on board and in a familiar space.

Letting out a small breath of relief as she stepped onto the boat, Marit was completely unprepared for the man who popped up from where he'd been crouched in the small cockpit. The only place anyone could've hidden from her view.

She opened her mouth to scream, in the hopes that maybe someone would be walking nearby and hear her, but she didn't get a sound out before the man rushed her and jammed something into the side of her neck.

It hurt.

That was her first thought.

The second was that she was going to die. That the man had stabbed her, and Eliot and Jonah would find her dead body on the deck of the *Wave Rider*, where she'd bled out.

The sudden sharp and intense pain of her muscles contracting was like nothing she'd ever felt before. Marit had no idea what was going on, all she knew was that she had no control over her body whatsoever. She fell to the deck like a sack of potatoes. Whatever the man had stuck her with, he kept it against her skin, and her muscles refused to do anything except spasm. It was as if she had an allover charley horse, and it freaking *hurt.*

"Fucking bitch!"

The words registered, but barely. She was too busy trying to breathe.

And then it was over. Except every muscle in her body felt like a limp noodle. Marit took a shallow breath and looked up.

Standing over her was Lucas Pearson. Apparently, he hadn't taken the Young brothers' words to heart after all. He'd just been stewing in his anger. He obviously knew her routine, the fact she got to the boat before Eliot and Jonah.

And her insistence that she didn't need an escort to and from the docks had allowed him ample time to make his move.

She had no idea how he'd managed to take out the light at the top of the dock, but she was certain that he was responsible. Probably something as simple as shooting it with a BB gun when no one was around.

Waiting for him to demand she quit, leave town, as he'd done every other time he'd confronted her, Marit prayed he'd say whatever he had to say quickly and then leave. Except this time, she was going to the cops. Filing a harassment complaint and charging him with assault. This had to stop. He'd gone way too far.

But in the back of her mind . . . she knew he wasn't going to simply stop with tasing her. He had something else in mind.

Something bad.

Lucas continued to stand there and sneer down at her. Just when Marit thought she could actually get her muscles to obey commands from her brain, he moved once more. He reached into his pocket and pulled out a bottle of something . . . and a handkerchief.

Marit had a feeling she knew what he was doing. She grunted as she attempted to roll over and get to her feet, but she'd only managed to get to her hands and knees before Lucas kicked her in the side of the head, knocking her back to the deck once more. He then dropped down, straddling her chest and putting one hand around her neck, the other over her mouth and nose. He was holding the bit of cloth he'd pulled out of his pocket and soaked with whatever was in the bottle.

A pungent scent filled her nose, making Marit panic and struggle against his hold. But he was a foot taller than her, and her muscles were still mostly useless from the tasing.

The substance on the cloth was making her woozy. Still, Marit had the crazy thought that whatever he'd used to try to knock her out, it wasn't working as fast as it did in the movies and on TV.

"Fucking pass out already, bitch," he growled, as the hand around her throat tightened.

Marit wanted to tell him that he was a complete idiot. That in order for her to breathe in whatever he'd poured on the cloth, he had to allow her to actually freaking *breathe* . . . but she supposed he'd get what he wanted one way or another. He'd either choke her out, or she'd succumb to whatever drug he was using.

The only consolation she had as the world began to go dark was that he'd said "pass out" . . . not "die." If he wanted her alive, he most likely had plans for her. Plans that wouldn't be fun, of that she could be certain. But as soon as Eliot and Jonah arrived, they'd know something was wrong. They'd call to ask if she was coming to work, and Zach would come running to find out what had happened to her.

The hate she saw in Lucas's eyes as he glared down at her was familiar. She'd seen it countless times in her own brothers' gazes as a kid. But this time it was different. She wasn't on her own.

She had Zach.

She wasn't going to die. Not when she'd just found him.

Her last thought before passing out was of Zach, and how he wouldn't stop looking for her. He'd do whatever it took to find her and make Lucas pay for daring to touch one hair on her head.

Chapter Fourteen

Zach had his hands deep in a bowl, hand mixing the ingredients to make homemade ravioli for the dinner he'd planned for Marit, when his phone rang.

Thankfully, he'd taken it out of his pocket earlier and it was sitting on the counter. But, still swearing at the timing, he looked down at the screen. He planned on letting whoever was calling just leave a message.

Upon seeing it was Eliot, Zach frowned.

He pulled his hands out of the bowl and grabbed a towel, quickly cleaning them enough so he could answer the phone. Eliot, Jonah, and Marit should've left by now. They should already be out on the water, preparing to haul their first pots.

"Hey, Eliot. What's up?"

"You know, just another day in paradise," the older man said with a small laugh. The easygoing tone of his voice made Zach relax. "Is Marit there? I'm guessing she overslept, since she's usually here before us."

And just like that, Zach was immediately tense again. "She already left. A little while ago. She should be there."

"Huh. She's not. We waited a bit to see if she'd show up and when she didn't, decided to call."

Zach was already on the move. If Marit wasn't at the dock, and she wasn't here at his apartment, she had to be somewhere between the two. "I'll head out and see if I can find her."

"I'm sure she's fine," Eliot said, trying to reassure him.

He was anything *but* sure of that. "I'll see you shortly," he told Eliot. "If I don't find her on the way to the dock, we'll need to expand our search. Call the police."

"Shit. You think something's really that wrong?" Eliot asked, confusion and fear in his own voice now.

"Yes. Marit takes pride in being the first one to the boat in the morning, you know that. When she left here, she was happy and healthy. She set off like she always does—on foot. If she's not there . . ." He let his words trail off, not wanting to say out loud all the awful scenarios rushing through his brain.

Then something occurred to him as he was jamming his feet into a pair of boots.

"She had any issues with Pearson lately? He been harassing her at work?" Zach wanted to think Marit would've told him if he had, but even though she'd sworn not to keep any further harassment from him, after she felt so bad about keeping the texts a secret, he still wondered if maybe she was downplaying anything happening at work.

"No. Nothing. We see him now and then, but he's been keeping to himself. He hired another new lobsterman, but I think the guy quit earlier this week."

The idea that Pearson might blame his own shitty leadership and fishing skills on Marit, making his lack of success her fault, flashed through Zach's head. If he was pissed and frustrated, it was possible he might take it out on the one person he blamed for all his "bad luck."

Marit.

But ultimately, he agreed with Linc. Something else *had* to be feeding his behavior toward Marit. There was no way he'd be this obsessed just because of her gender or an old fisherman's superstition.

But then . . . why?

"Is his boat there now?" Zach asked.

"Now that you mention it . . . I don't see the *Men At Work*. Lucas doesn't usually get up as early as we do to head out."

"*Fuck*," Zach swore. "Right. I'm on my way."

But he had a sick feeling that he wasn't going to find her knocked out on the sidewalk on his way to the dock. This involved Pearson. He felt it down to his bones. He'd done something to Marit, and all he could do was pray the man wasn't as deranged as he thought he might be.

"Okay, see you soon," Eliot said.

Zach clicked off the phone and grabbed a sweatshirt and threw it over his head before heading for his door. He clicked on Linc's name in his contacts as he slammed his apartment door behind him.

"Do you know what the hell time it is?" Linc asked in lieu of a greeting.

"Marit's missing."

"What?"

"Marit. She left for work this morning at the usual time, but I just talked to Eliot, and she never made it to the *Wave Rider*. Or at least, she wasn't there when he and his son arrived. I'm headed there now, but I have a very bad feeling about this, Linc."

"I'm on my way. It'll take me a bit to get there, but I'm coming, bro," Linc assured him. "I'll call Knox and Chad on my way in. What do you think happened?"

"Pearson," Zach said succinctly.

Linc swore long and hard on the other end. Then, after a short pause, "Fucking idiot!" He sighed. "But I think you're right. Wherever he is, that's where we'll find Marit. I'll send Knox to his house."

"He won't be there," Zach told his brother, as he walked the route through the streets of Rockville that Marit usually took to get to work. "His boat isn't at the dock."

"Shit. Okay. Who do we know with a boat?" Linc asked.

"Off the top of my head . . . no one personally, but Eliot does. I'll see who he can get together once I get to the docks."

"Keep me updated. We're comin', Zach. Marit's as tough as nails. She can handle Pearson."

"She's only five-two," Zach whispered, feeling sick. "It wouldn't take much to overwhelm her. To render her unconscious and take her somewhere."

"Be that as it may, if he managed to get the upper hand and took her somewhere, that means she's alive. If he wanted to kill her outright, he could've done it at the docks before taking off in his boat. So, that means he wants something from her . . . and I highly doubt it's anything sexual. He can't stand her."

His brother's words weren't reassuring. Zach took a deep breath, but it didn't help. His mouth watered uncontrollably, and he had to stop walking abruptly. Leaning over, he puked up the breakfast he'd eaten with Marit not that long ago.

"Damn drunk tourists," someone murmured a little too loudly from nearby. But Zach didn't give a shit if everyone thought he was hungover and puking his guts out from drinking too much. The thought of Marit being taken, possibly sexually assaulted, was more painful than anything he'd ever experienced in his life. Standing for days on end on the steel floor of a galley in an aircraft carrier wasn't as painful as this.

"You all right?" Linc asked.

"No," Zach said. "You and I both know rape isn't about liking someone. It's about control. And Pearson definitely feels as if he has no control when it comes to Marit. He'd want to put her in her place; what better way to do that than to take her somewhere, assault her to show her who's boss, then throw her body overboard?"

"Stop it," Linc ordered. "Wipe those thoughts from your head right this second. You think Marit would let that happen? Your woman would tear his dick right off if he dared even try to drop his pants around her."

Linc wasn't exactly wrong. But Zach didn't feel much better. She was vulnerable because of her size. Because Pearson believed she was beneath him.

"Get to the dock. Talk to Eliot, but more importantly, see what you can see. I like old man Sullivan, but if he's not thinking anything bad happened to Marit, he might miss even obvious clues. I'll have the cops meet you at the boat. See if Eliot can get in touch with any of his friends, so they can be on the lookout for Pearson's boat. We're gonna find her, Zach."

"Yeah." It was about all Zach could say. Nausea still swam through him, but he didn't have time to get sick again. He needed to get to the *Wave Rider*. See if he could find any trace of the woman he loved.

The fear and nausea slowly morphed into determination and anger. How dare Pearson touch Marit! Zach was positive it was him. Why the man thought he was so much better than *anyone*, let alone Marit, Zach had no idea.

There were countless examples in this world that made him wonder why people couldn't mind their own damn business. His own parents had reminded him to do that very thing more times than he could remember. When he tattled on one of his brothers, *mind your own business*; when he came home from school and tried to tell his dad about something a classmate had done, *mind your own business*; when he'd caught Knox smooching his girlfriend out at the lobster swing, *mind your own business*.

The world would be a better place if everyone would simply *mind their own fucking business*! Marit was a damn good lobsterwoman. And businesswoman. And friend. She'd do just about anything for Eliot and Jonah. Give someone the shirt off her back. It didn't matter what she had—or didn't have—between her legs. As long as she could do her job, that was enough. It *should* be enough.

But for people like Pearson, it would *never* be enough. He was of the mind that men should be in charge and women should know their place. And in his eyes, their place was at home, barefoot and pregnant.

Screw that. Zach had known too many female sailors who were excellent at their jobs to ever feel as if *any* job could only be done by just one gender.

As expected, Zach saw no sign of Marit on his way to the docks. People smiled and said good morning to him as he passed, but he barely heard them. All his concentration was on finding Marit.

He was practically jogging by the time he got to the parking lot for the harbor. He made a beeline for the berth where the *Wave Rider* was moored—but something made him stop and turn back around to face the long dock.

His gaze swept the area, trying to figure out what he'd seen in his periphery. What made him stop. Then he saw it. Glass on the dock.

Looking up, he saw a light atop a pole. A broken light. It could've been broken for days . . . but no. He had a feeling it wasn't. More so, his gut said it had something to do with Marit's disappearance.

If that light was out, it would've been very dark down by these boats at the hour when Marit arrived at work. The only other light coming from the parking area itself, at least until she got on board the *Wave Rider* and flicked on the boat's lights.

Spinning, he continued toward where Eliot was standing inside the *Wave Rider*. The man was frowning. "No luck?" he asked, stating the obvious.

"No," Zach said. "My brother is calling the police, they should be here soon. We know people in town, but with Pearson's boat missing, I have a feeling that's where Marit is. He took her, Eliot, and I need help from people with boats to find her." Zach was aware his tone was pleading, that he sounded desperate, but he was out of his league here. Even though he'd made his career and home on the water, he didn't know the fishermen in this area like he should.

He had no doubt Knox would get in touch with the Coast Guard, and they'd also be on the lookout, but the longer it took to mobilize people, the more time Pearson had to do something horrific to Marit. While he was talking to the cops, explaining why he thought Marit had been abducted by Lucas Pearson, he needed others to actively start looking for the woman he loved.

Eliot straightened. "*I* know people with boats. Lots of them. Lobstermen who are even right now out on the water. I'll call them. Tell them what's happening. Tell them to be on the lookout for the *Men At Work*."

Relief almost made Zach fall to his knees. "Do it. Call them. Call everyone."

"On it," Jonah said, already walking to the cockpit and picking up the mouthpiece to the radio.

As he listened to Marit's friend and fellow lobsterman put out the request to be on the lookout for Pearson's boat, and explain why, Zach swallowed hard. Marit was out there somewhere. She had to be all right. She simply *had* to be. The alternative was unacceptable.

~

Marit came back to consciousness in a flash. One second she was out, and the next she was fully aware of the sounds and smells around her. But she was smart enough to stay still, exactly as she was. To keep her eyes closed. She needed intel.

All the information she'd learned from the countless self-defense classes came back to her in a rush. Be smart. Think. Get away. Those were the tenets. She couldn't do that last one, not at the moment, but she could definitely do the others.

She was lying on her stomach and obviously on a boat. The rocking motion and the smell of the sea were so deeply ingrained in her brain and blood, she knew in a heartbeat that she wasn't on dry land.

Her head hurt, and her muscles felt as if she'd been lifting weights forty pounds too heavy for her frame.

Fucking Lucas. He'd tased her. Then rendered her unconscious. Had he stolen the *Wave Rider*? Hurt Eliot and Jonah? Panicked, she took a risk and opened her eyes a fraction of an inch. She saw worn and weathered boards in front of her face. Boards that had splinters.

So she wasn't on the *Wave Rider*. No way would Eliot let his boat deteriorate to this condition. Which meant she had to be on Lucas's boat, the *Men At Work*. He'd freaking kidnapped her. But where was he taking her? And what did he intend to do with her once they arrived at their destination?

Immediately, Marit's mind ran through scenarios. It seemed most likely he was going to throw her overboard. The water this time of year was frigid. She wouldn't last long if he *did* leave her in the water. She could swim very well, but her body would be no match for fifty-degree temperatures.

She couldn't think of any other reason why he'd have taken her on his boat other than to throw her into the sea. She had to prevent that at all costs. The water meant death and no future with Zach. No

Thanksgiving at his house. No first Christmas or birthdays or seeing Britt and Chad's baby being born. She wouldn't be able to see how Linc and Harper's relationship played out. Because there was definitely something between those two, even if no one wanted to admit it.

She wasn't going out at the hands of Lucas fucking Pearson. She'd have to wait to make her move. She was building the kind of life she'd always wanted, and she was going to fight for it. Do whatever it took to survive.

It was eerily quiet as they moved through the water. She couldn't see where they were or where they were heading from her prone position on the bottom of the boat, but she wasn't going to risk him knowing she was conscious.

The longer it took for them to get to wherever they were going, the angrier Marit became. She hadn't done one damn thing for Lucas to feel as if he had the right to kidnap her. She worked hard, didn't bother anyone. She should've let the Young brothers have free rein to do whatever they wanted to the man instead of insisting they back off.

Well, hindsight was twenty-twenty, as they always said. Marit wondered who "they" were. Who came up with these sayings?

Aware that her mind was wandering, she struggled to concentrate on the here and now. She needed to be ready for whatever Lucas had planned for her. For a moment, she worried that maybe he was going to meet up with Thorne, or another one of their buddies who had a thing against women working in the lobster industry. But she'd deal with that if and when it happened.

She had no idea how long she lay on the bottom of Lucas's boat, pretending to still be unconscious, but when the vessel began to slow, she decided it was time to "wake up." The last thing she wanted was to still be pretending to be unconscious when Lucas decided to make his move. She wasn't going to make whatever he had planned easy for him.

Groaning, she rolled to her back. She wasn't acting with that part. She was extremely sore from the jolts of electricity Lucas had shot through her body. It was also painful to swallow, most likely from where he'd wrapped his hand around her throat.

Pushing her aches and pains down, Marit opened her eyes fully as she sat up and looked around as if in a daze, trying to see if she recognized where they were, but also hoping to spot something she could use as a weapon in her immediate vicinity. She didn't see anything . . . but then she mentally smacked her head. She had a weapon on her own tool belt. She always carried a knife in case she needed to quickly cut a rope that may have gotten tangled around her feet.

She didn't dare reach for it; she didn't want to bring Lucas's attention to the fact that she had a weapon. But knowing she wasn't completely defenseless was a huge relief. Gave her a little more confidence.

"What . . . ? Where am I!?" she muttered dramatically.

"Oh, good timing," Lucas said with a sneer, as he stared down at her from his place behind the wheel of the vessel. "Have a good nap?"

What an asshole.

"Lucas? What happened?" Marit was doing her best to put on a show. To pretend she didn't even recall that Lucas had attacked her. Maybe if he didn't think she remembered what happened, it would give her a bit of time before he did whatever came next.

Lucas had steered his boat toward a small island. One Marit didn't recognize. Not that she knew the names of every island off the coast of Maine, there were way too many, but if it was one she passed every day, she would've recognized it. There was no telling how far away Lucas had taken them from Rockville. She didn't know how long she'd been unconscious, so it was impossible to know exactly where they were.

Marit's body lurched as Lucas ran his boat aground, jamming the front of his boat into the soft sand of the island. There was a tiny little beach of sorts. Just enough sand to serve as a kind of dock.

Lucas jumped out and grabbed a rope. He splashed through the shallow water toward shore, obviously planning on tying up the *Men At Work* so it wouldn't float away.

This was her chance! Marit quickly stood—and found she was surprisingly, irritatingly wobbly on her feet. She stumbled toward the controls of the boat, but to her dismay, Lucas had taken the key with him. Damn it! She'd been hoping to steal his boat right out from under him.

The next thing she tried was calling for help.

Marit grabbed for the radio and keyed the mike. But nothing happened. She frantically pushed buttons on the front of the radio, to no avail.

"You think I'm stupid?" Lucas asked as he stalked back toward the boat with an evil grin on his face. He launched himself back over the side and reached for her.

Marit attempted to dodge his grip. But still feeling the effects of being tased, she was too slow. He grabbed the front of her overalls and flung her away from the controls.

"I disconnected the wires to the radio so you couldn't call for help if you got the chance—not that I was gonna let you *get* that chance. And in case you were hoping someone could track us using the black box, I've disabled that too."

Marit stared at Lucas with big eyes. She'd managed to stay on her feet when he'd thrown her away from the radio, but she felt her legs going weak. She *had* hoped Zach would be able to figure out that it was Lucas who'd taken her, and that he'd know to contact marine patrol to check the GPS that was mandatory for all boats leaving the harbor.

"What's going on, Lucas?" she asked in what she hoped was a steady tone.

He grinned again, and the look of pure evil on his face sent shivers racing down her spine.

She'd messed up. Big-time. She should have reported his harassment weeks ago. But she never thought Lucas would actually *kidnap* her. The man was unhinged.

"You should've listened to me," Lucas told her. "And Thorne. You should've left Maine altogether. Because of *you*, I can't find good lobstermen. My catch has gone to shit. Having you on a boat is bad luck—and I'm done trying to be nice. Trying to get you to come to your senses. So . . . I'm taking care of my fishing problem. Once you're gone, I'll be able to find a halfway decent deckhand and my season will recover."

He was absolutely insane. That was the only thing Marit could think of. She had nothing to do with his skill as a lobsterman or why the people he hired kept quitting. From what she'd heard, he was a horrible boss. Skimped on safety, ignored the rules set forth by the state and other fishing regulatory organizations, and generally behaved like an asshole. Fishing in unsafe weather conditions, and sometimes even hauling other people's pots to check if the area was a good one or not.

In short, Lucas Pearson should have his license taken away by the state because of how reckless he was and how many rules he broke on a regular basis.

But instead, he was blaming *her* for his "bad luck"? What a joke.

"Seriously? *That's* why you're doing this?" She shook her head. "No. I don't believe it. It's not my fault you break industry rules. It's not *my* fault you're unethical, and you put everyone's safety at risk on your boat! So what's the *real* reason, Lucas?" Marit knew she was taking a risk, knew she should probably keep her mouth shut. But there had to be more to all this, to his months of harassment, than a silly superstition.

The look on his face when his grin turned to a scowl said she was right.

"You turned my dad in."

Marit blinked. *"What?"*

"You. Turned. My. Dad. In," Lucas repeated, enunciating each word, almost spitting them at her. "He made the huge mistake of hiring you. It was years ago, but you betrayed him in the worst fucking way a deckhand ever could. You turned him in to the Fish and Game Commission for a whole slew of ridiculous shit. You even claimed he was keeping breeding females and oversize lobsters."

"Oh my God . . . your father is Larry Welch?" She'd never made the connection. Why would she? They didn't share the same last name. She remembered Eliot saying once that Lucas's dad was shady. But she hadn't thought for a second that the man she'd worked for once upon a time—and turned in for some of the reasons Lucas cited—and the guy Eliot mentioned were one and the same.

The deep hatred Lucas had for her made sense now. It was still fucked up, but at least it wasn't just because she was a woman.

"*Yes.* And he had to pay massive fines because of you, bitch! He bought me the *Men At Work* before I moved here . . . and he couldn't believe it when I told him all about the stupid chick who thought she could hack it as a lobsterman in Rockville after already *failing* so spectacularly in Portland. He didn't even know you were still working in the industry. But after we made the connection, I made it my goal to fuck with your life as much as you did my dad's.

"Oh, and you should know, I've talked to Thorne about you. A lot. When he found out what you did, he's the one who encouraged me to pick up where he left off. To avenge my dad, and *all* lobstermen who've been turned in and fined simply for trying to make a living." Then he scowled. "But he thought my ultimate plan was *stupid.* That it wouldn't work. But fuck him! It will work—*has* worked. Now, get over here," he growled, pointing to a spot right in front of him.

Instead of doing as ordered, Marit took a small step backward. She was having a hard time wrapping her mind around what was happening. How Lucas was willing to hurt her, to do . . . she wasn't sure what, simply because his dad had to pay a fine for all the unsafe and illegal shit he was doing. She supposed she should be thankful Thorne wasn't in on this—whatever *this* was—otherwise she could be facing two captors right now.

But she was smart enough to know she was in deep shit either way.

Her gaze went from Lucas to the island, then back to him. She had no idea what he was going to do . . . but she certainly wasn't going to make it easy on him.

And she was secretly relieved that whatever his plan was, he was apparently going to execute it on this island and not in the middle of the ocean. If she could get to land, she had a shot at making it out of this. A small shot, but a shot all the same.

"Get. Over. Here. *Now!*" Lucas growled, barking each word out menacingly.

"Not a chance," Marit said—then launched herself over the side of the boat.

Chapter Fifteen

Zach glanced down at his watch and scowled. It was taking way too long to get the search for Marit going. The sun had come up fully, and all he could think about was the fact that she was out there somewhere, with a man who hated her for no good reason at all. No reason they were aware of, anyway. There was no telling what Lucas would do. But he couldn't think about that right now. Not if he wanted to stay sane.

"I can't stand here and do nothing anymore," Zach blurted.

All three of his brothers turned to look at him at the same time.

"She's out there somewhere. I need to find her! Need to do something other than just stand here and listen to people on boats talk about how they haven't seen any sign of Pearson. We don't know that they're even *looking*. They could just be going about their usual business of hauling lobster pots—not doing a grid search or anything!"

"The Coast Guard is out there," Knox said. "I've personally talked to some people I know from work, and they're on this."

"I know."

"And Eliot said everyone he knows is definitely not fishing right now. They're coordinating a search, so they're each taking a different section of the coast," Chad said.

"I know," Zach repeated.

"I called Rogers," Linc said.

Zach turned to his oldest brother in surprise. "You did? Why?"

"Because he's an asshole, but he's lived here his entire life. Knows this place like the back of his hand. He loves turning people in for illegal lobster pots. Telling tourists where they're allowed to boat and where they can't. And he ran that sightseeing and wildlife-spotting tour business for years before calling it quits. I found out that he hasn't arranged to have his boat stored yet, even though it's so late in the season. It's moored in Rockville Harbor. If anyone knows the nooks and crannies of this area, it's him."

His brother had a point. Their asshole neighbor had made a living basically tattling on others. He took great pride in calling marine patrol, the Coast Guard, basically anyone he could get to listen, and informing them of someone doing anything *he* decided was illegal.

"I think that's him now," Linc said, nodding toward a boat coming toward the dock at a high rate of speed. It was definitely going faster in the no-wake zone than was legal, which was a little ironic, but for once in his life, Zach was happy to see his neighbor.

"I'm going with him," he said, his voice full of determination.

"Me too," Linc agreed.

"I'll hop in with Jonah and Eliot," Chad said.

"And I'll stay and monitor the radio, coordinating the search as well as I can from the Sullivans' friend's boat," Knox said, pointing to the *Hull of a Catch*, docked nearby.

The police had been by to take a report. It wasn't until Zach pointed out the lunch he'd packed for Marit—which had been shoved underneath a lobster pot stacked on the deck of her boat—that they'd even agreed she'd made it to the docks and something had likely happened to her.

They'd listened to Zach's suspicions about Pearson, based on the months of harassment and texts, and promised they'd send one of their police boats out to look for the *Men At Work*. Thankfully, the officers did seem to be taking his report of a missing person seriously, and didn't blow him off by telling him Marit might have decided to take a break from the relationship and her job for a while.

Zach had said and thought lots of nasty things about Victor Rogers over the years, most well earned, but one thing that could be said about the man was that he was a hell of a boat pilot. He skidded into the dock as if he was in a Formula One race car.

"If you're comin', get on," Victor growled from behind the wheel.

Zach didn't hesitate. He jumped on board, closely followed by Linc.

"Thanks for coming," Linc told Victor.

The old man simply grunted. He nodded at Eliot, then maneuvered his boat so the bow was pointed back into the harbor and gunned it.

Thankfully, Zach was holding on. If he hadn't been, it was likely he would've been thrown overboard.

No one said much as the small but powerful boat zoomed out of the harbor toward the open ocean. After a minute or so, Zach stepped forward until he was standing next to Victor. "Any ideas on where to look?" he asked.

"Yes."

Zach gritted his teeth in annoyance. Would it kill the man to talk to him? Marit was in danger. It wasn't as if they were out on a pleasure cruise. Not that Zach would ever in a million years get on a boat with this man for a social outing. He'd probably find a way to kill him and dump his body overboard . . . one less Young to inherit the land Victor so desperately wanted to get his hands on.

"I'm not doing this for you," Rogers said after a moment. "I'm doing it for *her*. For Marit. She's a good girl. Not sure why she's with *you*, but . . ." He shrugged.

Zach was surprised to hear his neighbor say something positive about anyone. He wasn't even aware he and Marit had ever talked all that much.

As if he could hear Zach's internal confusion, Victor said, "She gave a tour of her boat to Kash. Took him out. Was the first time in a long time the boy's talked about anything other than stars. Then I saw her in town the other day, and she got me a discount on some seafood."

Zach wanted to tell Victor that Marit was nice to everyone, but especially to twelve-year-old boys who were desperate for some positive adult attention. But honestly, Zach didn't care what Victor's motivation was. It only mattered that he had a boat and was willing to motor around looking for Pearson.

"You know, when you aren't actively being an asshole, you're a good man, Rogers," Linc told their neighbor.

"Don't get used to it," he grumbled.

"Wouldn't dream of it," Linc reassured him.

Ten minutes went by. Then twenty. Then thirty. An hour passed, and they'd had absolutely no luck in locating Pearson or Marit. Zach felt as if he was going to go out of his mind. Standing on the deck of the boat, staring at the miles and miles of water, straining his eyes to see something, anything, that might lead them to where Marit could be . . . it was starting to get to him.

How in the hell were they going to find a tiny little boat in the middle of the ocean? Pearson could've taken her literally anywhere. There were thousands of islands off the coast of Maine that he could be hiding on or around. Or he could've hurt Marit, gotten rid of her body, and circled back around to Rockville, determined to play dumb about where she might be or his involvement in her disappearance.

Zach was well aware that thousands of people went missing without a trace every year. The thought that he'd never find Marit, that she'd become another statistic, made him want to puke all over again.

"Don't give up, boy," Rogers barked out of the blue.

Zach looked over at him in surprise.

"I can practically hear you thinking from over here. Any woman who can make it as a lobsterwoman isn't going down without a fight. Don't you disrespect her by giving up on her. My Carrie was much the same way. Tough as nails, didn't put up with any shit."

He was right. Damn it, Zach hated to agree with Victor on anything, but even though he hadn't had a lot of contact with Marit, the man knew who she was.

"Right. So . . . what's the plan? Are we just driving around blindly out here or what?" he asked, not willing to get into any kind of emotional conversation with Rogers.

"Should've left you at the dock," Victor muttered. "No, we aren't just driving around. I'm checking the places I think would be ideal for someone to do something nefarious. I've got a few other islands in mind to check. Out-of-the-way places. Uninhabited. Not on any damn tourist maps."

Chatter on the radio was nonstop. From the lobstermen in the area, communicating where they'd already looked in their own kind of grid search of the ocean. The Coast Guard was trying to organize the search, but the lobstermen weren't really listening. They were doing things their way, determined to find one of their own.

Eavesdropping on the captains talking about Marit was eye opening. Zach wished she could hear some of the things people were saying. Everyone respected her and expressed their disgust toward Pearson. *No one* liked the man. He was lazy, disrespectful, and word had definitely gotten around about what kind of captain he was, which was why he couldn't find or keep any decent deckhands.

But the most interesting thing he overheard was that Lucas's father was a lobsterman in Portland. And it sounded like the apple didn't fall far from the tree. No one liked Larry, which was apparently the man's name . . .

And when someone commented that Marit had actually worked with Larry in Portland years ago—and had turned him in for unsafe boating practices—everything clicked.

That *had* to be the reason Lucas was so determined to force Marit to quit. The reason for all the harassment. He was trying to make her pay for turning in his dad!

Oh, Zach had no doubt the man couldn't stand the fact a woman was able to work on a lobster boat, and do an amazing job to boot, but the real motivation behind his attitude, and very likely Marit's disappearance, had to be revenge.

Taking a deep breath, Zach tried to stay calm. Getting worked up wouldn't help the situation. Instead, he considered everything else the other lobstermen said about Marit. About how much they respected her, how impressed they were with her work ethic, her strength . . .

It seemed abundantly clear they thought little about her gender in regard to the job. She was simply a fisherman, just like them. And most captains and deckhands were simply doing what they could to make a living. Were too invested in their own schedules, their own lobstering, to care what someone else did.

Zach had a feeling none of them had shared their thoughts with Marit herself. So it wasn't too hard to believe how one person—maybe two, if he counted Deaton from Portland—could color her entire perception of a situation.

When he found Marit, Zach would make damn sure she understood that she was a welcome addition to the community. That she wasn't the pariah she thought she was. Maybe then she'd finally feel completely secure in Rockville.

As the small boat flew over the waves, clouds began to roll in. It was supposed to be a sunny day, but the weather was known to be unpredictable here on the coast of Maine. It was as if even the weather was weeping because Marit was missing.

The thought of checking out all the spots Rogers had in mind and *still* not finding Marit wasn't something Zach could stomach. It was looking more and more unlikely that they'd be able to track either of them down—but Zach wouldn't admit defeat. He'd stay out here for as long as it took to find her. Even if he had to steal a boat to come back out after Rogers gave up.

He wasn't giving up on Marit. Ever.

~

The second Marit jumped overboard, she wondered if she'd made a mistake. She landed on her feet, but she immediately slipped on the rocks and went down hard on her ass. Thankful for her waterproof overalls, she jumped up and, as quickly as possible, made her way toward the bank. But Lucas was right behind her.

As soon as she was on shore, she turned toward him, not wanting him to tackle her from behind.

She made the turn just in time to see him lunge for her, so Marit sidestepped, bringing her forearm down as hard as she could onto his arm.

He yelped in pain, stopping in his tracks.

Thrilled the move worked, Marit stepped backward, putting more space between them. The best-case scenario here would be that he'd decide she was too much trouble and get back on his boat and leave. It wouldn't be ideal, that was for sure, but she'd rather take her chances with nature than with the volatile Lucas Pearson. She could make a fire and signal any passing boats to pick her up. There was no telling what awaited her if Lucas stayed.

Well, she could guess. He wanted to see her dead. It was how he was planning on making that happen, exactly, that worried her.

"Now what are you going to do?" he asked with a smirk as he continued to stalk her.

For every step backward Marit took, Lucas took one forward. He wasn't closing the distance between them, but he wasn't letting it grow either.

"I'm going to make you regret putting your hands on me," Marit told him with all the sincerity she felt in her heart.

Lucas laughed. Actually stopped and threw his head back to cackle like a lunatic.

Marit took the opportunity he'd given her. Making a move when he wasn't paying attention. She rushed forward, hugging him around the waist and taking him to the ground. *Hard.*

He grunted loudly as he fell, and his head bounced off the hard-packed dirt. Since he hadn't been expecting to be tackled, he didn't do anything to keep himself from smacking the sand as hard as he did.

Keeping the words of her past self-defense instructors in mind, she didn't stick around to see if she could disable him further. Escape was the only thing she had in mind. Springing upward before he could wrap his arms around her and trap her on the ground, Marit turned and ran into the trees.

The island they were on was fairly large, with a ton of trees. This late in the season, all the birches had lost their colorful leaves, but there were even more spruces and firs to fight through, and Marit did her best to protect her face from all the branches that slapped her willy-nilly. She heard Lucas swearing as he pursued her through the densely packed trees and thick vegetation.

Surprisingly, the island also had a large hill basically in the very middle. It was difficult to climb, but at this point, she had no choice. Lucas was right on her heels.

She scrambled up the hill, hoping to lose him . . . with no luck.

Suddenly, she saw a small clearing ahead, at the very top of the hill, and even though she wasn't sure it was the right decision, she ran toward it. Desperate for a clear space to hopefully put some distance between her and Lucas.

At the last moment, she realized that she'd walked right into whatever Lucas had planned for her. And that he'd obviously thought this through a lot more carefully than she ever would've guessed.

She ran right into a booby trap.

Her brain had a millisecond to register big piles of dirt nearby. Then, running through a massive bed of fallen leaves in the middle of the clearing, she heard a loud *crack* before sticks under her feet gave way.

Marit screeched as she fell into a pit Lucas had obviously dug sometime in the previous days . . . weeks? She landed with a thud and felt a twinge in one of her ankles.

Looking up, she saw she was in a hole roughly ten feet deep and just wide enough for her to touch both sides if she spread her arms out. And there was water in the bottom. Shit. Fuck. *Damn!*

It had to have taken him ages to dig this thing. He'd obviously been planning this for weeks. Maybe even months.

Lucas laughed again, a triumphant one this time. "Got you!" he crowed. "Stupid bitch ran right where I wanted you to go! Stay right there, honey. I'll be back. Gotta get the boards I stashed near the shore to put over that hole." Then he laughed again, before leaning over the hole she was in and spitting.

Marit managed to dodge the loogie he'd hocked at her.

She heard him hiking back down the hill toward where he'd tied his boat. His words registered, and she shuddered. He was planning on leaving her here. After covering up the hole with boards.

And burying her alive.

There was no way anyone would find her if that happened. She wouldn't be able to signal anyone from the shore, and she was pretty sure Lucas would never, *ever* admit where he'd left her, even if anyone *could* prove he was involved in her disappearance.

Desperation swam through her veins. She had to get out of this hole before Lucas returned. Before he had a chance to follow through with his horrific plans.

Looking around, she saw the hole was muddy at the bottom but the sides were relatively dry. Thankful that it had been a fairly dry autumn, she reached up and tugged on one of the roots sticking out from the side of the hole. Marit was relieved when it didn't break off in her hand.

One of the good things about being so short was that she also wasn't very heavy. The gear she had on made her heavier than she was normally, but she really didn't want to leave any of it behind. If she had to evade Lucas on this damn island for any period of time, she'd need the clothes and gear for warmth.

Taking a deep breath, and ignoring the slight twinge in her ankle, she took hold of the root and tried to use it to climb up the side of the hole.

She immediately fell back down to the bottom with a small splash.

Adrenaline coursed through her body, giving her more strength than she might have had otherwise. She *had* to get out of here. Lucas thought he was so smart, but she wasn't about to roll over and give up. Thoughts of Zach filled her mind, giving her all the motivation she needed.

Using the root as leverage once more, Marit jammed the toe of her boot into the dirt wall of the hole, giving her just enough leverage to rise up enough to reach the next root she spied sticking out.

It was slow going, and her muscles were still recovering from being tased, but determination filled her the higher she climbed.

She reached the top after what felt like hours—but she knew was only minutes—and threw her hand over the edge of the hole with a grunt. She paused a second to make sure Lucas wasn't waiting at the top, laughing at her struggles, before wiggling and shoving herself up and over the lip of the hole.

She didn't pause to rest, she immediately scrambled to her hands and knees and then to her feet. She needed to get as far away from this hole as possible.

Marit had nothing in mind except to run. Escape. Hide.

She still had her knife on her, but she had a feeling if she tried to use it, Lucas would overpower her and take it away. She wasn't confident enough to gamble she'd get so lucky a second time with her self-defense moves. And she had no idea if he had a weapon of his own—he probably did—but she wasn't going to give him anything that he could use against her if she could help it.

So Marit ran. Away from the hole, away from Lucas. There weren't too many places she could go on an island, but she could do everything in her power to evade Lucas for as long as possible. Maybe until he gave up, deciding to leave her alone on the island in the hopes she'd die of exposure and hunger before anyone found her.

But there was an equal chance he wouldn't want to risk someone finding her alive, ensuring he went to jail for kidnapping and attempted murder.

Lucas had everything to lose here, but Marit was just as determined he wasn't going to succeed in his insane plan to get rid of her.

On the lookout for more booby traps, Marit made her way quickly and carefully down the other side of the hill, to the far side of the island.

She heard Lucas scream in frustration when he got back to the hole and found her missing. The sound echoed through the trees.

She grinned.

Served the asshole right.

But his next shouted words wiped the smile right off her face.

"You can run, but there's nowhere to hide!"

Marit took a moment to rest. She crouched down behind a large rock and tried to catch her breath. Tried to think. She needed to outsmart the asshole. He thought she was a dumb broad, but Marit was made of sterner stuff than Lucas ever dreamed. She was more stubborn, more determined to win this sick game he was playing.

No, not a game. He was playing for real. To get rid of her once and for all. To get revenge for her turning in his dad. It was so *stupid*! Larry had probably paid his fine and that was that.

Except, it obviously wasn't. Lucas viewed what she'd done as a betrayal . . . probably because his dad had taught him that it was all right to cheat the system. To skimp. To cut corners. It was no wonder deckhands didn't stay long on the *Men At Work*. Not if he was doing the same shit his father had done.

She wished she would've known about the connection between Lucas and Larry before now. The harassment would've made more sense, and she could've tackled the issue head-on. Or at least gone to the police with a *reason* why Lucas was behaving so irrationally. But none of that mattered right now. She needed to stay alive long enough for someone to find her, so she could tell the cops all about what happened and get Lucas arrested once and for all.

And Zach was looking for her. Of that she had no doubt. When she wasn't at the boat when Eliot got there, he'd have called, thinking she'd overslept, even though she'd never overslept a single day since she'd started working for him. And when Zach heard that she wasn't at the *Wave Rider*, he'd have raised the alarm.

Yeah, she was being looked for.

But suddenly Marit wasn't content to sit there and hide while waiting to be found. She had no idea where they were or how long it would take for anyone to find this little island. The longer she tried to stay hidden, the more chance there was of Lucas finding her.

And he wouldn't underestimate her a second time. He'd do something to knock her out again, maybe use that same drug he'd used the first time, then put her back in the hole while unconscious before sealing her in.

No, she needed to turn the tables on Lucas. Give him a taste of his own medicine. And the only way she could think to do that was to use herself as bait.

Thinking back to that hole, she realized how much dirt she'd displaced as she'd crawled up the sides. Even though Lucas was taller than she was, there was no way he'd be able to climb out like she had. He was too heavy.

Now she just had to figure out how to lure him back to the top of that hill . . . and get him into the hole he'd dug for *her*.

A small smile crossed Marit's face once more. She much preferred to be the cat than the mouse. And if Lucas wanted to play, she was more than willing.

Chapter Sixteen

Rogers had just circled what felt like the hundredth island, and Zach was second-guessing getting on the boat with his mom's neighbor. Did Rogers really know what he was doing? Where he was going? Every now and then, he muttered something under his breath and crossed something off on a list he'd made.

This felt more and more hopeless. There was no way they could search every single island off the coast of Maine. Besides, Rogers couldn't have any more knowledge than the Coast Guard or the police. Hell, the local lobstermen who were still actively searching for any trace of the *Men At Work* probably had more insider knowledge of where Pearson might have taken Marit.

Zach had always loved living on the coast. Found it beautiful. Rugged. Peaceful. But now looking out at the water made him sick. All he could think of was the fact that Marit was out there somewhere. Was she right this moment treading water, trying to stay afloat? Had Pearson hurt her? Had he done something more terrible, like weigh her down before throwing her overboard? It wouldn't be a stretch to think he'd tie a lobster pot to her ankles and push it, and Marit, overboard.

"Maybe we should go back," Zach blurted.

Rogers turned to glare at him. "You giving up on her?"

"No!" Zach said vehemently. "I just . . ."

"You don't trust me," Rogers said in a flat tone. He didn't sound offended though. "I get it. I'm not the nicest of guys. Neighbors. Believe it or not, boy, I actually liked your father. He was a good man. Worked hard. Minded his own business."

Linc snorted. "At least one of you did."

Rogers scowled. "As I was saying, I might be an asshole, but that doesn't mean I'm heartless."

"I'm not so sure about that," Linc said, crossing his arms over his chest and glaring at Rogers. "Sure, you let Harper and Kash come to live with you, but you're charging them *rent*. You disparage that kid so much, he's afraid to tell you about anything he's doing in school. He has to come over to Lobster Cove to get the praise he so desperately craves. That his own grandfather can't be bothered to give him."

"The kid is gonna be stepped on his entire life if he doesn't stand up for himself. If he doesn't man up and find an interest in something less prissy!"

"Science is prissy?" Linc asked incredulously. "You have got to be kidding me. Kash is smart as hell and kind to boot. And don't think I missed you avoiding me bringing up the fact that you're charging your own daughter rent. She's working her ass off just to make enough to pay for the things she and her son need, while you're bleeding her dry on the side."

"She needs to understand consequences," Rogers muttered.

"You really *are* an asshole," Linc said with a shake of his head.

This was getting out of hand, and it wasn't helping them find Marit. "I'm not sure if I trust you or not," Zach interjected, bringing the conversation back full circle. "I know you have a lot of knowledge about the various islands and coves and things, but it feels as if we've been out here forever, and we haven't found *anything*. I just think maybe the Coast Guard would have a better idea about where Pearson might be."

"He could be in Massachusetts by now," Rogers said. "Again, I know what you both think of me, and honestly, I couldn't care less—but I know what I'm doing. There are more islands near here that I think would be smart to check out. If we don't find the boat, I'll take you back to the dock and you can do whatever you want from there. I'll go home and continue to be the bad guy in all the scenarios you can think of in your little deluded world of sunshine and roses."

In any other circumstance, Zach might've found that funny. Anyone who thought the Youngs had lives full of nothing but sunshine and roses was seriously mistaken, but he wasn't in the mood to find anything amusing right now.

"Fine," he told Rogers.

"Fine," Linc echoed.

It was obvious to Zach that neither he nor his brother was happy, but it wasn't just that they were stuck with the neighbor they had a not-so-good history with. It was because they felt helpless. Because they were literally standing on the deck of a boat doing nothing but frantically, and uselessly, searching the endless waters of the ocean for a boat that wasn't there. Meanwhile, there was no telling what Marit was going through.

Zach turned his attention back to the water around them. Where *was* she? The longer it took to find her, the longer the search went on and they heard nothing from the dozens of lobstermen, the Coast Guard, or the police who were all on the water looking for her, the more dread rose within him. He needed Marit to be all right. Needed her back.

Marit was being hunted. It was an unsettling feeling. But that was what she wanted. Needed. Lucas needed to be able to find her, needed to think he had the upper hand. Couldn't have any idea of what she was planning.

The more time that went by, the more desperate the man was getting. She could tell by the increase in anger in his voice. He continued to yell threats as he stalked the island attempting to find her. Told her how useless she was, how the lobster community laughed at her behind her back, how she might as well give up because her fate was inevitable.

Marit ignored him as best she could as she tried to lead him back to the top of the hill. She thought of what she might say to him to make the man forget where he was, make him so desperate to get his hands on her that he wasn't even paying attention to his surroundings. It was a serious long shot, but it was all she had. So she needed him completely focused on *her*.

She couldn't help acknowledging the total absurdity of this situation. She didn't normally have to think of what she could say to infuriate someone so much, they'd *literally* want to kill her. But if she didn't distract Lucas, find some way to trap him in that hole, she might never see Zach again. Wouldn't get to live the beautiful life they were building.

But . . . she was tiring. And the sun that had been so bright and happy earlier was now hidden behind dark clouds, as if nature itself was affected by Lucas's vile intentions. There was a chill in the air that she hadn't felt before.

It was time to get this done. To lure the mouse into the trap.

Scrambling up the back side of the hill toward the makeshift grave, Marit cursed under her breath. The boots she wore to keep her feet dry and warm in the boat weren't meant for climbing up the sides of muddy hills. She lost traction and slipped back down about eight feet before she was able to stop herself.

"That's right, bitch! Get up there! Back to your hole. You're gonna end up there one way or another, you might as well make it easier on yourself. If you cooperate, maybe I'll have some mercy and just cover it with boards. If not . . . there's a lot of dirt that I can put back in that hole on top of you . . . after I make sure you're unconscious first!"

Looking behind her, Marit saw Lucas for the first time since she'd fallen into that hole. His clothes were dirty, he looked like he was struggling with the hill and out of breath . . . but he still had the evilest smile on his face. As if he was enjoying the chase.

Doing her best to block out his words and obvious excitement, Marit dug her fingers into the dirt and scrabbled on her hands and feet, moving upward. She hadn't come this far just to fail now. She wasn't letting this asshole win. He thought she was some weak, helpless girl? Well, he was about to learn that he'd underestimated her.

When she got to the top of the hill once more, she saw the boards Lucas had gone back to the shore to collect. They were lying haphazardly on the ground next to the hole.

Ignoring the shiver that went down her spine, and the loud cursing from Lucas as he attempted to get up the slippery hill—his heavier body weight was making it even tougher for him than it had been for her—Marit grabbed one of the boards and placed it across the hole. Then she did the same with another, and another, covering the hole as Lucas had planned all along.

She had just enough time to throw a few handfuls of sticks and leaves on top of her work before Lucas made it to the top of the hill.

The second he saw her, his evil grin returned. "There you are. You didn't seriously think you could get away, did you? You're on an island, *dumbass*. There's literally nowhere for you to go. And since I have the keys to my boat, you couldn't have taken it." He glanced at the hole he'd dug, laughing. "You think covering it up will make it go away? You're going in there one way or another, bitch. Make it easy on yourself, otherwise your death will be so much more painful than necessary."

"Fuck off!" Marit shouted. She was tired, cold, and sick of his shit. "Why are you doing this? What did I ever do to *you* to deserve your bullying? Made sure the authorities were aware that your dad was endangering the lives of everyone who set foot on his boat? Hurting the lobster industry by keeping breeding females and oversize males? What a joke! I don't deserve the lies and rumors you spread about me. Your *dad* deserves your disdain for being a shitty lobsterman, not me!"

"Screw you!" Lucas yelled. "My dad is a *legend* in the industry! You were lucky he hired you, and you spit his generosity back in his face. There's a rule—you don't narc on the captain! It just goes to show that women have no place in lobstering. It's a man's job. *Men* wouldn't run to the authorities because they don't have a life jacket. *Men* wouldn't cry because the captain wanted a little lobster roe for dinner. And if you were smart, you would've taken advantage of the awesome meat on those huge lobsters. But instead, you tattled on him. Ruined his reputation!"

"I had no idea I had to have a dick in order to haul pots," Marit taunted. "And I'm sorry . . . a legend? Give me a break. Your dad's a laughingstock. Everyone talked about him behind his back. *Everyone* knew he was an asshole. If it wasn't me who'd turned him in, it would've been someone else—some *guy*."

As they argued, they slowly circled the hole. He'd step closer to one end, and she'd counter the move. She'd step to the right, he'd go left. It was almost like a dance. Or like two boxers sizing each other up. Each looking for the right moment to strike.

Marit just needed Lucas to get impatient enough to make one vital mistake.

"My dad is ten times the lobster fisherman you are!" Lucas screamed, spittle spraying from his lips. His eyes were bugging slightly, and he looked deranged. "Look at you! You're *weak*! You don't even come up to my chest. How the fuck you ever thought you were strong enough to do a man's work is beyond me. Instead of telling lies about my dad, you should've been barefoot in someone's kitchen. Women aren't good for anything but lying flat on their backs and making sure their man has everything they want—food, pussy, and a clean house."

Marit snorted. She shouldn't be surprised that's how he thought, and yet hearing the actual words were still almost unbelievable. "It's the twenty-first century, not the seventeen hundreds, you moron. I think women have more than proven they're just as capable as men and can do whatever they put their minds to. *I've* proven it."

"You've proven nothing except you're a fucking tattletale little bitch!" Lucas yelled.

He was almost there. Almost so pissed at her, he was about to make a move. Marit kept circling, not letting him get close enough to lunge and grab her from either end of the hole. She needed him to take a step *forward.* Onto those boards. She had to keep taunting him. Pushing him over the edge he was standing on . . . literally and figuratively.

"I'd go so far as to say I'm a better lobsterwoman than you and most of your friends," she said, smirking. "*Including* your father. Since I'm shorter, I'm closer to the water, which makes it easier to haul the pots. My hands are smaller, so I can grab the lobsters out of the traps faster. I have more body fat, so I can handle the cold for longer periods. And I damn sure *know* my work ethic is far better than any man's I've ever worked with. I'm the first one to the boat in the morning and the last to leave every night.

"Your dad? He was lazy. Is probably *still* lazy. He breaks rules that are there to keep him and his crew safe—and you've learned to be just like him. You think everyone in Rockville isn't laughing because you can't keep any deckhands? That word hasn't spread that you not only don't know the first thing about lobstering, but you're willing to put everyone in danger just to make a buck? That you've got some hidden compartment on your boat for illegal hauls?"

She smirked again as Lucas seethed, his face getting redder by the second.

"Nope. The way I see it, in a few years, women will completely take over the lobstering industry. You *men* will stay at home, waiting on us, having dinner ready for *us* when we arrive. *You* can watch the kids while we go off and earn the paycheck for the family. Your boat will be renamed *Women At Work* . . . but hey, at least it'll finally catch some lobster, and in a shorter amount of time and in safer conditions . . . while you sit at home and twiddle your thumbs."

The sound that left Lucas's mouth was so unrecognizable, he almost sounded feral. If her plan didn't work, he would most certainly strangle her to death when he got his hands on her.

A flash of panic hit Marit as sparks practically shot out of his eyes. His hands fisted—and she tensed.

This was it. Either her plan would work . . . or she'd be dead. Taunting him had been part of the strategy, but now he was so furious, he wasn't thinking about anything except shutting her up.

Lucas lunged to the right, then to the left, as if trying to trick her, with Marit countering—then he did exactly as she'd hoped. He stepped forward, finally attempting a shortcut to get to her.

Right onto the boards that she'd placed across the hole. But instead of holding his weight, as he'd expected, they immediately tilted up on Marit's side before falling into the hole.

And Lucas went right down with them.

When Marit placed the boards across the hole, she hadn't centered them. Instead, she'd carefully placed each so the ends barely clung to the edge on one side . . . making them extremely unstable. Most of the leaves and sticks she'd strewn across the top were concentrated at that side.

Lucas simply hadn't noticed. He'd been too focused on her. Had assumed the boards were stable, that she'd covered up the hole so he couldn't shove her back in.

It had taken a bit of skill and a lot of luck to keep Lucas where she'd wanted him . . . on the side of the hole where the boards were unstable. She almost couldn't believe she'd managed it!

The swear words coming from the bottom of the hole were actually quite impressive. Marit stood at the top looking down for a beat, still hardly believing her plan had worked.

"You're dead!" Lucas screamed, as he tried to jump up and grab the edge of the hole.

Marit stepped back involuntarily, but she needn't have worried. He couldn't reach the edge. He then stupidly tried to scramble up the side, much as she had earlier, but he was too out of control, too out of breath, too heavy, too desperate. By clawing at the sides, all he managed to do was rain dirt down on top of him. He was actually widening the hole with his desperate attempts to climb out.

If he was smart, he'd use the boards that had fallen into the hole to help himself get out. But Lucas Pearson definitely wasn't a smart man.

He continued to swear at her, to describe all the despicable things he was going to do when he got his hands on her. Marit stood at the top of the hole, staring down at the man who would definitely kill her at his first opportunity, and tried to think about her next steps. She was afraid to leave, in case he managed to get himself out.

There were still a few boards lying on the ground; if it looked like he was going to reach the top of the hole, she could always bash him in the head to make him fall again. That option wasn't one she liked, as the thought of hitting him made her kind of queasy. But at this point, it was keep him where he was or die. And she kind of liked breathing, thank you very much.

He still had the keys to the boat in his pocket, so he was correct when he'd taunted her by saying she couldn't leave the island. But staying up here meant she couldn't signal any boats that might happen to go by. The last thing she wanted was to spend the night listening to Lucas's threats, but she was too afraid to take her eyes off him.

So it looked as if she'd be staying right where she was.

Someone would notice Lucas's boat at some point . . . she hoped.

She could probably risk heading back to shore to see if he had any emergency rations stored aboard that she could eat. But as soon as she had the thought, she mentally shook her head.

No. She had an irrational fear that the second she turned her back on Lucas, he'd somehow levitate out of that hole and come after her again. And he wouldn't be so easy to trick a second time.

Being on top of this hill wasn't ideal. The wind had picked up, and now that her adrenaline was waning, she was feeling the chill more than she had before. She needed to hunker down, wait for someone to find them. It could be twenty minutes or twenty days. She had no idea. But *someone* would find them. Of that she was sure.

Zach was out there. He knew she was missing, and he wouldn't stop until he found her. Even if everyone else thought she'd run, could no longer deal with the harassment, wanted to make a fresh start elsewhere, as she'd done in the recent past when she'd left Portland, Zach would know she wouldn't just up and leave. Not when she'd left him that morning happy and content and with plans for the upcoming holidays.

Marit picked up a few boards and arranged them together so she could sit on something other than the ground. She made sure to keep the heaviest one within arm's reach, just in case she needed to protect herself.

Lucas hadn't stopped threatening her. But at least now she couldn't see his desperate and wild attempts to climb out of the hole that he himself had dug. He'd done a little too good a job of making it escape-proof. At least for someone his size. He hadn't considered that her smaller height and weight would work to her advantage.

Sighing, Marit huddled in on herself, semirelaxing for the first time since waking on the bottom of the *Men At Work*.

Lucas was an asshole, yes. A misogynistic good ol' boy and a spoiled brat. But he also, unfortunately, wasn't the only one of his kind out there. Men who would go to any extremes possible to protect what they believed were their "rights." Their right to catch whatever lobsters they wanted and pick and choose which rules to follow. Plenty of men who thought women should stay home and let men do all the work.

Marit just wanted to make a living doing something she loved, the same way everyone else did. Being on the water made her feel at home. The repetitive motions of hauling pots, banding lobsters, rebaiting the pots, and throwing them back overboard were soothing to her. Her mind could wander if she wished, or she could simply be in the moment with the water and the work.

Suddenly exhausted, and sore as hell, Marit put her hands over her ears and closed her eyes, wanting just a moment of silence. Of course, her hands didn't completely block out Lucas's continued threats, but they were muted. She'd take it.

"Please find me, Zach. Soon," she whispered, wanting nothing more than to be in his arms, safe, warm. She was proud of herself for dealing with the situation she'd found herself in. But now that she was safe—well, relatively safe, as long as Lucas was in that hole—all she wanted was to give control of everything to the man she loved. He, and his family, would make everything all right again. He'd deal with Lucas and make sure he wasn't ever a threat again.

Chapter Seventeen

Zach was at the end of his rope. They hadn't seen anyone else out on the water, and there'd been no sign that anyone had been at or on any of the islands Rogers had passed by so far. He'd never felt this helpless in his life. And he hated the feeling. Marit needed him. He knew that down to his very core.

He wasn't a big believer in fate or psychic connections or anything of that nature, but about half an hour ago, he'd suddenly felt something deep inside—and it scared the shit out of him. He'd had to sit down before his knees completely gave out on him.

He couldn't explain what he'd felt when Linc had asked what was wrong. All he knew was that something happened. Something big. He was actually terrified that he'd somehow felt the moment when Pearson had killed the woman he was madly in love with. But he refused to say those words out loud or give up on the search.

"I've got three more islands I want to check," Rogers said. "They're long shots, since they're the farthest away from Rockville, and if this Lucas person brought Marit out here, he would've burned just under half a tank of gas. And before you ask how I know that, I just do. I know how big most lobster boats are, how much fuel they can carry. If he came all the way out here, he'd have just enough gas to get back to Rockville. Of course, he could've stashed some fuel on one of these islands if he'd planned in advance."

Premeditated kidnapping was horrifying. Shit, *any* kind of kidnapping was bad enough, but the idea of Pearson planning what he was going to do, where he was going to take Marit, made Zach's blood run cold.

"What then?" he asked. "If they aren't there?"

For the first time, Rogers looked at Zach with sympathy, and said with a shrug, "Then we head back and see what new intel everyone else has gotten. Figure out a new game plan."

Zach's first impulse was to yell *no!* He wasn't going back to Rockville. But honestly . . . did he *know* that Pearson had Marit? That he'd taken her out on his boat? No. It was a hunch. A hell of a good one, but there was a possibility he wasn't even involved. A tiny chance, but a chance all the same.

"Do these islands have names?" Linc asked Rogers.

"I'm sure they do. Probably at least some sort of number. Like Island 432-B or something. But I don't know or care what they are. Do you?"

"Not particularly. But if we find something, we need to know how to tell others to find us."

"Boy, we've got GPS. I can give everyone the exact coordinates as to where we are. They'll come running . . . so to speak."

"Right," Linc said.

Zach held his breath as they approached the first island. It was relatively flat and very rocky on the shore. There was no good place for a boat to tie up . . . although if Pearson was desperate enough, Zach supposed he didn't need an actual beach, he just needed to get close enough to shore to tie a line to a tree or something. That was *if* he even planned on getting out of the boat himself.

While on his neighbor's boat, looking for any sign of Pearson or Marit, Zach had had plenty of time to imagine all the different things that could be happening to the woman he loved. Horrible things he never wanted to think about ever again. But truthfully, Pearson didn't have to do much of anything. He could literally throw Marit overboard and leave her to die on one of these completely out-of-the-way and uninhabited islands.

"Best-case scenario is that he left her on one of these islands," Linc said, as if he could read his brother's mind. "She's resourceful. She can survive for as long as it takes to be found."

He wasn't wrong. Zach nodded.

"I don't see anything here," Rogers said. "I'm gonna move on to the next one."

Anticipation and dread filled Zach. He felt as if he were suffocating under the weight of the extreme emotions he was feeling. He needed Marit to be okay. To be found alive. He didn't even care who found her at this point. He just needed her found. He couldn't live the rest of his life not knowing what happened.

As they approached the next-to-last island Rogers wanted to check out, Zach saw that it was unusual in the fact that it had a high point right in the middle. As if sometime in the last millennium, there was some sort of earthquake or something that pushed the land up, as if someone had poked a finger into the earth from below. The trees were thick here, and there were fewer rocks around the shoreline.

Rogers slowly moved around to the back side of the island, the side facing away from Rockville. It literally felt as if they were in the middle of nowhere. Like this was an island more appropriate for a *Lord of the Rings* adaptation on TV or something.

For a moment, as Rogers motored around the island, Zach thought he was hallucinating. Just seeing what he'd been hoping and praying to see the entire time they'd been out on the water.

A boat.

And not just any boat.

The words *Men At Work* painted on the side of the hull were almost too good to be true.

"Holy shit. It's Pearson's boat!" Linc breathed.

"No one's on it!" Rogers added, sounding exhilarated that they'd actually found what they'd been looking for. As soon as the last word was out of his mouth, the man was on the radio, telling anyone and everyone that they'd found Pearson's boat, and giving coordinates to their location.

"They could be in the cabin," Linc said.

"Marit!" Zach yelled at the top of his lungs.

"Hush!" Rogers scolded. "You don't wanna warn Lucas that you're here if he doesn't already know. He could do something rash."

The man wasn't wrong, but Zach wasn't able to keep quiet. If Marit was here, she needed to know that help was on the way. To hold on. To stay strong for just a few more seconds.

"Get as close to shore as you can. We'll get out and tie up the boat," Linc ordered.

Thankfully, Rogers didn't argue, he simply did as asked. As soon as the hull of the boat hit sand, Zach didn't hesitate to jump out. His boots and pants immediately got soaked in the cold water, but he didn't even notice. All his attention was on the shoreline.

As his brother tied up the boat, then headed for the *Men At Work* to see what he could find there, Zach stood on the shore and let his gaze touch on every inch of ground, every leaf, trying to find any indication of where Marit and Pearson might have gone.

"Boat's empty," Linc announced, coming to stand at Zach's side. "Found some stuff I think will be interesting to the cops . . . bottle of some sort of liquid and a handkerchief nearby. Scuff marks that could be from a struggle or from lobster pots. Anyway . . . see anything here?"

Zach pointed to footsteps in the sand just past the rocks along the edge of the shore, then took a step forward to follow them.

But Linc grabbed his arm, holding him back.

"Let me go," Zach growled, struggling to throw off his brother's grip.

But Linc wasn't listening. "Not so fast, bro. You need to be smart! Use your head. You can't go tromping around making enough noise to wake the dead. Like Rogers said, warning Pearson that we're here could go very badly for Marit."

"This isn't Iraq, or North Korea, or wherever it was that you crashed, Lincoln! I'm not trying to be a dick, but if Marit is out there with an unstable Pearson, I need to get to her *now*!"

Linc stared at him for a beat before nodding. "I've got your back," he said simply, as he pulled out a pocketknife.

Zach wasn't a stranger to violence, but his entire being was focused on finding Marit. If Pearson was hurting her when they found them, he'd do whatever he needed to do to make sure the man never touched *anyone* again.

Apparently having words with the asshole wasn't enough to make him understand how serious the Youngs were about protecting one of their own. Now he regretted not making his point in a more physical way. Now he'd kill the man with his bare hands and deal with any consequences his actions brought down upon him.

Having Linc with him, with at least some sort of weapon, was reassuring, and it gave Zach the confidence he needed to stride into the trees.

It wasn't long before the land began to slope upward, and before they'd taken too many steps through the trees, they heard the first sounds of exactly what—who—they were looking for.

Pearson's loud and pissed-off rantings were easy to hear through the trees. His words carried on the wind that had picked up, now whipping all around them.

"Fucking bitch! When I get my goddamn hands on you, you're going to *wish* you were dead! Whore! Cunt!"

Zach's adrenaline kicked in. But even as he scrambled up the steep hill in front of him, it dawned on him that, aside from furious, Pearson sounded frustrated . . . almost desperate. As if he wasn't getting what he wanted—namely, Marit.

Zach glanced behind him and met Linc's gaze. His older brother nodded once, giving Zach permission to do what he'd been holding back from doing since they'd headed into the trees.

"Marit!" Zach yelled. "Where are you? It's me! Zach! Are you here?"

Silence met his call, and for a moment, his heart felt as if it had stopped beating in his chest.

Then he heard the most beautiful sound he'd ever heard in his life.

"Zach? I'm here! At the top of the hill!"

Zach moved even faster than before. It felt as if he were trudging through molasses though, not able to get to her as quickly as he wanted.

Interestingly, Pearson had suddenly gone quiet. When he'd been swearing at Marit nonstop before Zach called out.

The sight that greeted him when he arrived at the top of the hill was one he'd never forget. Marit was standing on top of a few boards that were extremely out of place in the pristine forest around them. There were piles of dirt in the clearing. She was shaking from head to foot . . . but she was alive and seemingly well.

Zach didn't hesitate. Didn't look around for any dangers that might be lurking, his only goal to get to Marit. The second his arms closed around her, his entire being seemed to sag in relief.

They both went to their knees, as if neither could stand a second longer. Zach was holding her too tightly, but he couldn't help it. He'd never been so scared in his entire life.

"Holy shit, that's one hell of a hole," Linc said almost nonchalantly from behind Zach.

"Well? Get me the hell out of here!" Pearson demanded belligerently.

Ignoring him, Linc walked over to his brother and squatted down, putting his hand on Marit's back. "Are you okay, Marit?"

She nodded against Zach but didn't lift her head.

"Hurt anywhere?"

She nodded. Then shook her head. Then shrugged.

"Okay. Take your time. Get your bearings. We aren't going anywhere."

Zach closed his eyes and held Marit even tighter, if that was possible. She was still shaking against him, and he felt a little shaky himself. He'd found her. She was okay. She was alive. That was all that mattered in this moment. Explanations about what had happened could wait. All he needed was to hold her, to feel for himself that she was in one piece.

How long they stayed there on the ground, he had no idea. But eventually, Marit lifted her head. Zach didn't let go of her, just loosened his grip enough for her to be able to meet his gaze.

"Hi."

He couldn't help it. Zach chuckled. "Hi," he echoed.

He watched as she took a deep breath. Then another. As she gathered her control and centered herself.

"I'm okay. He didn't hurt me. Well, that's not exactly true, but he didn't hurt me enough to keep me from turning the tables on him and giving him a dose of what he'd planned for *me*."

"The hole?" Linc asked.

Zach was glad his brother was there, for many reasons, but at the moment, mostly because all he wanted was to jump into that damn hole and kill Lucas fucking Pearson. Now that he was holding Marit, and knew she was alive and well, his anger toward the man who'd dared to touch her, who'd fucking *kidnapped* her, was overwhelming.

The only thing keeping him from doing exactly what he wanted to do was the woman in his arms. He didn't want to let go of her long enough to deal with Pearson.

Marit nodded. "He chased me right into the hole when we got here. Then he went back to the shore to get these boards—apparently his plan was to cover the hole so I couldn't get out and let me die here. But I climbed out while he was gone." She chuckled slightly. "My slight stature actually worked in my favor for once, and I got away.

"He wasn't going to just leave though. I knew that. So I led him around the island for a while as he tracked me, then came back up here. Antagonized him until he screwed up, ending up in the very hole he'd dug as my grave." She glanced toward the hole. "Since he's so much heavier than me, the dirt didn't hold up. He couldn't climb out. But I was too afraid to leave in case he figured a way out at some point . . . and then you guys arrived. What time is it, anyway?"

"Afternoon," Linc said distractedly.

"Wow, really? It's been that long since he took me?" Marit asked.

"It's been a lifetime," Zach told her quietly.

She turned her attention back to him as Linc wandered over to the edge of the hole.

"You came," she whispered.

"Of course I did," Zach said simply. "I knew the second Eliot called to see if you were coming to work today that something was wrong, and I immediately thought about Pearson. When his boat was missing from the dock, something all the lobstermen agreed was strange, since he was usually one of the last to head out each day, we called every resource we could to look for his boat . . . and you."

"How in the world did you find me? Wait—where *are* we?"

"We're miles from Rockville, and it's a pretty strange story as to how we found you. You know our neighbor? Victor Rogers?"

Marit frowned. "Of course. He can't stand you guys, and the feeling's mutual."

"Well, he has a boat and a ton of knowledge from years of being on the water in this area, and he didn't hesitate to come looking for you. This was actually one of the last couple of islands he thought to check before we were going to head back to Rockville and regroup."

"You fucking asshole! Don't just stand there! Get me out of here! I've got rope on my boat. Go get it and throw it down to me."

"Not happening, Pearson," Linc said. "I think I'll wait for the cops and the Coast Guard to get here first."

"What? *No!* Fuck you!"

"Come on, let's get you out of here," Zach told Marit.

He stood, and his knees screamed in protest. Not just because of the position he'd been in on the ground, but because of the hours he'd spent standing on the boat deck as they'd searched for her, and the climb up the hill.

"I'll stay here with pecker head to make sure he doesn't go anywhere," Linc said.

"Appreciate it," Zach told his brother.

"Wait, we need to call for help, don't we? Like the police? Lucas has the key to his boat in his pocket. And he did something to his radio so it doesn't work, and he disabled his GPS system."

"Rogers is waiting at the shore. He's called everyone."

"Everyone?" Marit asked.

"I think you're going to be very surprised by how many people were looking for you," Zach told her, as they slowly headed down the steep hill.

When they reached the shore, amazingly, the sun had come back out. It was almost eerie, but very appropriate all the same.

"You found her! You okay, girl?" Rogers called out from his boat.

Marit smiled at him. "I am. Thank you so much for knowing where to look."

"I'm old, not dumb," he told her.

"No, you aren't. And I owe you. Huge."

The older man harrumphed. And Zach was forced to come to terms with the fact that the neighbor he loved to hate had once again done the Young family a huge favor. The first was when he'd noticed Evelyn Young and Britt being kidnapped by Camden, their former employer, and was smart enough to call Chad.

And now this.

It might be extremely painful, as Rogers was prickly as hell and truly an asshole—one who was still after his mother's land—but Zach vowed to be friendlier toward him from here on out. It was the least he could do after he'd literally saved not only Marit's life, but Zach's as well. Because without Marit . . .

He didn't finish the thought. There was no need. She was here. Alive. And in his arms once more.

"Look!" Marit exclaimed, pointing toward the tip of the island, causing Zach to glance in that direction.

Boats. At least a dozen. And they were coming toward them at an extremely high rate of speed. They were lobster boats. Each and every one of them. They'd obviously come to the island as fast as they could, as soon as Rogers had given them coordinates. And they'd beaten both the Coast Guard and the police boats, to boot.

Marit looked up at Zach in awe. "It's the *Wave Rider*. And the *Shell Seeker*, *Northern Tide*, *Maine Event* . . . and even the *Crustacean Queen*!"

"It is," Zach agreed. "They've all been looking for you since they found out you were missing this morning."

The incredulous look she gave him both broke his heart and filled him with joy. But mostly the latter. She was finally realizing that not everyone felt about her the way Pearson did.

"I can't believe they were looking for me and not fishing," she said, her voice full of wonder.

Zach hugged her from behind, bending to rest his chin on her shoulder. "They were all appalled that Pearson did what he did. They respect you, Marit. They know how hard you work and have no issues with you lobstering right alongside them."

She craned her neck to look at him without pulling out of his embrace. "I had no idea. I thought everyone just tolerated me. Were maybe even waiting for me to fail."

"They don't. They weren't," Zach said simply.

"I'm going to cry," she whispered.

"Don't," Zach teased. "Tough-ass lobsterwomen like you don't cry."

She chuckled. "Yeah," she agreed.

"For the record? I'm so proud of you. I want to hear the entire story about what happened, because I have no doubt Pearson expected a meek and terrified girl that he'd enjoy bullying a little more before leaving you to die. But instead, he got a strong-as-hell woman who refused to go down without a fight."

"Turns out I worked for Lucas's dad once upon a time in Portland. Reported him for a lot of illegal stuff he was doing. Lucas didn't like that. It's why he was harassing me. Well, part of the reason."

"I know. I figured it out while we were looking for you."

"How?"

"Listening to the lobstermen talk on the radio."

"Oh. Zach?" Marit said, turning in his grip and hugging him tight. "I love you."

The lobster boats were circling the shore now, their crews calling out to Marit, saying how happy they were that she was all right and asking what was happening, wondering where Pearson was.

Zach ignored them for the time being. He stared down at the woman who had stormed into his life and taken his heart simply by being who she was. "I love you too. Thank you for being so strong. For not giving up."

The next sound they heard was a siren, as both the Coast Guard and the Rockville police arrived at the same time. A boat from the fire department was on their heels, as well. All three had their lights going, and the siren from the police boat echoed loudly on the water as it neared.

"Things are going to get crazy for a while, aren't they?" Marit asked.

"Yeah. You'll have to tell the police and Coast Guard what happened, the EMTs from the fire department are going to want to check you over, make sure you're okay. I need to contact my mom and Britt, and someone probably needs to call Harper and let her know that her dad's fine. And I have no doubt when we get back to the dock, there will be a ton of locals who'll want to see for themselves that you're okay, and some who're just simply curious as to what the hubbub is all about."

"Then we can go home, right?" Marit asked.

Home. He loved that she saw his tiny studio apartment as home. They wouldn't always live there. Someday he'd give her a bigger house. Maybe overlooking the water she spent so much time on.

"After you get checked out by a doctor, yeah, sweetheart. Then we can go home."

She wrinkled her nose at the thought of having to see a doctor but didn't protest, which told Zach a lot about how she was feeling. She was putting on a brave front, but she'd had a hell of a day.

"Maybe after we stop by Ruckus Donuts to stock up though? I'm hungry," Marit said with a small smile.

Zach chuckled. "Anything you want. And I'll see if I can't find someone with something you can eat in the meantime."

"The lunch you made for me might still be on the *Wave Rider*. That's where Lucas ambushed me," she told him.

Thinking of Pearson attacking her made Zach angry all over again, but he tamped the feeling down. His job was to take care of Marit right now. He'd let the authorities and his brother take care of Pearson.

"It was there when I left to look for you. I'll make sure you get it sooner rather than later."

Marit hugged him once more, then went up onto her tiptoes. "I love you, Zach Young."

He bent down and touched his lips to hers. "I love you back."

Then the shore was suddenly filled with people. All wanting to know if she was all right and where that asshole Pearson had gone.

Chad was there, as well, looking extremely concerned. He put a hand on Zach's shoulder. "You guys all right?"

"We are now," Zach told his brother, glad to see him among all the others.

"Marit Phillips?" a deep voice asked from beyond the crowd.

Craning to see over the lobstermen, Zach saw a young man in a Coast Guard uniform approaching from the water. The law enforcement boats had arrived, and everyone was coming ashore.

"Yes, that's me," she said, after taking a deep breath.

"We're going to need to know what happened here."

"Of course. But first you might want to go and relieve Lincoln Young. He's at the top of that hill"—she turned and pointed behind them—"guarding Lucas Pearson, to make sure he doesn't get away after kidnapping and attempting to kill me."

Her words were enough to cause a frenzy of action on the shore, as men hurried into the trees and started up the steep hill, with Chad in the lead.

It was going to be a long afternoon, but Marit was strong enough to handle all the questions that would be aimed in her direction. And Zach would be right there at her side. From here on out, there was no place he'd rather be.

Chapter Eighteen

Marit was exhausted and sore, and she wanted to be anywhere but in this hospital. She'd been brought to Pen Bay, the hospital closest to Rockville, to be checked out. She didn't want to go, and she *really* didn't like riding in the ambulance, but Zach had looked positively freaked out after hearing what she'd been through, and she'd hated seeing him so frazzled. So, she'd agreed to go with the EMTs . . . as long as he was able to go with her.

She'd expected to be looked over quickly and released, since she felt pretty good, all things considered. But she'd been delayed . . . for a very good reason.

Zach had stayed with her as long as he could, but at one point an officer showed up to question him, needing to know how Zach, Linc, and Victor had found Marit. The young man looked at him suspiciously, as if he actually thought Zach might have been in on her kidnapping or something, but she made sure the man knew before he left the room that Zach and the other men were heroes. That they'd had nothing to do with her abduction.

The officer nodded and said he'd be back to take her statement.

Marit wanted to roll her eyes. She'd already told the Coast Guard and someone else from the police department everything that had happened. But as soon as Zach exited the room, the doctor arrived to discuss what all her blood tests had shown. It was the perfect distraction.

To say she was surprised by the blood tests was an understatement.

And now she was waiting for the paperwork to come through so she could be discharged . . . and waiting for Zach to return. She took the moment or two of solitude to reflect on everything that had happened.

It seemed almost impossible to believe that Lucas hated her enough not only to want to kidnap her, but to bury her alive on that random island. His plan might have worked too, if Marit hadn't been so determined and stubborn. Too determined and stubborn to give up. But it was mostly luck that had allowed her to turn the tables on the man. If he'd gotten his hands on her again . . .

She shuddered.

Then she took a deep breath. He *hadn't.* And she was alive and well . . . or mostly well, that was.

It still blew her mind that so many people immediately began searching for her. She'd always thought when someone went missing, there was a mandatory twenty-four-hour waiting period before the cops could get involved. But that wasn't true. Apparently it depended on who was missing . . . how old they were, their mental state, and extenuating circumstances.

Since she wasn't depressed, and had made plans for later that day, and because she'd left for work as normal and wasn't at the boat when Eliot and Jonah had arrived, all that meant the report of her missing was taken seriously. Not to mention her history with Lucas and his apparent hatred for her, demonstrated in public on more than one occasion.

The curtain to her cubicle in the emergency room was pushed back, and Zach was there once more.

Marit hadn't realized how tense she'd been until he returned, and now she felt the muscles in her body relaxing. The doctor said she'd be sore for a while, but he reassured her that she wouldn't have any long-term effects from the drug Lucas had used to knock her out.

She also had a pretty nasty bruise around her neck from where he'd choked her, and more bruises all over her body from the rough treatment she'd experienced at his hands and from her time on the island. A mild concussion thanks to Lucas kicking her in the head. But overall, she felt pretty darn good for someone who'd been kidnapped and almost killed.

"Everything okay?" she asked with a frown.

"Everything's fine. He's just doing his job. Making sure to cross every t and dot every i. He needed more information for the report he's got to write up. Are you okay? I missed the doctor coming back in."

"About that . . ." Marit started, not exactly sure how to tell Zach what the doc had said.

The look of fear that crossed his face made Marit regret hesitating for even a fraction of a second.

"You know when we were talking about babies a while ago?"

"Yeah?" Zach said, now looking confused.

"Well, apparently your sperm is *very* determined and it took our conversation literally when I said I wanted kids," Marit told him with a shy smile.

Zach stared at her for a beat as her words sank in. "Are you saying . . ."

She nodded. "I'm pregnant. That's why the doctor wanted to do all those extra tests. The baby's okay though," she said quickly. "I'm not that far along, not enough to start showing yet. But your kid and Chad's are gonna be very close in age. They'll either end up best friends or super competitive throughout their entire lives, since they'll most likely be in the same grade."

"Holy crap," Zach whispered. "A baby!"

"You think your mom's gonna be happy?"

"Are you kidding? She's gonna lose her mind!" he exclaimed. Then he grinned. "*Pregnant.* Wait, you're on the pill. Is the baby okay? Are *you* okay? How did this even happen?"

"The doctor said we're both fine. And sometimes the pill fails." Marit shrugged. "We should probably buy a lottery ticket or two on the way home, considering how the last twelve hours have gone."

Zach sat on the edge of the bed and leaned over, putting his hands on either side of her shoulders. "Are you okay with this?" he asked quietly.

Marit nodded. "Surprisingly, yeah. I've been feeling off for a while now, and I couldn't figure out why. More tired than usual. I guess this is the reason."

"You should've said something," Zach scolded.

She shrugged. "I'm not going to cry about it every time I'm tired or have a splinter, Zach. That's not who I am."

"I know, but I still worry about you. A baby . . ." he said again, his voice full of awe. "I'm gonna be a dad. Shit—I don't know *anything* about being a father."

Marit chuckled. "I don't know anything about being a mom," she countered. "But we'll figure it out together. We have your mom to help us out and give us tips, along with probably everyone else we know. And I'm kind of glad that Chad and Britt will go first. Not by much, but still."

Zach smiled. Then he leaned down and put his forehead against hers. "I almost lost you today. Both of you. It was bad enough knowing *you* were out there somewhere, going through something terrible and there wasn't a damn thing I could do about it. But now, knowing that you were pregnant while he was drugging you, choking you, chasing you around that fucking island . . . it makes me want to go back in time and do things very differently. Make sure Pearson wouldn't even get the chance to do what he did today."

Marit put her hand on his arm and stroked soothingly. "It's done," she said firmly. "Pearson is locked up, he'll face the consequences of his actions. But more importantly, he's been humiliated. When he does get out, there's no way he can ever come back to Rockville. No one will tolerate that. Not the lobstermen, not the business owners . . . no one."

"What about Deaton?"

"What about him? The cops say he claimed no knowledge of what Lucas had planned. That he swears he wasn't involved in the kidnapping, and there's no evidence, no texts or phone calls that say differently. The man doesn't like me, but he flat-out said he's glad I'm no longer in Portland. I think as long as I stay away, he's happy."

"But he's friends with Pearson," Zach countered. "You said yourself that Pearson admitted to telling the man about his plans. So Deaton lied to the cops about that, at the very least. He could've also been an influence on what happened today."

"I know. But Lucas *also* admitted that Thorne didn't want anything to do with the kidnapping. Actually said that he called it 'stupid.'" She shook her head. "I overestimated what I thought Thorne might do to me, and fled Portland as a result. Then *underestimated* Lucas here in

Rockville. But I had no idea he was Larry Welch's son. Knowing that might've changed how I handled a lot of things.

"But honestly? Knowing how many people were out looking for me, and how many of them agree that Larry *and* his son are total slime . . . it's already changed my attitude in a lot of ways. We stick together. We might not always get along, but when push comes to shove, we're a family. I might never be a part of the 'in crowd,' might never get invited to hang out at the local pub and have beers with the guys, but I don't need that. Not when I have you and Lobster Cove . . . and our baby."

Marit's hand went to her belly. It was still hard to believe she was actually pregnant. It wasn't planned, but this baby was wanted.

Zach sat up and his gaze lowered, and he placed his hand over hers. "I still can't believe it," he whispered.

"When should we tell your mom?" Marit asked.

Zach chuckled. "I'd say in a minute or so, when she and the rest of my brothers and Britt appear in this cubicle."

"Wait, what?"

"They've been here the whole time," Zach informed her. "Waiting to make sure you're really okay and to escort us home. Britt stopped by Ruckus and got a dozen donuts. Knox called Jack, and he made us the lobster and white bean chili that was our special for this week.

"Harper and Kash arrived with my mom. I guess they weren't happy to just be sitting at home, with no idea of what was happening, so they went over to Lobster Cove and sat with my mom as they all waited for any kind of information. Then Kash insisted on coming to the hospital with Mom, when Linc called to let her know you were found and all right.

"Chad is hovering over Britt, of course, worried about how the stress of the day might have affected their baby. And Linc is probably standing around with his arms crossed, still pissed off that he wasn't allowed to have even one moment alone with Pearson after he was hauled out of that hole."

"Oh."

"This is what families do, sweetheart. They drop everything and show up when it counts the most."

"Where are they? I'm done waiting!" Evelyn's voice was easy to hear over the noise and chaos of the emergency room.

"Ready?" Zach asked.

Marit didn't have a chance to respond before the curtain was once more shoved back and Evelyn stepped toward the bed. Thankfully she didn't have the entire family with her. That would've probably been a bit much for the small emergency department.

"Are you all right, child?! I can't believe what that boy did! How dare he? But you're here now. I've got some cream I can give you for that bruise on your neck. It'll make it fade right quick. What did the doctor say? Can you leave yet? I think you and Zach should come home to Lobster Cove. Let me take care of you for a while."

"We're not going all the way out there, Mom," Zach interjected. "I'm taking Marit back to our place."

"But it's so small!" Evelyn complained.

Marit couldn't help but smile at the exchange between mother and son. She was still trying to get used to being treated as if she were one of Evelyn's chicklets. It was a new feeling, but one that made her heart grow every time she was around the older woman.

"What did the doc say? Can you leave yet? Are you okay?"

"I'm okay," Marit confirmed. She still wasn't sure how or when she should tell Evelyn about the baby. She was still processing it herself. But Zach took the decision out of her hands.

"Mom, you're the first to know, other than me and Marit . . . she's pregnant."

It took a moment for the news to sink in, but the moment it did, a smile spread across Evelyn's face and she actually clapped her hands gleefully. "You are? Oh my! That's amazing news! Wait—you mean you were *pregnant* when you were kidnapped?"

"Well, it didn't happen in the last hour, Mom," Zach deadpanned.

"That little motherfucker!" Evelyn swore.

Marit was genuinely shocked to hear such language from the woman's mouth, because if there was one thing she'd learned about Evelyn, she was strongly against swearing in general. Always, every time, she took her sons to task when they slipped and said a bad word in front of her.

"I can't believe he did all those things to you while you were carrying my grandbaby! If he wasn't already in jail, I'd do something drastic. I'm gonna make sure everyone around here knows how despicable he is. How he tried to murder a woman *and* a little baby!"

"Mom, relax," Zach said, trying to soothe her, but Evelyn was having none of it.

"I'm serious! If he even thinks about trying to fish in these parts or so much as shop here, he'll find not a single person will do business with him! We all know he's not going to be in jail nearly long enough—though if I had my way, he'd be in there forever. But he won't be settling around here. That's for damn sure. You two really *do* need to come back to Lobster Cove now. Your studio apartment is no place for my grandbaby to recuperate."

"It's fine," Zach told her.

"Zachary Young," Evelyn said sternly. "It's *not*. It's ridiculously tiny. It's no place to raise a family. You need to find a new place. You know you can always come home and live with me. The house is too empty, now that Britt and Chad have moved out. Or . . . oh! I think the old Barber place is for sale! I'll call my Realtor and see what she says."

"You have a Realtor?" Zach asked.

"Yes. Your dad and I contemplated selling Lobster Cove at one point, but decided to hang on for a little longer. Now that Otis isn't stealing us blind anymore, things don't seem so dire. Besides, you and your brothers are back, so there's no way I'd sell."

"Thank you," Marit said softly from the bed. "Seriously. Zach and I appreciate the offer to come stay at Lobster Cove with you, but we both need to be near town for our jobs."

Evelyn's eyes almost bugged out of her skull. "Don't tell me you're still going to go out lobstering?!"

"I am," Marit said firmly. "I talked to the doctor, and he said as long as I was healthy and taking care of myself, he saw no reason why I couldn't keep working, at least until I get too big to handle the pots safely."

"Mom," Zach started, trying to stave off the fit he could see his mom fixing to throw. "Marit's healthy, strong, and smart. She's not going to do anything to put our baby in danger."

Marit reached a hand toward Evelyn. Zach's mom took it and squeezed. "This baby was a surprise to both your son and me, but he or she is definitely wanted. Very much. I'm not going to do anything to jeopardize him or her, or myself."

Evelyn nodded. Then surprisingly, her eyes filled with tears. "My babies are having babies! It's all Austin and I ever wanted. To see our boys happy with women who cherish them, who they cherish just as much. And to see them with families of their own. To experience all the joys we did when you boys were growing up. I'm proud of you, Zach. Of all you've done. And will do. You too, Marit. I'm probably going to be overbearing, and nosy, and way too interested in your body and what's happening inside it for the next several months. But it's just because I'm so happy and excited for you both. For you *three*."

"I can live with that," Marit told her.

Evelyn squeezed Marit's hand once more, then turned to Zach, propping her hands on her hips. "You're going to make an honest woman out of Marit, right, son?"

"That's such an antiquated term, Mom," he said with a shake of his head. "And sexist. Why wouldn't you ask Marit if she's going to make an honest man out of *me*?"

"Fine. Marit, when are you going to make an honest man out of my son?"

Marit chuckled. "We haven't talked about that at all," she admitted.

"Kids these days," Evelyn huffed with a shake of her head.

"Got your discharge papers," a nurse said as she entered the cubicle, holding them aloft and waving them around.

"Thank goodness," Zach said under his breath.

"I'll go tell Knox to bring your Explorer around front," Evelyn said, as she turned to leave. But she stopped before stepping out of their little space, looking back toward the bed. "I'm glad you're all right. That you outsmarted that jerk. That you're stronger than your size would suggest. People always underestimate us small-statured women. Welcome to the family, Marit. We're all better for knowing you."

Before Marit could thank her, or burst into tears, Evelyn was gone.

But everyone in the emergency department heard her exclaim as she walked back toward the waiting area, "I'm gonna be a grandma again!"

"So much for telling everyone individually, on our own time," Zach said with an exasperated sigh.

"I'm actually glad. Makes it easier," Marit said, with a little smile and shrug.

"If you want to get dressed, I'll be back with a wheelchair. I know you probably don't want or need it, but rules are rules. Be right back," the nurse said with a huge smile on her face. She'd obviously heard Evelyn's announcement as well.

The second they were alone again, Zach leaned down and kissed Marit. His lips were warm, and the excited little tingles she got whenever he touched her sparked once more. It was no wonder she was pregnant, considering they couldn't keep their hands, or other body parts, off one another.

"Will you marry me, Marit Phillips? Will you join my crazy family, protect me from my mom's shenanigans, continue to help make The Lobster Buoy successful, let me cook for you, take care of you, put up with my overbearing and overprotective ways, and allow me to be your biggest cheerleader for the rest of our days?"

Marit stared at him with her mouth open.

"It's not a fancy proposal like Chad had for Britt, but it comes from the heart. My heart. You own it, Marit. It's yours. And I'm handing it over gladly. If this is all too fast, we can wait as long as you want to actually get married. And before you ask, I'm not proposing because you're pregnant. If marriage isn't something you want, we can simply be partners for the next hundred years or so."

Marit swallowed, ignoring the pain in her throat. "Of course I will," she told him. "Marry you. You are literally everything I've ever dreamed of in a husband."

Zach beamed down at her. "I forgot to ask the doctor when you might be cleared to make love."

"I didn't. He said as long as I'm not hurting, there's nothing preventing us from being together," Marit told him with a huge grin.

"Awesome. But not tonight. Tonight, I need to get you home, pamper you, feed you, hold you, and simply revel in the fact that you're okay. That you and our little babe are *both* okay."

"Sounds perfect."

"Tomorrow though . . ." Zach said with a glint in his eye.

Marit chuckled again. "Are we telling your mom we're engaged, so she can let the rest of the family know in an inappropriate way in a very public ER waiting room?"

"Hell no. She can wait. I need to find the perfect ring for you first. One that's not too big, that you can wear while you're lobstering. Maybe one with inset diamonds so it won't catch on your gloves or something."

This man really was perfect for her. Some men would probably demand she quit. Insist that lobstering wasn't safe for her or their baby. Or maybe want to get her a huge-ass ring to make some sort of "claim" on her. But Zach wasn't like that. He was happy if she was happy, and he understood that she was happiest when she was on the water.

"I love you," she said, feeling more content than she'd felt in a very long time. Maybe ever.

"And I love you back," he replied.

"You said Britt picked up Ruckus Donuts? You think she has them with her now?"

Zach chuckled. "You and your donuts. Yes, she has the box with her now. The owner threw in an extra half dozen because he knows you so well and was horrified about what happened."

"Awesome," Marit breathed.

"Yeah."

"Here we are!" the nurse said cheerfully as she wheeled the chair into the room. "Your ride out of here."

"I've got her," Zach said, as he stood and held out a hand to Marit. "Let's go home."

"Home," Marit repeated. Anywhere this man was felt like home to her, but she couldn't wait to see the four walls of his tiny little studio. She already had such great memories there. Evelyn was right, eventually they'd need to find a bigger space . . . but for now, Zach's place was just perfect.

Epilogue

Linc sat up in bed and gasped. His hand immediately went to his shoulder, and it took him a few moments to realize that he wasn't sleeping under branches and leaves, his arm wasn't almost torn from its socket, and he wasn't on the run from enemy forces determined to find and kill him . . . after interrogating him, of course.

He was breathing hard, as if he'd been running. Sweat dripped down his temple, and he'd soaked his sheets once again.

Damn nightmares. The head docs he'd been to all said the nightmares would fade. Said that once he'd mentally dealt with everything he'd been through during that week after crashing his fighter jet, he'd be able to sleep through the night once more.

That was a crock of shit.

Linc had dealt with the mental aspect of what happened. He'd actually received training before the crash on what to do if he was ever captured by the enemy. He'd gone through "interrogation training," and he didn't recommend it to anyone.

Afterward, he'd had physical therapy for his shoulder . . . and yet he was still medically chaptered out of the Air Force.

His entire identity had been tied up in being a pilot. Not just any pilot . . . but a hotshot top gun fighter pilot. He'd been one of the best of the best. And now what was he?

Nothing. It sucked.

Looking at the clock, Linc saw it was one in the morning. He hadn't been asleep that long. He'd long since gotten used to only getting two or three hours of sleep each night. He swung his legs out of bed and quickly gathered up the sweat-soaked sheets. After throwing them into the washer, he went down to the kitchen in nothing but his boxer shorts.

He made a cup of hot chocolate—he didn't care how childish it was, he loved the stuff—and walked over to the large windows in his living room to stare out at the night.

Linc loved Maine. Always had. One of the reasons he'd enjoyed living out West was because there weren't as many people around, very similar to his home state. But here, he had a lot more water and trees.

The house he'd bought needed a ton of work, but he liked the place and had nothing but time on his hands. He wasn't working, had saved and invested wisely while in the Air Force, and now he received disability since being discharged. So he spent all his time working on either his own house or his mom's.

Thoughts of his mother made Linc smile, forgetting his nightmare. Evelyn was a firecracker. He hated that his dad wasn't here anymore, but at the same time, he was grateful he hadn't lived to discover the appalling things his oldest friend, Otis, had done. He would've been so proud of his sons though, for coming home to help their mom when she needed them most.

He also would've been thrilled about the two grandbabies that were on the way.

Linc shook his head. He still couldn't believe Chad and Zach had both found women to put up with them, who were now *pregnant*. Their mom was in heaven with the fact that in the next year, she'd have not one, but two grandchildren to spoil rotten.

As Linc stared out into the darkness, imagining how beautiful the ocean would look if the moon was bright enough for him to see it, he realized his feet were cold. There was a chill seeping in from around the windows.

Sighing, he realized resealing the windows—or maybe even replacing them—was on his list of "must do" things for the house. Of course, every day it felt as if he found another "must do." The house was old, but he'd fallen in love with its location—on a hill overlooking the Atlantic—and hadn't hesitated to buy it, especially because he'd gotten it for a steal.

It was big, with five bedrooms, an office, a dining room, two separate living areas, a small but cozy kitchen, and of course, those huge windows letting in the light and warmth in the summer and highlighting the view. His brothers had helped him with the roof earlier in the summer, while it was still warm, and he'd rebuilt the deck off the back of the house so it wouldn't collapse when someone walked on it.

He still needed to gut the kitchen and put in all-new appliances, as well as redo the floors in the entire house. Painting was up next on his task list, though.

He should do that now. Might as well get something done since he was awake. There wasn't a chance in hell of him being able to fall back to sleep.

His family wasn't aware of the extent of his insomnia or the nightmares connected to his PTSD—or that he had PTSD at all. And he wasn't about to tell them. He was the oldest Young brother. The one everyone looked to when they needed something. Admitting to a weakness like not being able to sleep because of one damn week of his life? Wasn't going to happen.

Looking into the now-empty mug in his hands, Linc sighed, then turned toward the kitchen. He'd just finished washing the mug, putting it in the dish rack next to the sink, when he heard his phone pinging.

Looking around, he realized that he'd grabbed it off the nightstand out of habit when he'd left his bedroom on the second floor, leaving it on the counter when he'd made his hot chocolate.

Frowning, Linc grabbed it from the linoleum countertop. Concerned about how late it was and hoping nothing was wrong with one of his family members, he looked at the screen.

His frown grew. The text wasn't from any of his brothers or his mom. It was from Kash. The twelve-year-old kid who lived next door to Lobster Cove. The grandson of the curmudgeon who'd been a thorn in their side for as long as he could remember.

The son of the girl who'd made his high school years almost unbearable.

Linc had befriended Kash that spring, and they'd gotten even closer when he'd helped coach him for the annual Great Crate Race. Obviously desperate for some positive male attention, the boy had latched on to Linc in a big way.

He was a good kid. Smart as hell. A little nerdy. At times, he seemed like he was twelve going on thirty, and other times, he was more like a seven-year-old. But Linc liked him. A lot. Told him that if he ever needed anything, no matter what it might be, to let him know.

The second Linc read the boy's text, he tensed.

Kash: r u up im scared

Linc was moving toward the stairs even as his fingers flew over the keyboard.

Linc: I'm here, Bud. What's wrong?

Even before Kash started typing a reply, Linc was getting dressed. He didn't know what was happening, but if the kid was texting him at—he looked at his clock on the table next to the bed—one thirty-four in the morning, something was very wrong.

Maybe his grandfather had finally kicked the bucket. Lord knew the man hadn't made many friends in all the years he'd lived in Rockville. But he was still Kash's grandfather. There was at least *some* decency inside the man, because he'd invited Harper, his daughter, to live with him when she had nowhere else to go . . . even if he was charging her rent. And he'd done the right thing and reached out to Chad when he'd realized Britt and their mom were kidnapped by Camden Calvert.

And then there was the fact that he'd been the one to find the island where Marit had been taken after being attacked by that shithead, Pearson.

Victor Rogers was still an ass, but Linc was starting to see that the man had some redeeming qualities. If something had happened to him, it would affect Kash and . . .

Linc's thoughts wanted to stray to Harper, and he tried to lock that shit down—but failed.

The woman had made his life a living hell when they were teenagers. He wasn't sure he could ever forgive her for what she'd put him through . . . even if she was obviously struggling hard now. It was karma, Linc had thought, when he'd first found out how low she'd fallen. From the popular, beautiful runner-up for homecoming queen, voted most likely to succeed in high school, to single mother working at Walmart and living back at home with her dad, in the town she couldn't wait to escape.

But the thing was . . . Linc found that he reluctantly respected the woman she was today. She kept to herself, worked her ass off, and did what she had to do to give Kash what he needed. A roof over his head, food, an education . . . family.

But it hadn't always been that way. Linc was well aware of the rumors about how mother and son had lived in a car for a while, right before she'd come back home to live with her dad in Rockville.

It was time he let the past go once and for all. He knew better than most how people could change. He wasn't the boy he'd been back in high school, just as he was no longer the man he'd been while in the Air Force. Harper obviously wasn't the same mean girl she'd been when they were kids.

Linc's phone dinged again, indicating he had another text. Pushing thoughts of Harper and their past to the side, he concentrated on the here and now.

Kash: mom got in another fight with granddad I think he kicked her out and she doesnt have anywhere to go she told me she was going to sleep in her car at Walmart im scared what if she doesnt come back what if someone hurts her while shes sleeping what do i do

Linc frowned. Harper and her dad had a volatile relationship for sure. But the fight had to have been *really* bad for her to decide not only to leave Kash at the house, but also to think her only option was to sleep in her car.

Linc's mom had offered to let her and Kash stay in the rental house on Lobster Cove, and Harper had declined at first, then finally agreed. Kash had been so excited . . . then a couple of days before they were supposed to move in, the dishwasher leaked, and no one had discovered it for a full twenty-four hours. The floors were ruined, as well as the drywall in not just the kitchen, but the rest of the small house.

When Linc pulled up the soggy mess, not only was mold already growing, he'd discovered asbestos in the subflooring. As a result, he'd had to pass the job of making sure the cancerous material was removed to a professional contractor, one who was licensed to do that kind of thing. And of course, all the contractors were booked up for weeks, if not months.

Harper had been gracious, and she said she understood, but it was still a blow not only for her and Kash, but for Linc's mom as well. She'd been so looking forward to them moving in.

Kash: linc?

Shit, he needed to get his head out of his ass and deal with this. Not leave the poor kid hanging.

Linc: I'll take care of this, Bud. I'll go find her and make sure she's safe. Are *you* safe? Are you scared of Victor?

Kash: no hes a grump but not to me just to mom i dont like when they fight

Linc: All right. I've got this. You need to get some sleep, you have school in the morning. I'll let you know when I have her and what's up, and you can read the text when you wake up. You trust me to take care of you and your mom, right?

Kash: yes

Linc: Good. Then go to sleep. You have that science test tomorrow.

Kash: i could pass it without any sleep its easy thank you linc i knew youd help

Linc: Anytime you need me, I'm here. Thank you for trusting me.

Kash: ttyl

Linc now knew that meant "talk to you later." It had taken him a while to understand the shorthand Kash used, and to get used to him not using any punctuation whatsoever when he texted.

He threw a sweatshirt over his head and leaned over to pull on his boots. Thanksgiving was next week, and winter was finally rearing her head here in Maine. The first snowfall of the year was supposed to come in a few days.

He and Harper might have a lot of mutual baggage in their past, but Linc would be damned if he sat around and let her continue to live in her car. He didn't know what he could do to help her situation, but he'd do *something*. Maine was no place to be homeless . . . not that *any* state was ideal for it. And he wasn't the kind of man who sat around and did nothing when a twelve-year-old kid reached out for help, admitting he was scared.

Harper may not have been the one to ask for his assistance, but she was damn sure going to get it all the same. She always did what was necessary for Kash—and Linc was fully prepared to pull on those heartstrings to get her to agree to accept his help.

One way or another, Harper Bates would be safe for Thanksgiving . . . and beyond.

RETURN TO ALPHA COVE IN THE PILOT

Sparks fly when a former bully moves in with her former victim in *New York Times* bestselling author Susan Stoker's tantalizing third foray into Alpha Cove, a spicy military romance steeped in emotion.

Ex-fighter pilot Lincoln "Linc" Young is a survivor, masking his PTSD and nightmares behind a calm exterior. When his father's death brings him back to Maine to help his mom, he never expects to cross paths with his former high school tormentor. But the woman who once made his life hell now stirs completely different emotions in Linc, and when he finds Harper in need, he impulsively offers her and her young son a place to stay.

Harper Bates thought she'd hit rock bottom after returning to her childhood home in Rockville, Maine. Then her father begins judging her every move—and worse, her son Kash, when they discover he's being bullied at school. The last person she expects help from is Linc, the boy Harper herself had bullied years ago. Now a commanding presence who makes her and Kash feel safe, Linc inspires both a growing attraction . . . and lingering shame over her past actions.

Temporary cohabitation quickly turns into something more as Harper and Linc reveal intimate secrets that put them both on a path to healing. But they're unaware someone else has a secret. And it's about to impact the one person the couple can't live without—Kash.

CONNECT WITH SUSAN ONLINE

SUSAN'S FACEBOOK PROFILE AND PAGE

www.facebook.com/authorsstoker

www.facebook.com/authorsusanstoker

FOLLOW SUSAN ON INSTAGRAM

www.instagram.com/authorsusanstoker

FOLLOW SUSAN ON TIKTOK

www.tiktok.com/@susanstokerauthor

FIND SUSAN'S BOOKS ON GOODREADS

www.goodreads.com/susanstoker

EMAIL

susan@stokeraces.com

WEBSITE

www.stokeraces.com

ABOUT THE AUTHOR

Photo © 2015 A&C Photography

Susan Stoker is a *New York Times*, *USA Today*, and *Wall Street Journal* bestselling author whose series include Badge of Honor: Texas Heroes, SEAL of Protection, and Delta Force Heroes. Married to a retired Army noncommissioned officer, Stoker has lived all over the country—from Missouri and California to Colorado, Texas, and Tennessee—and currently lives in the beautiful wilds of Maine. A true believer in happily ever after, Stoker enjoys writing novels in which romance turns to love. To learn more about the author and her work, visit her website, www.stokeraces.com, or find her on Facebook at www.facebook.com/authorsusanstoker.